C.E. Maras

Burgundy

For my family, who are the foundation I have built my dreams upon. From the first grader who wanted to be a writer, to the woman who found her bravery to publish a novel, thank you for loving me, supporting me, and encouraging me to take the leap. I could not have done this without you.

Preface

Emergency – noun, often attributive: an unforeseen combination of circumstances or the resulting state that call for immediate action; an urgent need for assistance or relief.

Panic – noun, a sudden overpowering fright; a sudden unreasoning terror often accompanied by mass flight

Adrenaline – noun, a substance that is release in the body of a person who is feeling a strong emotion (such as excitement, fear, or anger) and that causes the heart to bear faster and gives the person more energy; commonly used in describing the physiological symptoms that occur as part of the body's fight-or-flight response to stress, as when someone is in a dangerous, frightening, or highly competitive situation.

Deranged – adjective, mentally unsound; wildly odd or eccentric

Fate – noun, the will or principle or determining cause by which things in general are believed to come to be as they are or events to happen as they do; an inevitable and often adverse outcome, condition, or end.

Revenge – noun, a desire for vengeance or retribution; an act or instance of retaliating in order to get even; an opportunity for getting satisfaction.

Words. They are only words. Important as they may be, they could never convey the overwhelming emotions and physical exhaustion she was feeling in the moment. The persistent pounding of her pulse in her ears, the pace at which her lungs worked to push fresh oxygen to her overworked muscles—save for the few times her breath caught in her throat. Any time the thought of one of them dying at the hands of that lunatic crossed her mind, her breath faltered. Her feet moved at almost too quickly a pace for her body to keep up. Even on the unforgiving and ever-shifting terrain of the sand, she persevered.

In the distance, the wail of police sirens broke through the soundscape of the ocean. Her ears perked at her name being shouted from behind. She did not dare to look back; she knew who was pursuing her—there was nothing he could do in this moment. She remained focused ahead, making out the silhouettes of her destination in the evening's twilight. Three figures huddled together, one of them a few feet away from the others.

The solo figure, aggressive in its stance, slowly approaching the others. The antagonist's arm reached down, removed something from its pocket, and raised it straight ahead. Her eyes narrowed on the glint of the gun; her target acquired.

Hurtling herself forward, she heard the pleas and cries from the victims. The vicious words being spat from the assailant's mouth formed a trail of hate. With the remanence of energy, she sprang forward on the verbal trail, and collided with her destiny.

One

The blare of a car's horn shook Jodie from her trance. She parted her eyes slowly, in preparation for the sun's blinding glare. She held her hand in front of her face to shield her eyes from the blaze, then looked outside to discover that they only moved a quarter of a mile in the last twenty minutes. She closed her eyes once again, hoping to sleep through the bumper-to-bumper traffic, but the sun burned through the passenger side window and slowly cooked the epidermis of her right arm, making it uncomfortable to get any rest. Sighing, she turned her head and looked at the on-ramp where a line of cars waited to get their turn to pack onto the highway. Heat rose up from the hoods of the cars in waves, which mesmerized her as she watched the heat's ballet until she heard a grunt from the back seat.

Her ex-boyfriend was slouched in the back seat, his head supported by the window. His mouth open with a dried line of saliva at the corner, and his hat pulled down so only the tip of his nose and gaping mouth were visible. His shoulders attempted to push deeper into the corner between the car seat and the door. A smirk found its way onto her face as she visualized him push himself through the car and out onto the highway. She shook the thought from her head as she watched his hand reach for his groin and adjusted himself with a satisfied smile, then began to snore. Her eyes rolled back into her head with disgust as she thought *this is what I dated*.

In the side-view mirror, Jodie spied Doris Sullivan, one of her sorority sisters, with her long blonde hair in front of her face as she furiously filed at her left ring finger. Her long lashes covered her blue eyes as she bit on her overly-glossed lower lip. Doris took great pride in her appearance and loved the attention she got because of it, and the power she wielded over the opposite sex. Jodie and Doris were in the same pledge class of their local sorority, Tri Omega, and that was where their similarities ended. Doris was uninhibited with a wild streak a mile long and the capability to party all night, indulge in a one-night stand, and then appear back at the dorm looking as good as she had left it the night before. She had a lust for life and was unapologetic for her behavior. She always went after who or what she desired, never allowed anything or anyone to stop her, and could care less of what people thought of her. Jodie envied her laissez-faire attitude.

The boredom of sitting in traffic began to wear on her as she pulled her seatbelt away from herself, then let go to allow the mechanism pull it back into place. After a few pulls of her seatbelt, she let go and looked down at her hands. She studied her short stubby nails and picked at her cuticles, then pushed them away from the nail bed, and gnawed at any piece of skin that she could get her teeth on. She pulled too much skin back on her thumb, which caused it to bleed. She sucked in a breath at the sudden jolt of pain and shook out her hand, disgusted with her bad habit. Her attention returned to the window again, as she studied her new surroundings. The cement wall on the side of the road was cracked and speckled with green moss and weeds that poked through. An illegible scribble in spray paint decorated the bottom. She did not understand how someone could deface the wall in such a highly congested area.

As she tried to decipher the graffiti, a red twenty-year-old Nissan pulled up next to her. Two men sat in the car, nodding their heads in sync while the bass vibrated the street. The driver, who wore a blue bandana around his mostly shaved head looked over at her and smiled, then hit the arm of the passenger, who wore a white tank and a backwards blue cap. The passenger looked over at her, smiled slimily, then shouted, "Hey baby, where you goin' lookin' so good?" Jodie's eyebrows furrowed into a scowl and tried to find something to distract herself from the catcalling neighbors. She pulled down the visor and looked at the mirror, where her deep brown eyes stared back at her. Her dark-brown hair fell in front of her right eye as she studied her smile. Her teeth were not as white as she would have liked them to be, but they would do. She sucked her teeth and made sure they were clean.

Amanda Walker watched her life-long friend study her teeth in amusement, and could not help but giggle when she heard the sucking. Jodie shifted her eyes toward the driver's seat and saw Amanda trying to cover up her giggling with a frown.

"What are you doing?" Amanda asked as her eyes grew with laughter.

"Don't you have to watch the road or something?"

"Well, normally if we were actually moving, yeah, but the road doesn't do stupid things like you do!"

Jodie closed the visor and crossed her arms, then turned her head to find the red Nissan a few cars ahead of them, calling out to the next unfortunate car. She began to stare out of the window, trying to study the heat waves again, but the reflection of Amanda's forced frown in the passenger side window made Jodie start to giggle. Within seconds, the two girls erupted into a fit of laughter. Doris barely noticed, looking up from her nails for only a second as Ben snored slightly louder, which shocked the front seat into silence. Amanda looked back at Ben through the rear-view mirror as Jodie looked over her shoulder. Ben pushed his shoulders into the seat a little more and adjusted himself again. The girls looked at each other and began to laugh again.

"Ok, enough... we don't want to wake cranky pants back there," Amanda said as she tried to calm herself. Her honey-colored eyes were wet with tears of laughter as she pulled on her short, golden-brown ponytail. Amanda had an athletic build, very slender and toned, with a small nose and a huge smile, who attracted men all the time, but she hated the attention. She was another opposite of Jodie in the sense that she was very opinionated and loud, especially during arguments or playing sports. Jodie would rather hide her face in a book than go out and party or play sports.

"We've been in this car forever, where are we?" It was the first thing Doris said since the Billy Joel sing-a-long over an hour before.

"Navigator?" Amanda asked as she turned to Jodie.

Jodie opened the map app, and watched it struggle to refresh. After thirty seconds of wrestling with it, she cleared out of the app and took out the directions she printed before they left.

Amanda rolled her eyes when she saw the paper come out of Jodie's bag. "You laugh, but the app isn't loading. Make fun of my archaic ways, but at least we have some information." Jodie defended herself as she scanned over her printout.

"According to this, we should have been there over an hour and a half ago. We're still on the parkway. We're at exit... one-twenty."

"And we are going to?" Doris asked as she tapped her file on the back Jodie's seat.

"Thirty-eight." Ben mumbled as he yawned and stretched.

"Look who finally woke up!" Jodie said sarcastically as she grabbed his knee. "You were in such a deep snore… I mean sleep. I didn't think you would ever wake up."

Ben smacked her hand off him and sarcastically laughed. "You're so funny Jodie! I can't imagine why I broke up with you."

"Nice, asshole," Amanda said as she looked in the rear-view mirror.

Ben waved her away. "I'm kidding, I'm just tired. You all know that I was out with the boys last night."

"Well, who told you to stay out late Ben?" Amanda chimed in to protect her best friend.

"Seriously Ben, why did you bother coming? I could have easily given your place to someone else." Jodie said without looking back at him.

"Because we are friends, and we planned this trip months ago. I'm not missing a chance to play poker. I'm sick of the guys at home. Can't tell if they like playing like morons or they just don't know how to play. They piss me off."

"Here we go with the poker talk again." Jodie said as she rolled her eyes.

"Just because you don't know your ass from your elbow when it comes to cards," Ben said as he began to sit up.

"Oh yeah, that just makes me so inferior to you in the whole spectrum of life." Jodie said as she looked back at him.

"Jodie, get over yourself." Ben raised his voice and rolled his eyes towards the window.

"No, Ben, you get over yourself. Geeze, you're such a pain in the..." Jodie started to raise her voice back as she was interrupted.

"Ok children, can we stop? Seriously. We are probably going to be stuck in this car for another two hours. Can we just relax?" Amanda asked as she pulled into the left lane.

The traffic started to break up. About a half mile ahead there were flashing lights and a billow of smoke. The smoke was a never-ending black cloud that filled the sky like a biblical swarm of insects. Five state trooper cars, two ambulances, and a fire truck surrounded the source of the smoke in a semi-circle.

"There's the source of the traffic. Freaking rubber-neckers. I hate people." Amanda said as she weaved the car through the traffic.

Jodie turned her attention to the side of the road to see what happened and tried to look around the emergency vehicles, but nothing was visible. She began to shrug her shoulders until her heart caught in her throat. Beyond the third trooper vehicle, the remnants of a small car were visible. The frame was charcoaled, the inside of the car impossible to make out. There was one thing that popped out of the car, the teeth of the victim in the driver seat. The skeletal structure of driver looked as though it was pointing out of the window frame in her direction.

"What? What is it, Jode?" Doris asked when she saw Jodie jump.

"In the car, there was a body. I could see its teeth, and it was pointing at me." Jodie said as she pressed her finger against the hot glass.

"That's creepy." Doris said as she looked out towards the burnt car. They watched the officers move around the scene like a choreographed masterpiece.

"Nothing adds to the already wonderful trip like seeing a burnt dead guy," Amanda said as she stepped on the gas and flew down the highway.

The next hour was passed in silence. The car veered onto exit thirty-eight as Ben woke up again. Oblivious to the accident, he rubbed his eyes and re-adjusted his Giants hat. Looking out of both windows, he cheerfully said, "Hey we made it... Atlantic City baby, woo!"

Two

Doris leaned into the front seat and pointed her long, freshly manicured finger out past Jodie's nose. She shook her finger and said, "There, Amanda. That's the hotel. I booked it before we left, it was really cheap."

Amanda pulled the car up in front of the Burgundy Motor Inn. The hotel looked as if it had passed its prime in the nineteen-sixties and was never updated. The boardwalk was just down the block, but shady characters surrounded the front of the building. The girls looked at one another, a sudden wave of anxiety crashed over them simultaneously. Doris began to open her door as a taxicab flew up behind them and frantically honked, causing her to pull her legs back into the car.

"What are you doing? Go get our room." Ben said as he looked at Doris, who shook her head. "Don't be an idiot, just go."

Doris attempted to leave the car and the taxicab's horn began to blare again. "What the hell...," Amanda began to say as she looked in her side-view mirror. The cab driver got out of the car and started to bang on the entire side of Amanda's car. He yelled at them in another language and his spit hit against the window.

"No park! No park! Out of here... damn bastard... move!" He yelled as he hit against her car.

"We are just checking in you freaking psycho!" Amanda yelled back as she stepped on the gas and pulled away from the hotel.

Doris looked back at the crazed cab driver and gave him the middle finger. He shook his fist in return and jumped up and down in the middle of the street as he continued his tirade. "Wow. Maybe we should look somewhere else." Amanda said as she pulled onto another block.

"Yeah, good idea. That place was swarming with the rejects of life." Doris said as she flipped her blonde hair over her shoulder.

"Let's get as far away from the boardwalk as possible." Amanda said, driving down North Carolina Boulevard.

The boulevard merged and ended at a large hotel and casino, towering over everything surrounding it. The sign in the upper corner of the building danced in fluorescent lights, changing colors constantly. Jodie's eyes lifted as much as they could, trying to count how many floors there were. Without turning her head, she said, "There has to be vacancy here."

***

Amanda sat in front of the Borgata with the car running as Jodie hung her arm out of the window as she waited on hold with a local motel. Amanda's hand tapped against the steering wheel as she played with her ponytail and glanced around at the garden around them, wondering how this place could exist just mere miles from a dive. Her eyes shifted over to the doors as they waited for either Ben or Doris to come out. The song in her head continued as she bobbed her head and tapped on the wheel. From the corner of her eye, she could see Jodie shooting her a look with her eyes bulging out of her head.

"What?" Amanda asked as she continued the tapping. Jodie could feel her head begin to pound between the slow, moaning hold music coming from her phone, the endless hours baking in the car, and the rhythmic tapping of the fingers. The noises clashed, and she felt as though there was a two-year-old screaming at the top of his lungs while banging two pots together. She gently covered her forehead with her left hand and softly rubbed her temples with her middle finger and thumb.

"That... please just stop." Jodie said, strained, as she looked at the drumming fingers.

"Oh, sorry. One of those headaches?"

"Yeah. What is taking them so long anyway- hello? Yes hi, I am looking for a hotel room for three nights." Jodie said as soon as the torturous music ended on the other end of the phone.

Amanda watched Jodie as she spoke and tried to read her facial expression. Her dark eyes were scrunched into a nervous scowl as she continually nodded her head.

Why did people do that when they are on the phone? It's not like the other person can see them? Amanda thought with a smile. In the corner of her eye, she finally saw Doris and Ben exit the hotel.

Ben walked up to the passenger side of the car, shaking his head as he lifted the door handle. Doris stopped behind him, waited for him to move, and then walked behind the car to get in on the other side. Ben slid to the driver side when Doris opened the door. "Um, I was sitting on this side." Ben said with a lopsided smile. Doris rolled her eyes and exhaled loudly as she slammed the car door shut and walked back around the car to get into the passenger side.

"Child." Doris said under her breath as she adjusted herself in the seat. "So?" Amanda asked as she turned in her seat to face Doris.

Jodie's hand flew up and shook in Amanda's face. "Uh-huh, yes, ok. Well, thank you for your time. Bye."

Jodie ended the call and dropped her phone in her lap. All eyes fell on Jodie as she pushed her dark hair back from her face. She looked back at all of them and said, "Well they have an opening for the rest of the week."

Everyone smiled and sat up a little in their seats. "Really that's great!" Ben said as he rubbed his hands together, leaning into the center of the car.

"Yeah, great... if you have five hundred dollars a night to stay there."

"Oh. Not great." Ben said as he fell back into the seat. He removed his blue and red Giants hat and rubbed his floppy light brown hair. He squinted his emerald eyes and put the hat back on. "Well Jode, you were always the smart one, what should we do?"

"What about this hotel? Didn't you two go in there? What'd they say?" Amanda asked Doris.

"Well, they had no vacancies, but apparently Ben and I are married."

Jodie's eyes shot up and looked at Doris through the side view mirror. Although Jodie and Ben had broken up over three months ago, and then a year ago before that, the thought of one of her friends dating her ex-boyfriend bothered her. Honestly, the thought of him with anyone else bothered her. She had dated a few guys since they broke up, but she never told him about them. Why would she? It would just cause unnecessary jealousy or arguing. That is what the two of them seemed to be the best at. It was the basis of their relationship, which is why they never lasted very long. They challenged each other on everything, both headstrong and passionate. Emotions always ran high between them, from hatred to lust. But no matter what their relationship status was, there was always an undeniable attraction that bound them together.

Jodie could feel Ben's gaze on her. "Jode?" He asked as he tapped her elbow with the front of his sneaker. He knew what she was thinking; he could see the storm brewing in her dark eyes. He knew that expression very well, it was usually the look that she had before she started to yell. He smiled to himself, aware that he still had some effect on her emotions. She slowly turned her head, so he could only see her left eye.

"Don't be jealous." He said with a smirk as he winked at her.

Jodie wanted to smack the smirk off him; along with the smoldering stare he was giving her. She hated the emotional pull on her belly when his stared at her. The way her body burned from the heat of his eyes. "Go to hell."

"I was there, remember? I dated you."

And just like that, the butterflies in her stomach were set ablaze with anger. "You son of a... "

"Enough!" Amanda yelled out. She could not stand them fighting, it was all she ever heard for the past three years. They were in love, they hated each other, they were friends, and then they were dating again. It was the same thing over and over. Their infatuation with one another was unhealthy. She hated that he was on this trip, she hated that her best friend was still in love with him, and she hated the snapping that came from Doris and her gum.

Fingers twirling in her golden hair, Doris sighed. "It was an old guy, Jode. He thought that we were married because we were asking for a room. He said that there were none but wished us the best of luck and hoped that we had many children."

Amanda started to laugh. The thought of Ben and Doris was ridiculous, especially the two of them reproducing. *God save us the day that happens,* Amanda thought. Jodie looked over at her, completely un-amused. Amanda coughed to cover the laughter and looked down. "So, what do we do?"

"I was checking hotel apps, but either everything is sold out, or completely out of our price range," Ben stated. "The guy behind the desk mentioned that there is some big convention going on, so there is an issue with vacancies across the board."

"I guess we have to go back to the Burgundy. I have called every hotel that said there were rooms available and there is nothing. Why didn't we plan for this?" Jodie said as she rested her head on her hand, as she looked longingly out at the doors of the Borgata. The trip just seemed to go deeper and deeper down the drain.

"This was your trip, Jodie. You were the one who *had* to get away this weekend." Doris said.

"It was your responsibility to get the room, Doris," Jodie said as she snapped her head around.

"Yeah, and I did. Not my fault some crazy cabbie chased us away." Doris snapped back.

"Did it ever occur to you to do some research on the place Doris? Never mind the cabbie, did you see the scum of the earth hanging out around the place?" Jodie said, the pounding in her head increasing.

"Okay! We're going back to the Burgundy. We'll just park in a not so shady looking lot and walk over." Amanda said as she pulled away from the Borgata. She shook her head as she drove back down North Carolina Avenue, wanting to smack Doris for not being responsible for her part of the trip. Amanda knew why Jodie needed to go away this weekend, why they both needed a reason for fun and distractions. She parked in the small dirt lot next door to the hotel. The four of them got out of the car and stretched as Amanda circled her new cherry-red Ford Focus and checked for any damage. She turned in a full circle, her eyes searching the lot, then scrunched her face and looked at Jodie. "I don't want to leave my car here. I don't think it's safe."

"Well, I don't think the hotel is safe, but we don't have much of a choice," Jodie said as she threw her overnight bag over her shoulder and held her pocket book.

She looked up at the hotel and shuddered, the cloud over this dark weekend was getting darker. She started to walk to the entrance and tried to avoid the stares and hollers of the men standing across the street.

Ben followed Jodie's lead and threw his bag over his shoulder. Doris coughed to get Ben's attention. Looking over his shoulder, he asked, "What's up Doris?"

"Well, this bag is a little heavy for me. And I don't want to hurt myself at the beginning of the trip. Could you grab mine for me?" She asked as she batted her eyes and twisted a little from side to side. Ben hated it when women acted like they needed a man to do everything for them, but Doris then made a little pout with her lips, which caused Ben shift slightly in his pants. As annoying and desperate as she was, she was attractive, and he is only a man. Clearing his throat, he bent down to get the bag and walked straight into the hotel lobby.

"Thank you," Doris said with a small, sultry voice.

Ben saw Jodie standing at the decrepit counter as she waited for an employee to help her. She tapped her toe against the desk as she crossed her arm and leaned on the counter, her chipmunk cheeks partially covered by her dark hair. The rest of it was tossed over her shoulder and cascaded down to her mid back. He studied her hair, remembering how it felt to run his fingers through its thick smoothness, which forced the thought of Doris' pout out of his head. A pang of guilty struck him in the chest, knowing it was wrong to be attracted to one of Jodie's friends. He could have his pick of any girl, but her friends were off-limits. He would murder any friend of his if they tried anything with Jodie, same for her if she went along with it.

He approached her and placed his hand on her shoulder, causing her to jump from the unexpected contact and looked over at him. He smiled at her as he yelled over the counter. "Yo, a little help out here!"

Amanda and Doris walked into the hotel lobby when a small, rotund middle-eastern man with a white turban on his head waddled out of the back room. He reminded Amanda of the sultan from *Aladdin*.

"Yes, yes, I am right here. How can I help you?" The small man asked with a heavy accent as he hoisted himself on a stool. He adjusted his eyeglasses and looked at the four of them.

"Hi, we have two rooms—adjoining preferably, for the next three nights, reservations should be under Sullivan." Jodie said as she reached for her credit card and ID.

"Okay room 324 and 325. That will be six-hundred and fifty-five dollars please." The man said as he filled out the paper work.

The four of them took turns signing waivers and paying their part of the bill. Jodie grabbed one of the keys and turned around. It was the first time she got a good look at the lobby.

It was small with a white ceiling fan that was barely turning. The walls were a soft peach with mirrors covering one of them. The wall with the entrance was a large window, and there were very old, once white verticals covering the entirety of the space. The floor was covered in gray imitation tile linoleum. A small coarse welcome mat the color of dirt laid crooked in front of the door. The counter covered one corner of the room in a shell-colored Formica semi-circle, with yellowed pieces of paper hanging behind it, which included a hand-written sign stating checkout was at eleven.

Past the counter was a small pink elevator door. A Coca-Cola machine lit the far corner of the room, along with an old vending machine, whose food looked like it was older than they were. Jodie's eyes were drawn to another door that seemed to open to a darkened bar. She could make out a few bar stools and some bottles of alcohol lining the wall, but the rest was shrouded in shadow. She started to walk over to the door to get a better look when the small man stopped her.

"Miss, miss. You get to the room through the elevator."

She paused, her attention still pulled to the dark room, and unnerving feeling tickled the base of her neck. Still unable to make out the figures in the room, she pried her eyes away from the darkness and joined her friends at the elevator.

Three

Amanda and Ben loaded into the elevator together and barely fit, although the sign stated that the elevator held four. They looked from the sign to each other and began to laugh.

"There is no way four people fit in this little thing." Amanda said as she pushed herself into the corner.

"Well, there's one way to find out," Ben said as he made his way to the back. Doris entered next and placed herself directly in front of Ben, then pressed herself against him and yelled for Jodie to hurry. The doors began to close as Jodie stuck her left foot in. Ben reached past Doris and pried the door open, so she could get the rest of herself in there. Jodie's eyes grew wide as the door closed on her backside.

"Wow. This elevator waits for no one huh?" Ben said as he winked at Jodie. Jodie blushed as she averted her eyes down to her feet and tucked her hair behind her ear. Ben smiled, acknowledging one of her nervous ticks.

The door on the other side of the elevator opened, and they poured out into a mint green hallway. The old red signs on the wall had room numbers on them.

"Rooms 300 to 310 are this way." Doris said as she pointed to the left. "311 to 320 are this way." Amanda said, looking to the right.

"And we are 324 and 325." Jodie said, looking at her key. The girls shared a confused look as they searched for where their rooms would be in the halls.

Ben noticed an exit door straight ahead and walked to it. He opened the door, the fresh air doing little to clear the musty smell of the hallway. Seeing the rest of the rooms, he turned to the left and started walking. The girls shrugged as they watched the door close, then followed him.

The hotel had a motel setting in the back. White cement banisters lined the bright blue walls with large windows and deep blue doors. There was scaffolding lining the floor surrounding an empty in-ground pool with a puddle of mud floating in the deep end, the door of the chain-linked fence surrounding the scaffolding was unlocked and squeaked in the hot summer breeze.

The group made their way to the rooms as Ben opened his door and disappeared. Amanda took the key from Jodie, opened the other room, and stepped back. A musty odor filled her nostrils and dust particles danced in front of her. She sneezed and fanned her hand in front of her face, then reached for a light switch, but there was none. Slowly, she made her way into the room where she encountered two full size beds covered with a dark purple and pink flower pattern and brown velvet headboards attached to the wall on her right. The carpet, a thinning brown color with green leaves and purple and pink flowers, met the cracked plaster of the cream-colored walls. A small refrigerator was hugged between a green chair and the short brown dresser. An outdated large silver television sat on the other side of the dresser, next to a pink chair. The large mirror covered the wall and ran the length of the dresser, reflecting the depressing room. Amanda placed her bag on one of the beds and turned on the light between the two beds. A shaky Formica table served as the nightstand, where a telephone and an alarm clock sat.

Jodie walked in after Amanda turned on the light. Looking around in shock, Jodie mumbled, "What the fuck did we just get ourselves into?"

A knock on the adjoining door made Jodie jump. She opened the door to see Ben's stupid grin. "Nice place," he said as he walked into the room, "Did you see the bathroom yet? Doris is freaking out in there right now."

Doris' squeals were audible from the other room. She stood at the bathroom door way, wailing, "it's pink and green and dirty. I can't bathe in here!"

The bathroom was tiled in a maroon tile from the middle of the walls to the floor, where it collided with light pink tile. The top part of the wall and ceiling were light green. A radiator hung from the bottom of the wall and there was a dirty shower curtain hanging off the shower rod.

Doris walked into Amanda's room and threw herself on the other bed. She laid there and kicked her legs like a child having a temper tantrum. As she dramatically whimpered on the bed, Ben poked Jodie's lower back with his finger. He leaned his head up to her ear, his breath warm on her neck, "so sexy, where are you going to be sleeping?"

Frustrated, Jodie rolled her eyes at him. "I'm staying in here with Amanda."

Doris picked her head up from the bed, her whimpering ceasing immediately. "I guess that leaves me in your room, Ben." She wagged her eyebrows at him as she supported herself on her elbows.

"I hope you can behave yourself. You're twenty-six, act like an adult." Jodie said as she walked away from him.

"Hey, I can't help it sometimes." Ben said with a huge smile on his face.

"Can we go get dinner? I'm starving." Amanda asked as she walked over to the front door.

Doris jumped off the bed and ran out of the door, her excitement for food was palpable. Doris was a tiny thing, but she loved to eat, and could eat a five-course meal and still be hungry, yet she would not gain a pound. Jodie followed as Ben shut the door behind them. They opted to take the stairs, deciding it would be safer than attempting to all fit into the elevator again.

They headed towards the boardwalk, avoiding the locals that lined the street, who hollered at every woman that walked near them. Jodie stepped onto the boardwalk and welcomed the warm sea breeze enveloping her face. Her hair whipped around behind her as she shut her eyes and deeply inhaled. This is why she came here; to escape the everyday, to run away from her mundane job and to forget what this weekend was. She wanted to run away from her friends and into the waves. Happiness filled her soul as the setting sun glowed on her face. She walked to the edge of the sand, kicked off her flip-flops, and sunk her feet into the cooling sand and dug her toes in deeper. She loved the beach and the ocean. When she was a little girl, her mother would bring her to the beach once a week over summer break. She would go with her two best friends and they would build sand castles and jump over the little waves that collided with the sand. At the end of the day, they would sit at the edge of the surf and let the water rush over their legs while they dug in the sand with their little fingers until the sand crabs surfaced. But that was many years ago, a long time before the accident that ripped her apart.

Five years ago, when Jodie was eighteen, her best friend, Lisa Parker, died. Lisa, Amanda, and Jodie all met in girl scouts when they were entering elementary school. Lisa was as brazen as her hair was red. At their first meeting, Lisa grabbed a gummy worm out of Jodie's snack bag and put one end in her mouth.

"Hey! That was mine!" Jodie said as she tried to grab the worm back from Lisa. Lisa bit it in half, then took the remainder from her mouth and said, "Well you shared your snack so, I guess we are friends then." She then walked over to Amanda, gave her the other half of the worm, and said, "That girl told us to share this. She said that we will be friends forever if you eat it." Amanda looked over at Jodie, who watched the scene in confusion, then back at the red-headed girls with freckles and a mischievous smile. She eyed the gummy worm half and ate it from Lisa's fingers. Lisa put her arm around Amanda, approached Jodie with her other arm, and stated as they walked over to the reading area, "We are going to be best friends." And from that moment on the girls were inseparable.

That was until the accident—the accident that split them up forever. The memory flashed into Jodie's mind like a movie preview. She saw Lisa's smile, an empty liquor bottle, a letterman's jacket, taillights, a phone ringing, cop lights, and a casket.

"Yo, Rogers... Rogers...Jodie!" Jodie heard as she fell from the memory. Amanda ran up to Jodie and studied her face. "Are you okay?"

Jodie nodded her head and wiped at her eyes, unaware that she was crying. She forced a smile on her face, "I'm fine."

Amanda tilted her head and put her arm around Jodie. "I know, the beach reminds me of her too." Jodie nodded her head again and sniffled. "Food?"

Jodie shook her head. "No, if you don't mind, I want to just sit here for a while. You know, think."

"Gotcha. Do me a favor," Amanda said as she grabbed her shoulders, "don't get too depressed on me okay?"

Jodie nodded, forcing a smile to her best friend. Amanda nodded her head and put her forehead against Jodie's. "You know we came here this weekend for a reason. It's been five years; you know she would want us to be happy."

Amanda kissed her on the cheek and rubbed her arm. She turned around and headed to the edge of the sand. Jodie watched her run back over to Ben and Doris. They all waved at her and started to walk down the boardwalk.

Four

Jodie sat down on the sand, so the water would only hit her feet when the waves crashed. She closed her eyes and breathed slowly. She heard something to the right of her and looked over.

There were three little girls chasing after each other, one with a bucket on her head, another with a shovel held out in front of her. The third girl fell on the sand, laughing and kicking her legs in the air. The two girls helped the third one up and they walked over to the end of the water. The water ran over their little feet, the same way they ran over Jodie's. One of the girls pointed over at Jodie and whispered into the other girl's ear, who in turn, whispered to the third girl. The third girl looked at Jodie and waved. Jodie smiled, waved back, and looked out at the sunset across the water.

The three children sat down a few feet away from Jodie. The girl that sat next to her had long dark hair in two braided pigtails, brown eyes, and little bucked teeth. Her belly stretched out her pink one-piece bathing suit. The second girl wore a bright blue bathing suit. Her light brown hair was held back with a headband and her golden eyes shone like the sun as she sat down next to her friend. The third girl stared at Jodie with her brilliant green eyes. Jodie felt like the girl was staring into her soul. Through her fire-red hair a smile formed, spreading the spray of freckles on her nose and cheeks. She sat down, and the four of them looked out onto the water in silence.

After some time, the one with the red hair stood up, and her two friends looked down at the sand. She hugged the girl with the brown hair and whispered something to her. The girl nodded in response. She then hugged the girl with the dark hair and whispered in her ear as well. The girl with the braids nodded.

From her peripheral vision, Jodie saw the girl approach her. The girl patted her on the head and brushed her milky-white hand across Jodie's tanned face. Jodie sat there with her arms hugging her knees, not wanting to touch the random child. The girl whispered, "I miss you, Jodie."

Her voice sounded like a lullaby and her arms snaked around Jodie's neck. The moment felt like warm cocoa on a freezing winter's day. Overwhelmed by her senses, Jodie inhaled and smelled the pureness of the little girl, mixed with the scent of Lisa's perfume. "I have to go now." The little girl said as she loosened her arms. She turned to face the ocean, and silently walked into the water, submerging herself until all that stuck out of the water was the top of red hair floating behind her.

Jodie tried to yell out to the little girl to stop, tried to launch herself into the water, but she could not move, and her voice came out as a whisper. The little girl was gone before Jodie could blink, like she was never there. Paralyzed, she shifted to the left to see the girl with the brown hair stand and hold out her hand to the other girl, who limply accepted and stood. In a matter of a few breaths, the sadness left the girls faces and they were smiling as they had been just minutes before. Hand in hand, the little girls skipped off together to the far end of the beach. Jodie sat there, staring as they ran off, another set of footsteps running after them.

***

Ben walked to the edge of the boardwalk, balancing the gyros and sodas in his arms. He looked out to the beach and found Jodie. He paused before leaving the boardwalk, just taking her in. She looked so peaceful, sitting there staring into the distance. He saw her turn her head occasionally, but she was mainly looking off at the horizon. He had bought her dinner, knowing that she would be starving, and approached her slowly, not wanting to startle her.

Ben stopped short, startled by what he saw. Out of nowhere, Jodie's head jerked to the left and stare up at something. He watched her following something with her eyes and stare out at the water again. Her body jerked a little, as if she was stuck. After a pregnant pause, her head turned back to the left, and she stared off into the distance.

He walked over to her right side and looked down at her. "Hey."

"Oh, hey." She said, not looking up at him, but rather returning her gaze to the ocean.

"Anyone sitting here?" He asked as he began to lower himself to the sand. She hesitated for a moment, blinked a few times, and then shook her head. He grunted when he hit the ground and handed her a gyro.

"Oh, thanks. I'm starving." She said as she unwrapped the gyro and sunk her teeth into it.

"I figured," he said with a laugh, as he handed her a drink. "It's diet. I know you too well."

She smiled with a mouth full of food and took the drink from him. She was going to ask him for a napkin, but he took a few out of the pocket of his shorts and stuffed them into the crook of her elbow. She tried not to laugh with her mouth full of food as she acknowledged how well he knew her. She briefly looked to the left, where no footprints were to be found. The smile faded from her mouth, realizing there was a lot he did not know about her.

He saw the expression cast over her face and knew that there was something wrong, but she was trying to hide it. He nudged into her with his shoulder. "What were you staring at?"

She paused for a moment and shoved more food into her mouth. Buying herself some more time, she took a long sip of her soda and continued chewing. She could not tell him about the vision, or whatever it was, could she? Ben took another bite of his food and watched her. A piece of yogurt-covered onion hung from the corner of his mouth.

She racked her brain, thinking of something to say. "I, uh...", she began to say, but saw the food dangling on his face and started to laugh. She took one of the napkins from her elbow and wiped his chin. He locked eyes with her and she felt butterflies in her stomach return. She absolutely hated that he still had this effect on her. She coughed and looked down.

"Did I ever tell you about my friend, Lisa?" She asked him. He furrowed his brow, pretending to place the name. "Lisa Parker? I met her back daisies? Close with Amanda and me?"

Ben nodded his head as he took another bite of his food. Of course, he knew who Lisa was. He spent many nights letting Jodie cry on the phone or on his shoulder when she was having a weak moment. He knew all about Lisa.

"Well, this might sound weird, but I think I saw her."

Ben let the straw rest against his bottom lip as he looked over at her and absorbed the information. He knew that she had some issues when it came to Lisa; a few therapy sessions, some notebooks of thoughts, but never hallucinations.

"I know, it sounds crazy. It was just that there were these girls, and the red hair and..." she rambled until she realized that Ben was looking at her as if she belonged in a strait jacket. She shook her head. "I'm kidding, it's nothing. It's just the beach makes me think of her and I saw some little girls playing before. It's the anniversary of her death, she just on my mind, that's all."

Ben took a long sip of his soda and looked out to the water. He then looked around him, looking for the little girls playing, but he could not see any. The sand around her did not took unsettled, just the impression of his walking over. He returned his gaze to Jodie watching her dissect her gyro. Her fingers were covered with the tzatziki sauce and shreds of lettuce. She witnessed him studying her from the corner of her eye. Without a second thought, she wiped her fingers on his cheek.

A wide smile broke across his face as he grabbed a napkin and wiped the sauce off his cheek. He looked down at the soiled napkin and smeared the remanence onto her cheek. "Oh, it's on," she laughed, putting more sauce on her finger, stretching her arm back in his direction. Laughing, he grabbed onto her wrist, examining finger. He lowered his head to her hand, and put her finger in his mouth, slowly licking the sauce off. He swirled his tongue around her fingertip and kept his eyes locked on hers.

The butterflies she felt earlier suddenly felt hotter, falling deeper than her stomach. Her body reacted to him; he could see the lust drape over eyes. He took great pride in knowing that she wanted him, but he was a little surprised by how he was reacting.

He removed her finger from his mouth and rested his forehead against the top of her head. She sat still, save for her deep breathing. He inhaled deeply, and exhaled slowly, clearing his mind and trying to calm himself down. "Do you want to go back to the room?"

She slowly nodded her head. They stood up, brushing the sand off themselves. Ben took Jodie's hand, and led the way back up to the boardwalk. He stopped at a garbage can, letting go to collect her trash. He grabbed onto her hand again and started to head towards the hotel.

She stared down at his hand, unsure of what she was doing. She looked up at him, slowing down as he dragged her behind him. He looked back at her with one eyebrow raised.

"Um," she cleared her throat, "I want to go back to the room, because I, uh, don't feel well."

Five

Doris and Amanda sat outside a small pizza place attached to one of the many arcade halls lining the boardwalk. Amanda looked up to the sky and watched the seagulls dance above her head to a tune only they could hear. The sky's reddish hue seemed to fade away as the night sky began to dominate the heavens. The seagulls reminded her of angels floating overhead, minus the noise.

She looked across the table to find Doris stuffing a gigantic piece of barbeque chicken pizza in her mouth. The slice was larger than her head, but she had no problem devouring it. A smile formed on Doris' face as she struggled to chew and swallow her last bite.

Amanda looked down at her own slice and pushed it off to the side. It tasted like rubber, and the pepperoni slices were congealed with oil. She took a drink of her water and looked over to the basketball game. There was a tall man, about six foot three, with spiked blonde hair. His tanned calf muscles bulged out from the bottom of his khaki shorts. The hem of his navy-blue shirt just touched the top of his maroon boxer shorts when he arched up to shoot the ball. He turned his head to the dirty blonde-haired woman with a little boy hugging her leg. She caught a glimpse of his smile and she spit out her water.

"Whoa, Amanda! Are you ok?" Doris asked as she wiped her mouth with a napkin. Amanda stared at the man dribbling the basketball and shook her head.

"I can't believe it." She said as she tried to close the water bottle, not looking at what she was doing. She missed three times before Doris grabbed the water bottle from her and closed it herself. "Do you know who that is?" Amanda asked in a hushed squeal.

Doris looked over and studied the man. She shook her head. "Nope, but he has a nice ass."

"Oh my God! That's Pete." Amanda said, searching for some recognition in Doris' face. "Pete Erickson?" She asked when Doris failed to give her the acknowledgement she was looking for.

"I didn't go to school with you Amanda." Doris said as she chewed the remainder of her pizza. She reached for Amanda's plate and asked, "Can I have this?"

"Wow, I dated him back in our sophomore year of college. We were inseparable. That summer he went home to Connecticut and visited almost every weekend. Then junior year he never came back. His dorm room was empty. I tried to call him and message him, but he never responded." Amanda said, not taking her eyes off him.

"That was three years ago Amanda. Look, he has a wife and a kid." She said as she pulled a piece of pepperoni off the pizza.

"I have to say something, right?" Amanda asked, chewing nervously on her lower lip.

"I don't know about that, it's kind of awkward." Doris said, wiping pizza oil from the corner of her mouth with a crumpled napkin.

Amanda stood up and pulled her hair out of its ponytail. She shook her head and smoothed out her white tank top. "How do I look?" Amanda asked Doris as she adjusted the top of her jeans.

"You're really doing this?"

"Yes, how do I look?"

Doris gave her thumbs up and she took a drink from Amanda's water. Amanda nodded her head and walked over to Pete and his family. Doris sat there, watching Amanda try to be calm as she approached her former lover. She nodded her head and almost coughed up her water when Amanda tripped on a loose board.

What are you doing you idiot? Amanda asked herself as she crossed through a group of people, deciding what to do. *If he wanted to see you, he would have kept in touch.*

The little boy hanging on the woman's leg watched Amanda as she walked over. Amanda avoided the boy's stare and tapped Pete on the shoulder.

Pete turned his smiling face towards the tapping, his brown eyes twinkling with laughter. The twinkle in his eyes faded a little when he recognized Amanda, but he kept his smile intact. Amanda plastered her most brilliant smile on her face and stated, "Pete Erickson."

"Amanda Walker," he said as he nodded and rubbed the back of his neck, "It's been a long time." His eyes raked over Amanda and then nervously shifted over to the woman standing next to him. The little boy, who looked to be three years old, tugged on Amanda's pant leg. She looked down at him and smiled. The little boy waved up at her and whispered hello through his bowl-cut brown hair and sparkling brown eyes. Then he hid his face in the back of the woman's knee and giggled.

Amanda looked back up at Pete. She forgot how much taller he was than her. Her head just reached his shoulder. He shifted his feet a bit and dug his hands into his pockets. "So, um, how've you been?"

"Good, good," she said as she exaggerated her head nodding. "You know, graduated from New Paltz, of course after a very shocking and depressing junior year, which I'm sure you knew about. I took a year off after, worked a few temp jobs, and come fall I am attending LIU for my masters. But enough about me, you look like you've been busy." She said as she slightly nudged her head toward the woman and little boy.

Damn that felt good!

Pete's face went from shock to anger as she spoke. He laughed with a sneer before he started to speak. "Well, first off, congratulations on graduating. That's quite the accomplishment. See, I didn't get to graduate because my parents split up during that summer right before junior year. Yeah, and there wasn't enough money to send me back, so I enlisted in the Navy. My four years are almost up, and right now we are docked not too far from here. My *sister* drove here to visit me. You remember my sister, Andrea, don't you Amanda?"

Amanda's face fell, and she wanted to bury her head into the sand and have a wave crash over her and drag her out to sea. Amanda looked over at the woman and recognized that she was once the little fifteen-year-old girl that stayed up all night in Amanda's dorm room, giggling at the dirty texts her roommate showed them on her phone. "Hi Andrea," was all Amanda could choke out, accompanied by an abrupt wave.

"Hi, Amanda," she said smiling, "this is my son Andrew. He will be three in October." The little boy twirled in circles as he held his mother's hand. He fell, and he looked up at them. Noticing all the attention was on him, his bottom lip started to quiver, and tear brimmed his eyes.

Andrea picked Andrew up and said, "Ok my little actor, I think it is time for sleep." She looked up at Pete and smiled. "We are going to go back to the hotel room. Don't hurry back, unless *Peppa Pig* excites you."

Pete nodded and kissed Andrea on the top of the head. He rustled Andrew's hair and patted him on the butt. "It was nice to see you again, Amanda." Andrea said as she turned around.

The two of them watched Andrea until reached the door to the hotel. Pete and Amanda nervously looked over at one another. "Wow Pete, I'm so sorry. I had no idea. I just had this whole thing in my mind about you and what happened, and I just thought...," she said and then shook her head, "I mean, I'm sorry."

Pete smiled and nudged her with his arm. "I can't blame you. I never really gave you a reason for me leaving. But I must admit, I'm very impressed with the attitude you had going on there."

"Well, like I said, I had a lot of time to think of why you left and what you were doing all of these years."

"You know Mandy, I never stopped thinking about you. It broke my heart to not tell you what happened."

Hearing him call her Mandy brought back the memories of the happiest she had been since Lisa's death. She remembered the first time they met, in line at the cafeteria. He made a comment about the wet trays being more appetizing than the food sitting on them. She remembered their late-night study sessions for the petrifying pop quizzes in their trigonometry class, and then not going to class to spend the morning in bed together. They were in love back then. She looked at him, realizing that the man that stood next to her was no longer the same boy who ran out to get her coffee at three in the morning.

As if reading her mind, Pete started to reminisce. "Do you remember Professor Cowell, bald guy with bad breath?"

Amanda smiled and nodded her head. "World History, Seven AM. Turtle neck with the plaid vests. Always humming the theme song to *Knight Rider*."

"He was awful." Pete said as he started to laugh.

"Yeah, he was." Amanda said as she looked over to where she left Doris. An old man with a loaf of bread sat at the table, throwing it to the dancing seagulls. She looked around the boardwalk, but she could not find her. Pete's eyes followed Amanda's.

"Did you lose something?" He asked as he turned in a full circle.

"Someone. My friend, well my friend's friend. She was sitting at the table there." She said as she pointed to the old man.

"Well, we can look for her." Pete said as he offered Amanda his arm. Amanda shook her head and smiled. "You still have the charm."

He smiled cockily and started to walk. "So, what does this friend of a friend look like?"

Six

"Ben, this really isn't necessary, I'm fine, really." Jodie said as she walked into her hotel room and shut the door. She laid down on the bed and stared up at the ceiling. Ben walked through the adjoining doors and stood next to the bed and leaned over her with his arms crossed. He studied her prone figure, his eyes drifting from her shimmery pink-painted toenails the peered out from her black flip flops, up her partially tanned legs to her gray linen shorts, lingering briefly at the swell of her breast under a black t-shirt, and finally her unfocused brown eyes. He cleared his throat, causing her to shift her eyes from the ceiling to his and crossed her arms.

"You don't look well. You should stay here and rest."

"That is what I intended on doing. I don't need you here to baby sit me." She said as she raised her head slightly from the bed.

"How are you feeling? Are you sick? Was it the food? Or the car ride? You seemed okay when we first got here."

"No, I don't think it was the food. I think I'm just tired, I had a lot to do at work to prep for my vacation."

"But what if you need something? Or you want the TV channel changed. This piece of shit hotel doesn't have a remote. I'm staying." He said as he turned down the other bed. He grabbed her arm and lifted her up as she rolled her eyes. "Get changed."

"No. Seriously, I'm fine."

Ben walked over to the green chair with the luggage piled on top. He unzipped her overnight bag and dug through it.

"Give me a break, Ben." Jodie said as he took her pajamas out of her overnight bag and held them up. Jodie shook her head in protest.

Ben nodded his head and threw the pajamas at Jodie. The clothing hit against Jodie's stomach and landed on to the bed. She looked down at them and scowled. "Stop fighting me and get changed."

"You know, I came on this vacation to get away from my parents, thanks."

"Jodie, get changed."

"You can't tell me what to do. We aren't a *couple* anymore." Jodie said, emphasizing the word couple with finger quotation marks.

"Yeah, whose fault is that?" Ben asked as he propped himself against the dresser and crossed his arms. The moment on the beach feeling like a distant memory.

"Yours." she stated as she shot him a cold stare.

"Bullshit. It was yours." He said waving his hand at her, as though he was shooing the idea away.

"Oh, that is such garbage and you know it, mister I want to spend all my time playing poker with my friends." She said as she rolled her eyes.

"Oh yeah, okay miss I'm obsessed with my sorority that I cut time with my boyfriend to go to pledge events."

"Oh, let's talk about that. If I remember correctly, your poker game got cancelled, so you decided to spend some quality time with your girlfriend, who you knew had plans already. But since I never got to see you, I went to my event two hours late," Jodie said, hardly pausing for a breath.

"It's a sorority Jodie, grow up! You're in a cult!" He yelled, throwing his arms out at his sides. He hated that damn sorority. She was nothing like the other girls, she was intelligent, sweet, and innocent. From what he saw, the rest of them were like Doris, party girls who went from guy to guy without a care in the world. He always worried that something would happen to her when she was with that crowd, someone slipping something in her drink or taking things too far with her.

"You're addicted to gambling!"

"It's poker, not gambling. And I'm not addicted."

Jodie scoffed at his rationale. She understood that he was enrolled in a stressful cooking institute back in the day, and that he worked most nights at the restaurant, but she could not for the life of her understand why he would spend his free time with those idiots that he called friends, wasting hours and money for nothing. She always felt like an afterthought with him. And it only got worse when he graduated and began working as a sous chef full time.

"See, this," Jodie said as she moved her finger in a circle between them, "is why we don't work."

She grabbed her pajamas and stormed into the bathroom, slamming the door behind her. She sighed and looked up at the ceiling, then pressed her ear against the door, half expecting him to follow her. All she heard was silence. She figured that he left, and it was better that he did. Her headache worsened from the yelling match. She unbuttoned her shorts and let them fall to the floor, kicking them away from her feet. She put on her gray sweat shorts and folded her shorts, replaying the argument in her head. *Why do I still bother with him?* She asked herself as she pulled her shirt off and removed her bra. She sniffed her armpits quickly and put a little more deodorant on. She checked her teeth in the mirror and then rinsed her mouth with mouthwash. She pulled the black tank top over her head and turned to the side. The black did not do much to hide her small belly. She sucked in a little and hit her stomach.

Running her fingers through her hair, she opened the bathroom door and walked out. Expecting the room to be empty, she found Ben laying in the other bed, television on, with an open bottle of water on the night table for her. His floppy light brown hair fell in front of his eyes as he watched the television as he laid on his right side with his back towards her.

His white shirt clung to his muscles as his midnight blue boxers hung around his waist and thighs. Jodie tried to look away from him, but she was like a moth drawn to light. He felt her eyes on him and he smiled. He looked over his shoulder and watched her walk to the middle of the room. Her black tank top revealed almost too much of her for his comfort.

"Why don't you go play poker or something?" Jodie said as she grabbed the bottle of water.

He nudged his head over to the television without taking his eyes off her. "Next best thing." She looked over and saw that there was a poker marathon on ESPN.

"A shitty place like this and we get ESPN." She said as she shook her head and took a drink of water. She looked over to the wall, trying to avoid eye contact with him. He sat there with a smug look on his face, just as he did after every fight. She refused to be the first one to apologize, since she always was.

Jodie's awkwardness subsided when Ben's hotel room door flung open. Doris walked in, throwing her bag on the bed. She saw Jodie standing in the middle of the room and walked over to her. "Jode, this place sucks. Can we go do something?"

Jodie looked over at her, mid drink. She held up a bottle of aspirin. Doris looked over at Ben lying on the bed. "Another headache?"

Ben nodded his head. Doris looked at Jodie, then Ben, and then Jodie again. She could feel the tension in the room and knew that she entered in the middle of something. "Am I interrupting something?"

Jodie almost spit out her water. "Oh God no! I was just telling him to go play cards. And it seems to be the weirdest thing, now that I want him to leave me alone and play cards, he doesn't want to. I just want to lie down for a while."

The two girls looked over at Ben. He sat there, trying to ignore their stares. His blood was still boiling from the previous fifteen minutes. Doris cleared her throat, catching Ben's attention. Doris beckoned him with her finger as he grunted and began to get up from the bed.

"You know what, that is a great idea. I think I will go play some poker, since I'm addicted and all. You better get some sleep." Ben said as he stood up and put his shorts on.

Doris jumped up and clapped, glad to know that this trip was not a mistake. She originally did not want to go on the weekend excursion, but she figured that if there were casinos and alcohol, there would be fun. The addition of Ben did not hurt either. She ran into the other room and yelled back to Ben, "One minute! I just want to freshen up."

Ben looked over at Jodie, who was lying on the bed with her arm draped over her eyes. He could not help the mix of feelings he had whenever he thought of her. She made him so angry, always pushing his buttons. He swore that she enjoyed fighting with him, why else would anyone act the way she did. Ben looked around the room, unsure if he should say something to her. One minute turned into five minutes and Doris finally stepped into Jodie's room wearing an extremely short denim skirt and a red halter-top that pushed her breasts so far together; she looked could have defecated out of her shirt. She flung her long blonde hair over her shoulder and said, "You ready to go, hottie?"

Jodie lifted her arm a little, so she could see Doris. She shifted her eyes to Ben's face, and chuckled. Ben looked like a cartoon with his eyes bulging from his head. Doris turned around in a circle, modeling her strategically planned outfit. Jodie was used to seeing Doris like this, it was her typical good time attire. It meant either she was not coming home or she was not coming home alone.

Ben followed Doris out of the door and turned to take one last look at Jodie. Jodie sat up a little and looked at him. He felt a pang of guilt leaving her without resolving anything, but they were in Atlantic City and he did have a lot of money burning a hole in his pocket.

He pointed at his two eyes and then pointed at her. Jodie rolled her eyes and turned onto her side as he shut the door.

***

Jodie was asleep for about an hour when she heard the hotel door open. She rolled over and looked at the door, hoping to see Ben.

"Jode? Jode... are you awake?" Amanda whispered as she shut the door. She tip-toed over to the bed and turned the light on.

Jodie shielded her eyes with her arm and mumbled, "Huh? What's up, Amanda?"

"Are you awake?" Amanda repeated as she sat down on the bed.

Jodie shook her head and rolled over, pulling the covers over her head. Amanda shook her head and giggled, freezing Jodie in place when she heard it. It was not Amanda's giggle; it reminded her of Lisa. Amanda pulled the covers off Jodie and pulled her arm to get her out of bed.

"Come on, Jode, I have to show you something." She walked over to the foot of the bed and picked up Jodie's flip-flops as Jodie studied her movements. Amanda felt Jodie's eyes on her and looked over. "What, Jode?"

"It is you, right?" She asked as she stood up and slid her feet into her sandals. Amanda paused and looked at Jodie, as if she had another head sprouting from her neck.

"No Jodie, it's the boogie man. Who else would it be? What is with you? Let's go." Amanda said as she walked to the door and opened it. Jodie looked outside, unsure if she wanted to leave. "Come on!" Amanda yelled as she grabbed Jodie's arm and pulled her out of the room.

"Where have you been? I haven't seen you since the beach." Jodie asked, realizing that her friend disappeared for the remainder of the evening. She power walked to keep up with Amanda, who seemed to have an unlimited amount of energy pouring out of her. Amanda turned the corner and ran down the stairs.

"Jode, come on. I need to show you something." She yelled up the stairs, ignoring the question. Jodie followed her down three flights of stairs until they were at the door of the lobby. Amanda put her hand on the doorknob and put her finger to her lips, gesturing to be quiet. She slowly opened the door and crouched on the floor. Jodie, unsure of what her friend was doing, followed her lead.

They made their way across the lobby without the little man on the bench seeing them. Amanda dove into the darkened door that Jodie earlier believed led to a bar. She followed, trying to make things out in the dark. She was right; it was a bar. She held on to the bar stools for balance as she crouched through the room. Amanda waved her over to a small black leather couch. They both kneeled on the couch and peeked their eyes over the top.

Behind the couch, Jodie saw an exact replica of Lisa's room. Jodie shook her head and looked over at Amanda, who smiled at her and nudged her head forward. She could not believe her eyes; the lavender walls were still covered posters of boy bands. The fluffy white bed spread, which always reminded Jodie of a cloud, was lined with the stuffed animals that Joe Rappaport won for her out of the claw machines at the bowling alley. She heard muted talking coming from the side.

Jodie lowered her head down as the bedroom door with the slightly faded Imagine Dragons poster swung open. She watched in amazement as she saw Lisa walk in with her red curls piled on top of her head. She had on a green facemask and an oversized Rangers jersey with bright white socks. She turned around and faced the door talking to whoever was behind it. Jodie watched a sixteen-year-old Amanda walked in, wearing a blue and white-striped tank top and matching pajama pants. Her hair was past her waist, hanging in a single braid down her back. She was carrying a huge bowl of popcorn and three dvds under her arm. Lisa yelled out, "Jode, let's go slow poke!"

Jodie jumped when she heard her name. Amanda put her hand on Jodie's shoulder and shook her head. Jodie looked back to the girls and saw herself when she was sixteen. She came walking in with cotton balls between her toes and an oversized purple tee shirt. Her dark hair was short, hanging right below her neck in two little pigtails. Her eyebrows were bushier than she remembered. She closed the door behind her and sat down on the pile of pillows on the floor with her friends.

"Ladies, tomorrow is the big night," Lisa began to say as she took a box out from under her bed. "Who is with me?"

Amanda shot her hand up in the air and gave Lisa a high five. Jodie looked down to the floor. The other girls shot her a look and Lisa stood up. She spread her stance and placed her hands on her hips.

"Now Jodie, tomorrow night will be the perfect night. We'll be at Tiffany Henson's house, no parents, lots of boys."

"And, Lisa has something in the box for us." Amanda said with a huge smile on her face. Lisa sat back down and opened the box. She held a bottle of Vodka in one hand and a row of condoms in the other. Amanda and Lisa threw their legs up in the air and kicked as they squealed with delight.

Jodie remembered this scene in front of her all too well. It was the night before Lisa lost her virginity to Joe Rappaport. They all slept over Lisa's house that night, preparing to look glamorous for the party. It was the night that Jodie believed began the chain of events that led to Lisa's death. Jodie sat there and watched as she mouthed the words her sixteen-year-old self said out loud.

"I'm not ready for that yet. The first person I sleep with is the man I am going to marry."

The other girls looked at each other and then continued their squealing. Jodie sat there shaking her head. Lisa put her hand on her shoulder and said, "Well then Jodie, when do you plan on getting married?"

"When I'm twenty-three." She said matter-of-factly. Amanda sat up and looked at Jodie. Amanda and Lisa shared a look and faced Jodie again.

"Okay, Jode. Tell you what. You wait until twenty-three. And if you don't have sex by then, I'm coming after you!" Lisa said before she busted out laughing.

Jodie nodded her head, "Fine. And we will be happy together. Just you wait."

"What if he cheats on you, Jode?" Amanda said as she tried to cover her smile with a serious scowl.

"He wouldn't. But if he did, I would seriously hurt whoever seduced him." Jodie said as place the DVD into the player and started the movie, *Pitch Perfect*.

"Would you kill her?" Lisa asked ten minutes into the movie.

"Who, Anna Kendrick?" Amanda asked with a mouthful of popcorn. "No idiot, the seducer. Would you kill her, Jode?" Lisa asked again.

Jodie looked up at Lisa and shrugged her shoulders as she shooed her away with her hand.

Darkness fell over the bedroom, and all that Jodie could make out was the silhouettes of the girls and the glow of the television. She inhaled deeply and shut her eyes. She felt Amanda's hand on her arm.

"Twenty-three, Jode."

Jodie opened her eyes and looked at Amanda. Amanda's face morphed into Lisa's sixteen-year-old face. Jodie's eyes grew huge as Lisa said, "Twenty-three. . . I'm coming for you, Jode."

***

The grip on her arm tightened and shook her. Jodie jumped up to find Ben staring at her, the light on the nightstand was on and the other bed was undone. Ben stood over her, petting her head.

"Jodie are you okay?" He asked her as she threw her legs over the side of bed. She tried desperately to catch her breath, but she felt like all the oxygen was sucked from the room. Ben sat next to her and rubbed her back. Her eyes darted back and forth as she looked around the room.

"Where is Amanda?"

"Amanda?" Ben asked as he looked around the room. "I haven't seen her since dinner. Why?"

"When did you get back here?" She asked as she jerked back from him. Ben dropped his arm.

"Around twelve-thirty. I was worried about you."

"Did I leave the room?"

"Urn, I don't think so."

"What time is it?"

"About three o'clock. What is wrong, Jodie?" He asked as he gently placed his hand on her back.

"Nothing. Bad dream." She said as she shook her head. The truth was she was scared out of her mind. In all these years, she never had such a vivid dream about Lisa.

I went through therapy for this, I shouldn't have these dreams anymore. She thought as she hugged herself.

"Maybe you should just lay down." Ben said as he started to stand up. Jodie's hand flew out like a reflex and grabbed his shirt.

"Can you lay with me?" She asked, her eyes wide with fear.

He slowly nodded as he sat back down on the bed. She laid down on the edge of the bed. Ben climbed over her and lay down next to her. They laid there, not touching, for about fifteen minutes.

The vividness of the dream haunted Jodie as she stared up at the ceiling. Something felt off, she could feel it in her chest, the dream was completely different than the ones she had after Lisa's death. The old dreams felt as if Lisa was just coming to visit, this one felt sinister. As if Lisa was reaching out from the other side and actually made contact. She felt as though something she buried deep inside years ago was unlocked, old memories and new sensations flooding through her system simultaneously.

A level of unease settled into her bones as she felt herself fighting off an unfamiliar essence. The top of her spine tingled and the sense of dread rushed through the veins in her body, slowly spreading down her spine, through her limbs, and out of her extremities. The moment passed with little fanfare, but a strange sensation of cold and heat fluctuated through her as she tried to focus on her surroundings.

Ben reached over her to turn off the lamp. His chest brushed against hers as he turned off the light. Jodie placed her hand against his stomach, her touch surprising him. He froze for a moment and looked down at her. She stared up at him, eyes filled with lust, as she moved her hand under his shirt and splayed her had on his stomach for a moment. He slowly put his hand against her neck and rubbed his thumb against her cheek. He watched as she reacted to his touch, slightly biting on her lower lip, and felt electricity flow through his body. He lowered his face to hers and kissed her. She pushed her body against his, her hands clasped his face, and wrapped her left leg around him. Her hand traced down his body to the elastic of his boxers for a moment and then pulled it down.

He looked down at her, knowing that she never wanted to do this before. He sat back for a moment, putting some space between them, trying to straighten out his thoughts. She sat up and removed her tank top. He stared at her for a moment, "Jode, I, uh" he stammered. She nodded her head and pulled him down on top of her.

***

Sunlight flooded into the room from under the curtains. Ben placed light kisses along Jodie's shoulder and neck holding her tightly against him, replaying the moment he desperately wanted and patiently waited for since he met her years ago. Jodie kissed his hand, taking comfort in the warmth of his embrace, and continued to stare at the light. She had just lost her virginity in the dirtiest hotel room she had ever seen, and all she could hear in her head was "Twenty-three."

Seven

Doris sat at a small bar on the far wall of the poker room Ben had chosen. She placed her chin on her hand and re-crossed her legs, shaking her sandal against the bar and studying at the ceiling. She knew every nook and cranny of that section of the gold covered ceiling; she had been staring at it on and off since Ben left. She looked down at her watch and realized that he left over an hour and a half ago.

What is the deal with these guys? All they want to do is sit at those stupid tables and play poker. And why the hell did Ben leave me here alone... fucking Jodie. She thought as she scanned the room. The men in the room, all different ages, were completely consumed in the poker games. *I'd probably get more attention at a gay bar.* A smile formed on her face and she returned her gaze to the bar. An older man was staring at her with a towel thrown over his shoulder. He wore a crisp white shirt with black buttons running down the middle. The black bowtie and vest were a stark contrast to the shirt. His shaved head shone from the dim lighting of the bar. He smiled and winked his bright blue eye as he walked over to her.

"You know, that's the first time I've seen you smile since you planted yourself there over a half an hour ago." He reached over the bar and removed the martini glass from her semi-closed hand, purposely brushing his fingers against her. Doris liked him immediately; just bold enough, and he was the only man paying any attention to her.

"Let me guess, apple martini?" He asked as he turned his back.

"You're good." Doris said as she tossed her hair. He looked back at her and she gave him a seductive smile.

"Yes, I am," he confirmed as he poured the martini into the chilled glass.

He returned to Doris, ignoring the overly done-up older woman, who frantically waved her hand trying to get his attention. Her bra strap slipped down over her saggy-skinned arm and her wrinkly breast popped over the top of her shirt as she leaned onto the bar. The man shook his head slightly as he delivered the drink, allowing his female counterpart to handle the desperate woman in the middle of the bar.

"Why thank you," Doris said as she looked at the bright red name tag, "Charlie."

He smiled and extended his hand. "You are welcome..." he said, waiting for her name.

"Doris."

"Doris. And where would you be from Doris?" He asked, not letting go of her hand.

"Long Island. Well, Huntington to be exact."

"Well Doris from Huntington, it is a pleasure to meet you." He kissed her hand and winked before he turned to help another customer.

Within five minutes, Doris pushed her empty glass towards the edge of the bar, signaling her need for another drink. The female bartender went to grab the glass, but Charlie stopped, "I've got this one, Dina."

Doris smiled as Dina walked to the other end of the bar. As he mixed her drink, Charlie initiated another conversation. "So, are you meeting someone here?"

Doris sighed, propping her chin on her hand, and sinking into the position. "No, I came here with someone, but he ditched me."

"Boyfriend?" He asked, raising an eyebrow.

"It's… complicated," she said, looking up for a moment. "We are totally into each other, but we are being cock-blocked by his ex. She's a nuisance."

Doris received her drink and slowly sipped it, raising the glass from her mouth, her body still slouched. Her lips were loosening with every drink she consumed.

"And get this one Charlie, she crashed our getaway this weekend. Can you believe it? Her and her friend had to tag along. And she demanded adjoining rooms. Like, get off my dick, bitch, move on!"

Charlie chuckled and shook his head, "Well, he's an idiot. And she is obviously threatened by you, but let's be honest, who wouldn't be." He smiled as he pushed himself away from the counter and helped a couple a few seats away.

Doris sat there for another half hour, feeling more confident and aroused by the minute. Charlie looked over at her seductively as he spoke with the other customers. Doris knew exactly what, and whom she would be doing tonight.

"So, Charlie, tell me, how old are you?" She asked when he delivered her sixth martini.

He stood up straight and smiled. "Way older than you, sweetheart."

Doris nodded her head as she took a sip of her drink. "I doubt that."

"I'm thirty-eight."

Doris took another sip of her drink. She had just turned twenty-four a few weeks ago. "You're not that much older, I just turned thirty-three," she responded with a twinkle in her eye.

"Thirty-three huh? I don't have to check your ID, do I?" He asked as he leaned over the counter.

Doris smiled and replied. "Age is just a number, and they say you are only as old as you feel. Tonight, I am feeling thirty-three." She winked and then downed the last of her drink.

He raised his eyebrows and nodded his head. "When you are right, you are right."

He leaned over the bar, his mouth mere inches from her ear, and whispered, "I get off in twenty minutes."

She smiled and whispered back, "Then I should be getting off in thirty."

***

Doris stood in front of the employee entrance, pacing back and forth then leaning into the wall for support. She could not remember how many drinks she had while she was sitting at the bar. Charlie kept handing them to her, she didn't pay for one. She paused against the wall and let the room spin around her.

The black door with the employees only sign opened, and Charlie's head poked out. He looked over at Doris and waved her over. She stumbled over to the door took a moment to focus on his bright blue eyes. They were stunning, an unique ice-cold blue.

He smiled and touched her long hair. "Listen. There is a whole bunch of people in here. I know somewhere else we can go, for more privacy."

Doris nodded and tried to force a serious look on her face. Charlie pulled her against him and whispered in her ear, "I can't wait to fuck you." He bit her ear lobe and crossed the hallway to a small door in the corner. Doris followed him, trying to keep her balance as she walked. He opened the door and let her in first.

She looked around and saw bright white walls and a tiled floor. A line of chrome sinks lined a wall under a long mirror. She could make out a few solid oak doors to one side. He opened one of the doors and stepped in. She followed him in and saw a white porcelain toilet in the corner. *Classy,* she thought as he shut the door behind her. *Not the worst place I've done it in.*

She turned to him and pushed him up against the wall. It was a good thing he chose the handy-capped stall. She ran her hands down his washboard stomach and undid his pants as she dropped to her knees. His moaning filled the bathroom as she took him in her mouth.

Right before he was about to finish, she stopped and stood up. She pushed him onto the toilet and straddled him. He pushed her skirt up and slid into her. Doris gripped the metal bar in one hand and his shoulder in the other, trying to keep her balance as she ground her hips into him. She let go of the bar and tried to grab onto the tiled wall in front of her, but it was too smooth and slippery for her to grip. She grabbed onto Charlie's shirt as she climaxed, and then everything went black. Charlie watched her neck go limp, she swayed back, and then she slipped off his lap when he released her waist.

Charlie stood up and pulled his pants back on after she hit the floor. He looked down at her and nudged her side with his foot; she was out cold. He knelt and checked if she was breathing. Her breath was slow and steady. He studied her face and traced her jaw line with his finger. Her reddish lips were swollen from kissing. He bent his face and licked them, pushing his tongue between her lips.

He then trailed his finger from her cheek to her neck and then to the top of her red halter. He pulled one side of it down and sucked at her nipple. He felt himself go hard again. He put his hand under her skirt explored. When he was ready, he played with himself and finished on her face.

Charlie looked back at her when he opened the stall door. He smiled to himself and walked out of the bathroom, leaving her sprawled out on the floor.

***

Doris' eyes fluttered for a few moments as her eyes focused on the ceiling. *What the hell? Where am I?* She asked herself as she held her head. She sat up to find a toilet bowl staring her in the face. Lifting herself up by the handicap bar, she pulled her skirt down and walked out of the stall. She looked at her surroundings, then paused when she saw her face in the mirror, Charlie's remnants drying on her cheek. She began to heave and threw up in the sink on which she was supporting herself. She washed her face, letting the cool water remove the souvenir of the night and rinsed the sink out. She stumbled out of the casino and headed back to the Burgundy Inn. The night sky was beginning to dissipate into morning. She checked at her phone and saw that it was five o'clock.

Doris quietly opened her hotel room door, carefully trying not to wake everyone. She shut the door behind her and pressed her back against it. She kicked off her sandals and started to walk to the adjoining door but stopped short when she heard moaning. Peaking her head into the room, she saw Ben's white, muscular rear straining and slowly moving at a rhythmic pace. Jodie's thighs hugged his waist as her hands clung to his back.

A wave of nausea crashed over Doris. She ran into the bathroom and threw up every apple martini she consumed that night. She passed out hugging a towel, with her head hanging in the toilet.

Eight

Amanda waited at the edge of the boardwalk as Pete ran to his car. She hugged herself for warmth. The midnight breeze drastically dropped from the ninety-six degrees of the afternoon and early evening. She examined the sky, staring at the diamonds shining on the dark blue velvet of the night. There was a romantic feeling in the air that reached deep down into her bones.

Fate brought her on this trip. Not Jodie's need for an escape, or Ben's poker addiction, or the anniversary of her friend's death. Someone wanted her to come here. Something dragged her to Atlantic City on this specific weekend for this specific reason. Her reason came walking up with a few blankets in one arm and a lantern in the other. Amanda's soul smiled when she saw him approach her. It was her destiny to be here.

"Shall we?" He asked as he headed to the beach. Amanda nodded her head and followed him, kicking off her sandals when she reached the sand.

Pete walked over to the edge of a dune and laid out a blanket. He signaled for Amanda to sit down and wrapped another blanket around her shoulders. She snuggled into the warmth of the blanket and watched Pete as he turned on the lantern. The dim glow of the lantern highlighted his chiseled jaw line. His hair had a golden glow to it, but his brown eyes looked darker, more intense and alluring.

Pete caught Amanda staring at him and smiled. Her face turned a shade of pink as she shifted her gaze to her hands. She looked back up at him and smiled nervously, the act pulling at his heart. He leaned over and gently kissed her cheek. "This is really nice," he said as he pulled another blanket over his shoulders.

Amanda nodded her head and changed the subject. "So, Pete, what happened with your sister?"

"Well, it happened in my first year of the naval academy. I received an email from her once a week. It was probably early January when she wrote to me telling me that she was pregnant. The father was some guy she met at a sweet sixteen party or something. I think he worked at the country club it was at or something. I never met him.

"She kept it a secret for as long as she could, but once she was about five months into the pregnancy, my parents found out and all hell broke loose in both Erickson households. She moved in with my father, because my mother found comfort in the liquor cabinet. She never saw the father of the baby again, but she heard that he was arrested for statutory rape. Freaking bastard. If I ever met him, I would kill him."

Amanda sat there watching a mix of emotions dance across Pete's face as he unfolded the story. He looked over at her and smiled. "At least I got the cutest nephew out of it."

Amanda nodded her head. He really had changed since the last time she saw him. She was not sure if it was the Navy that made him harder, or everything life had threw at him.

"Tell me Mandy, any men in your present?"

Amanda shook her head and laughed. She had not been able to have a serious relationship since her junior year of college. "No. There haven't been many in the past either."

"Why? You are a beautiful girl. I can't imagine men not throwing themselves at you." Pete looked out to the ocean and watched the waves as he waited for an answer.

Amanda wanted to smack him upside the head and yell at him that it was his fault. Instead, she started talking about a few of her bombing relationships.

"Well, there was a guy named Mike. I met him at a coffee shop in my senior year. We dated for a couple months. It was ok, until he had to be right about *everything*. Then there was Keith, I met him at my first temp job. He was one of those muscle heads, totally not my type. I don't know. There were a few others, but nothing great." She said as she shrugged her shoulders.

"But yes, you are right, I still have all those fuck boys pretty much throwing themselves at me. Just like back in the day." Amanda said as she started laughing. "What about you?"

Pete nodded his head and smiled. "Yeah, I've got all those fuck boys throwing themselves at me too."

Amanda busted out laughing, but Pete looked up at her without a smile. Amanda calmed herself down while she watched him look down at the sand and draw circles in it. Amanda touched his shoulder, causing him to look up at her and say, "Listen Mandy, I need to tell you something."

Amanda sat up a little straighter. "Um, I don't know how to tell you this. Actually, I haven't told anyone yet, but um, I'm gay."

Amanda paused, a thoughtful look settling on her face. She cracked the smile she was trying to hide and pushed his arm. "You're a nut."

Pete started laughing and pushed her back. After a few moments of laughter Pete stopped laughing. "Seriously though Mandy, I am gay."

Amanda looked up at him and stopped laughing as well. "What are you talking about, Pete? You're not gay."

Pete nodded his head. "Well, I wasn't back then, I mean, with you, I didn't know."

Amanda shook her head in disbelief "What are you talking about? We had something, I mean, we were in love... we made love. How the hell are you gay?" Confusion setting in as her voice grew in intensity.

"Mandy, it had nothing to do with you. Seriously, I realized it about two years ago. I was docked in Virginia and I met this guy, Pat. He had the most stunning blue eyes that I had ever seen. We had a few drinks, and things kind of happened. Mandy, I think I am in love with him."

Amanda stood up and stared him down. "I can't believe it. Why would you tell me this?"

"Because I love you."

"You love me? You love *me*? You haven't even seen me in years!" She yelled. "You love me, but then you love Pat. Pat the gay guy with the blue eyes that you had a magical evening with in Virginia!"

"Mandy, wait..." Pete said as he stood up.

"Fuck you!" Amanda yelled. She turned and ran to the boardwalk. She spun to face him and gave him the finger.

***

Amanda wandered the boardwalk for a while, not wanting to be around people. There were so many thoughts running through her head. She played back her memories of their relationship, trying to remember if there was something that she overlooked. Maybe there were clues. Maybe it was her fault, maybe she did something wrong.

She finally decided to head back to the hotel, she was physically and emotionally drained. She passed a parking lot in route and saw Pete from the corner of her eye. He was packing his blankets into the trunk of his car. She watched him from the end of the lot, pulling the blanket from off her shoulders and began to fold it, her feet pressing against the gravel lightly as she approached his car.

He turned his head and stared at her as she held out the blanket and gave him a half smile. He took the blanket from her and focused on the trunk. He was extremely quiet as tears fell from his eyes, landing on the blankets. Amanda's heart broke for him and she hugged him as tight as possible. She knew that no matter how hard everything was for her, they were ten times worse for him. He buried his head in her neck and began to sob.

Nine

The water pelting against Jodie's skin did nothing to wash away the memories of last night. Lisa's face was burned into the back of her mind as the words she had spoke echoed in her head, the memory of that party replaying in a loop. The dull throb between her legs reminding her of something lost that she could never regain, but she was so consumed with her memoires, she could not begin to process her feelings or relationship with Ben. She placed her palms against the wall of the shower and let the water beat on her face, wishing the water could clear her mind.

She lost herself in her thoughts, remembering the beginning of that party: the pine green door with the half-moon window at the top, the loud music vibrating through her veins, the smile on Lisa's face when she saw Joe Rappaport standing by the stairs. *Why did I let her go with him?* She thought to herself as lifted her face to the showerhead.

That party was the catalyst for Lisa's demise. It was the beginning of her two-year secret relationship with mister popular. He wanted to remain on the market, as he told Lisa, and she went along with it because she was infatuated. She grew more distant over those two years, colder, and more dependent on his approval. She remembered how Joe approached Lisa, whispering into her ear, Lisa's head nodding eagerly as they walked up the grand staircase of Joe's sprawling home by the Great South Bay in Brightwaters.

Had she known what he was doing to Lisa, or at least what she strongly speculated, she would have done more to stop it. The coroner's office was unable to determine the exact time she received all the bruises, but there were old ones and fresh ones when they found her. If Lisa hadn't been so distant for that two-year span, Jodie would not have been so excited to go with her best friends to that graduation party Lisa invited her to. She would not have caved into drinking with the rest of her classmates, wanting to experience the feeling of being a carefree teenager celebrating the end of an era. She would have never stepped foot onto the Rappaport's beautiful multi-million-dollar property again.

Lost in her thoughts, she did not hear the door to the bathroom open. Ben walked in fully naked and closed the door behind him. Pulling back the curtain, he stared at Jodie, smiling to himself, still amazed that he slept with her. They had been involved with each other for years, but she never allowed them to go all the way. He stepped in and possessed her in his arms.

Jodie's eyes flew open as she turned around to see what grabbed her. Ben gave her a lazy smile with half closed eyes. He kissed her forehead and snuggled into her shoulder. She pushed away and turned to face the showerhead again.

"What are you doing in here?" Jodie asked as she grabbed the washcloth and started scrubbing her arm.

"It's too early to be out of bed. I've come to drag you back." He said as he tickled the base of her spine with his finger.

"It's almost eight, Ben. We overslept."

"We didn't sleep much last night." He said as he moved his finger up her spine. Her body reacted against her will. She wanted to be left alone. She needed to think about what happened. Ben's hand cupped one of her breasts as the other slid between her legs. She melted into him, allowing the feelings of ecstasy to build and the thoughts of Lisa to subside to her desire for Ben. She wiggled in his grasp, then turned around to kiss him.

She pressed herself against him, wanting him again, felling a little more clear headed. He pulled her leg up around his waist and entered her. Jodie held onto Ben's shoulders, relishing in the sensations new to her body. He kissed her neck and nipped at her ear, her eyes closing, her mind focusing on him. Her pulse raced as she grew closer to her climax. Suddenly, Lisa's pale, dead face flashed into her head, her eyes flew open as she panicked and pushed Ben away from her. She evacuated the shower and hastily adorned a towel.

"Jodie, what the fuck?" Ben yelled out in frustration, looking from his abandoned erection to the flung open bathroom door. He turned off the shower, wrapped a towel around his waist, and followed her as she ran into the hotel room. She collapsed on to the bed and grabbed her cell phone. She searched for the one contact in her phone that she swore she would never use again, her therapist. She tried to dial number, but her phone rang in her hands, the caller id unknown.

The ringing startling her, she began to cry as she answered the phone, no longer able to hold the tears back. "Hello?"

"Jode?"

She heard Lisa's voice on the other end, taunting her. She could feel the hysteria beginning, the shallow breathing making it hard for her to respond. "What do you want from me, leave me alone!" Jodie screamed into the phone.

"Jodie, can you hear me? It's Amanda."

Ben sat down on the bed across from her cautiously, unsure what to do. She looked like a cornered animal, scared and on the defensive. He witnessed her breathing normalize a bit, the wild look in her eyes receding.

Jodie calmed herself down a bit. "Amanda?"

"What? Yeah, it's me Jode. Sorry, my phone died. Listen, I can't hear too well. Meet me at the main entrance of the boardwalk by the Burgundy in half an hour. Bring Ben, Doris, and a portable charger. I have a surprise for you."

"Amanda, I have to talk to you." Jodie said in a strained whisper. Her muscles tense to the point of snapping.

"Jode, what? You're breaking up. Half an hour." Amanda said before she hung up the phone.

Jodie sat on the edge of the bed, hunched over with the phone in her hand. Ben reached out and gently touched her knee.

"Jodie, what is going on?"

She looked up and wiped at her eyes. "Nothing, I'm just an emotional mess right now."

"Does it have to do with Lisa? I know this weekend is a tough one for you." He asked as he sat up and crossed his arms.

His words struck a chord in her that she could not explain. She could not let him or anyone know what she saw last night, they would put her on medicine that did not make her feel like herself. They would make her sit in the therapist's office for hours and make her unearth painful memories about her best friend. As weak as she was moments ago, she knew better than to ever speak to that therapist ever again.

"It was Amanda, she wants us all to meet her down at the boardwalk in a half hour." She avoided the question as she walked to her luggage, picking out her outfit.

"Does it have to do with Lisa, Jodie?" He pressed, following her. "I'm concerned, I've never seen you..."

"I lost my fucking virginity last night, Ben. Can you let me deal with it in my own way?" She yelled, interrupting him. She did not know what else to say, so she went for the obvious.

"And it was amazing babe, and I'm so happy that we did. And I think that we can finally..." He said softly as he stood close, not yet touching her.

She could not handle this; she was more of a basket case than he knew, and she could not get him involved in her level of crazy, especially after last night. She looked down at the floor, her forehead almost touching his bare chest. "It was a mistake," she whispered.

Ben paused for a moment as he processed her words, they dripped through his ears, a slow, steady poison that worked through his veins until it reached his heart, which seized and broke. The feelings he was allowing himself to feel for her again were walled up in an instant. It was how he always dealt with his feelings, wall them up and walk away. He stepped away from her, nodded his head and put his arms out. "Yeah, hey fine. I get it. But just remember, Jodie, you wanted it." He said as he pointed at her and walked into the other room.

***

Ben ran his hands through his hair in frustration, unsure how to handle the rollercoaster that was his and Jodie's relationship. He buried his face in his hands a sighed, interrupted by the sound of a throat clearing.

He looked over his hands and saw Doris sitting on the edge of one of the beds. She was looking at him and smiled, her eyes shifting back to the adjoining door.

"I'm guessing you heard all of that," he said quietly. She nodded her head and pressed her lips together. "Great," he stated with a slight head nod and an eye roll.

"Look, it's none of my business, but I've been a spectator to this highly volatile relationship of yours since the get-go. You two are like two moths attracted to a bug zapper. The closer you get to it, the more dangerous it is for the two of you."

Ben rested against the dresser and crossed his arms, not wanting to hear Doris's words. "I get it, you two have always had this will they, won't they, intense and extreme relationship, but you two aren't good for each other."

"You don't know anything, Doris." Ben replied.

"But I do. I was there the night you met. I was there when you two started dating. I witnessed the highs and lows. I was there when you broke up with her the first time, I was the one who watched her wilt into herself. I tried to help her during those six months, I got her to go out and meet new people. Then you somehow weaseled your way back in." She paused for a moment.

"And I watched and waited, because I knew it was only a matter of time before it all imploded again. And this time, she realized how wrong you two are. And yet somehow, three months after your breakup, you are here with us on our trip." Doris stood and approached Ben. She stood inches from him and leaned in to deliver what he expected be the final blow to protect Jodie. He braced himself for the impact of her words, as she said in a hushed tone, "when are you going to realize that you deserve better?"

Ben furrowed his brows and looked at Doris. "What?" That was not what he was expecting to hear.

"Oh, look at the time!" Doris said, backing away from Ben and looking at her watch. "Didn't I overhear Jodie say we had to meet Amanda soon?"

Doris poked her head into Jodie's room to see her sitting at the edge of the bed, her elbows on her knees and her chin supported by her fists. "Sweetie, are you ready to go?"

Jodie smiled half-heartedly at Doris and slightly nodded her head. She overheard her berating Ben. She always thought that Doris had a crush on Ben, but she always supported Jodie when they broke up. And it was nice to hear her stick up for her.

***

At nine-fifteen in the morning, Amanda saw Doris and Ben walking up to the boardwalk in silence. Jodie was trailing them by about three feet. Ben approached Amanda and pulled her away from the others. "Something is up with Jodie."

Amanda looked quizzically at him. Ben rolled his eyes and pulled her a little further away. "Listen, this morning she flipped out, crying and whatnot. She says it is because we slept together, but I think it…"

"You what?" Amanda exclaimed as her eyes popped out of her head. "Shh…" he said as he looked around, "we had sex last night."

Amanda shook her head in shock. "Whoa, how the hell did that happen? She was waiting, you know, for marriage. No wonder she was flipping out."

Ben studied Amanda's face and asked, "Really?"

Amanda nodded her head furiously. "Yeah, there was a time that we all decided to lose it the same night, and well, needless to say she didn't. Dude, how did you not know that?" Amanda looked incredulously at Ben as she walked over to Jodie.

Ben paused, thinking about Amanda's revelation. Jodie had always just said that she was not ready, that it had to do with her past. She was always uncomfortable around the topic of sex, and never wanted to talk about it. They had done plenty of other sexual activities over the course of their relationship, but she never told him the reason why she really shied away from having sex with him. A feeling of guilt flooded him, now knowing her true reason.

Jodie forced a smile on her face as Amanda approached her. She grabbed Jodie's hand and walked her over to the corner of a building, a large smile on her face as she put her hands over Jodie's eyes.

"What are you doing? I really need to talk to you."

"Shh, it's a surprise."

Jodie's heart began thumping in her chest as Amanda nudged her forward, the hysteria building again. Jodie held her breath when Amanda lifted her hands, expecting to see Lisa's deathly pale eyes staring back at her, but instead saw Pete standing in front of her with five bicycles. The tension in her body melted away as she squealed and jumped on Pete.

"Hey kiddo!" He said as he hugged her.

"Oh my God! Pete! What are you doing here?"

"Visiting." He said as he saw two other people turn the corner. "Hey, I'm Pete."

He extended his hand to Doris and then to Ben. Ben looked at Jodie hanging from Pete's waist, a genuine smile on her face, like this morning meant nothing. "Pete was like the brother I never had, well when he was around. He dated Amanda forever and I got to visit with them every weekend." She explained, feeling the weight of Ben's stare.

"Yeah, that was a long time ago." Amanda said as she smiled up at Pete. Pete walked over to the bicycles with Jodie in tow and gestured to them.

"We rented out one for each of you. They are allowing bikes on the boardwalk until noon today." Pete said as he held the bike handle on Amanda's bike. "That is, if you don't mind me tagging along."

***

Amanda rode her bike ahead of everyone. She loved the feeling of the afternoon breeze on her face. She pedaled faster, increasing the rush of the wind. As her speed increased, she raised her arms out to her sides and soared like a bird. She weaved in between the tables lined on the boardwalk and circled around a man dressed as a clown.

Amanda looked back at the others. Ben was coming up behind her. Pete and Jodie kept a lackadaisical pace together as they talked and laughed. Doris was struggling behind them on her bicycle. Amanda biked back over to Doris.

"You look like you need an oxygen tank." Amanda said as she slowed her pace to match Doris'. Doris looked up at Amanda and shook her head.

"Seriously, are you okay? You look like crap."

Doris tried to remember last night's events, but they only came back to her in pieces: the bald guy at the bar with the blue eyes, apple martinis, the golden ceiling, and then waking up on the bathroom floor. "It was a long night."

Amanda nodded her head, relating to the long night explanation. Amanda and Pete hardly slept last night. And his car was not very comfortable for the few times they did doze off. She smiled at Doris and patted her arm. Doris looked ahead. "Looks like I get a break, they are stopping."

Ten

Pete and Ben stood in front of a pop-up fun house, sizing one another up. "So, how do you know Jodie?" Ben asked as he crossed his arms.

Pete smiled at the question. He knew exactly the type of guy Ben was, the tough guy who had a weakness for a woman, but would not admit it to anyone. And to prove his manliness, he will not keep a steady relationship with the woman, for fear that she would get too close or he would become too vulnerable. "I dated Amanda in college."

"Right. So then how do you know Jodie? She didn't go to college with Amanda."

"You've done your homework." Pete said laughing. "Jodie used to come up and visit Amanda almost every weekend of sophomore year. After she finished pledging, she used to stay away from the college as much as she could."

Ben nodded his head. "So, you two were close?"

Pete nodded. "Yeah, she became my little sister while I was away from home."

"So, you two never...?" Ben started to ask as he stared Pete down.

"No."

Ben nodded his head in approval. He went to turn his head and look at the beach when Pete interrupted him. "So, how do you know Jodie? I never heard of you."

Ben looked over at Pete, who had a sly smile across his face. "We met at a party in the beginning of her junior year. My brother had pledged a fraternity and he made me go to a party they were having. I saw her sitting outside, so I went out and started talking to her, and that was it."

***

The last thing he wanted to do was go with his younger brother to a party. Between working full time and culinary school, his free time was few and far between, and he didn't want to waste it at a kegger, it wasn't his scene. But he couldn't deny his brother when he begged him to drive him there, promising to pay for gas and do Ben's share of chores for the next week. Plus, it was Jimmy's freshman year, and his first college party, and everyone needs that experience.

They arrived at the Long Island University campus and headed over to the dorm where Jimmy's friend of a friend lived. They walked in and found people in the hallways, wandering from room to room. Ben and Jimmy followed the crowd to the dorm at the end of the hallway, where the keg and punch bowls were housed. Jimmy grabbed beers for them, and they made their way back out to the hall. Each room they walked past had some different theme. Some had music playing, others had drinking games setup, another you could smell from a few doors down that it was the designated drug room.

"Yo, Thatcher!" Jimmy's friend shouted and grabbed his shoulder as he walked past and dragged him into a game of flip cup. Jimmy called out to Ben, "I'm just gonna play a quick game, bro."

Ben nodded his head and kept wandering through the crowd. Hearing an old favorite, he leaned against the doorway to the room playing club music from the early 2000's.

He observed some people sitting on beds, singing along to the music. A group of girls were sitting on the floor, swaying along to the music as they sang. One of the girls on the floor yells out over the music to her friends, "I can't just not dance!" She stood up, drink in hand, and began to dance. She gyrated her hips, making her way back down to the floor to grab the hand of the blonde girl next to her and pull her back up with her.

The two of them danced like no one was in the room. Their bodies in sync to the beat, rubbing against one another. They were like a ying-yang, the Mediterranean features of the one girl with her dark hair and eyes against the blonde hair and blue eyes of the Nordic girl. The initiator yelled down to the others to get up, and then continued to sing at the top of her lungs, only pausing to drink from the red solo cup in her left hand.

Ben chuckled to himself and he watched the drunken fools' party. He was going to leave to find his brother, but he could not keep his eyes off the brunette dancer. Her long hair cascaded down her back and she moved her hips from side to side. She smiled at her friends with her large eyes as they sung the chorus together. Raising her cup in the air as they sang the last part of the song, she hugged the blonde and laughed.

"I need air," she shouted to the group as she separated from them. The blonde grabbed her by the waist and smooshed her lips into her cheek. The blonde then let her go and shouted, "Don't take too long, I need my partner-in-crime!" She smiled and nodded as she exited the room, brushing past Ben as she left. She made eye contact with him as she walked by and continued down the hall to the exit.

Ben pushed off the doorway and followed the beautiful brunette. As he was making his way to the exit, his shoulder was grabbed, and he was turned. Jimmy smiled at him and shouted, "Ben, beer pong, let's do it!"

"Um, can you give me a minute?" Ben asked, looking towards the exit.

"Come on, bro, one game! The other team are hotties!" Jimmy exclaimed as he pulled Ben's arm, leading him to the room next to the exit.

"Oh shit, the Thatcher brothers are up!" Jimmy's friend announced as they walked up to their side of the table. A cheer coming from the spectators in the room.

Ben rolled his eyes in exacerbation, grabbing the ping pong ball and sunk the first shot. The girl standing across from him pouted as she drank while Jimmy cheered in Ben's ear. Jimmy took his turn, the ball rolling around the rim of a cup and falling out. "Ugh," both Ben and Jimmy grunted.

The girls took their time to set up, more concerned about how they looked in their outfits, and flirting with the spectators. Ben was getting impatient. While the two girls were talking to someone behind them about their technique, Ben grabbed a bunch of ping pong balls on the side of the table. He began to throw them into the cups, sinking almost every one of them. Jimmy laughed as the girls turned. "Hey," they shouted when they realized what Ben was doing, "that's not fair!"

Ben walked over to their side of the table, looking at the cups to see that all but one had a ball in it. He pointed at the target cup, and Jimmy threw a ball. It landed, and Ben bowed to the girls. "I bid you adieu, ladies."

"What was that?" Jimmy yelled over the crowed of laughter as Ben headed to the door. "Are you leaving? Dude, it's only been like an hour."

"No, I just need to go outside. Text me if you need me." Ben said as he patted Jimmy on the back.

Ben walked out of the dorm in a hurry, looking around for the brunette. He saw a few groups of people standing around, some sitting on the grass. A larger crowd formed on the side of the building, where he found another keg hidden behind some bushes.

He walked amongst the college students, searching each group for the girl. She was gorgeous, and he would hate himself, and his brother, if he missed the opportunity to meet her. He finally spotted her by the parking lot, her back facing him while sitting on the back of a car. He approached the car as another guy walked over and began making out with her.

"Figures," Ben mumbled and as he rolled his eyes and turned around. He shook his head and headed over to the keg. He chugged a solo cup full of beer and grabbed another, while some of the guys started chanting "Chug, chug, chug!" After the second beer, which was consumed in a matter of seconds, he took one for the road, and walked back to the entrance of the dorm.

He leaned against the wall of the building, next to the door. Pulling out his phone, he continued to consume his beer. He did not have any messages from his brother, and there was nothing interesting on social media to look at. Sighing, he put his phone back in his pocket and looked over at a bench a few feet away from the entrance. Figuring he could just camp out there for the rest of the party, he began to push off the wall when he noticed the brunette sitting on the bench, cup in hand, intently looking at her phone.

"Oh my god, you're here!" Ben exclaimed as he approached her. He looked back to the parking lot, the girl on the car still making out with the guy. *It wasn't her,* he thought with a smile.

She did not acknowledge his presence and continued to stare at her phone. Her hair providing a privacy curtain for her face.

He sat down next to her and smiled, "Hey! I saw you dancing before. You're a really good dancer."

She sat there, completely still, not disengaging from her phone.

Wow… rude bitch, Ben thought as he studied her, his patience growing thin from his alcohol consumption. *Doesn't she know how long I've been looking for her?*

He tapped her on the shoulder, and she jumped, looking over at him wide-eyed. She set her phone down on her lap and her cup between her knees. She moved her hands to her ears, removing the wireless headphones that were not visible through her hair.

"I'm sorry, were you talking to me?" She asked, studying his face. She was very attracted to him. His emerald green eyes burrowed into hers, his light brown hair kissed with blonde was unruly, begging for her to run her hands through it. His full bottom lip slightly pulled by perfect white teeth.

He stared at her, studying her face, unsure of what to say next. His emotions just ran the gambit from excited to extremely insulted to nervous. He was at a loss for words, staring deep into the melted chocolate pools that were her eyes.

She slightly nodded her head, pressing her lips together. "Okay... good talk," she said as she started to collect her things and get up from the bench. *Another winner... what a shame. Why do I come to these things?* She thought as she removed herself from the situation.

Oh my god, idiot, say something to her. She's walking away! Something, anything! He thought to himself, mustering the courage to speak. "Uh, ah, dancing?" He stammered. *Wow, smooth asshole,* he thought as he shifted his eyes from her to the trees behind her.

"What?" She asked, turning back in his direction. Her face a mixture of amusement and annoyance. She knew she should walk away, but she could not help herself, she wanted to look at him. She watched as his eyes shifted away from her, while he ran his right hand through his hair, and noticed the definition in his arms. He shrugged slightly, raising his arm, gesturing with a party cup in his left hand.

Ben nervously chuckled, making eye contact with the beautiful girl. "I, uh, saw you before, dancing."

"And?" She asked. *'Oh god...'* she thought, feeling embarrassed.

"You looked like you were having fun." He said with a half-smile.

"At the moment, I was." She responded, looking down at her phone.

"What are you listening to? Not enjoying the selection of music here?" He asked, trying to make conversation.

"Huh? Oh," she said, putting her phone in her back pocket, "I was listening to an audio book."

"Anything good?"

"The Canterbury Tales? It's for my medieval lit class, I just listen to it as I read along." She said, shrugging her shoulders.

He laughed. "Wow, partying and studying at the same time? How much do you think you will remember?" He asked her, lightly patting the bench next to him.

"What do you mean?" She asked as she slowly walked back over.

"I never knew studying and drinking to be a good combination. It never worked for me."

She sat down and tilted her cup towards him to show him the contents. "It's water. I'm not a big drinker, and these parties really aren't my thing."

"Yeah, me neither." He said looking at the cup. "Wait… so you aren't drinking. Like, at all?"

She shook her head in response.

"So, what I saw in there before, the singing and dancing, that was done sober?" Ben asked, his eyes showing his amusement.

"Like I said before, I was having fun in the moment," she said with a shrug as she rested her back against the bench. *He smells so good.*

This girl is something else, Ben thought as he followed her lead and sank into the bench. He leaned his head against the brick wall of the building and smiled.

"I'm Ben," he said as he extended his hand to her.

She looked down at his hand, eyebrow raised. She looked at it for a moment, smirked, and shook it, "Jodie."

***

Pete listened to Ben's story and could picture Jodie sitting on the bench outside of the party, either holding her ears as shields from the loud music or escaping the cigarette smoke cloud. "So, I'm assuming that you two dated?"

Ben nodded his head. "Yeah. We dated for about a year and then broke up."

"Oh. I'm surprised that she is still hanging around you. She never seemed the type to keep an ex around."

"We dated again." Ben explained. He was getting a little annoyed with all of Pete's questions.

"Are you two are still together?"

"No. We broke up a few months ago. Our relationship has always been... intense." Doris' words flooded his mind as he responded.

Pete nodded his head and smiled.

Amanda and Doris made their way over to them. Pete gave them a brilliant smile as Ben scowled a little, arms still crossed. Amanda looked around them. "Where's Jodie?"

Ben nudged his head in the direction of the fun house. "She's in the bathroom." The two men said in unison.

***

Jodie entered through the doors of the fun house and looked around for the main counter. A seventeen-year-old girl with highlighted hair sat behind the glass counter. She sat there snapping her gum as she scrolled through her phone. Jodie approached the counter. She waited for the girl to notice her, but she was too engulfed in the glow of the phone.

Jodie cleared her throat, but the girl just ignored her. "Excuse me?"

The girl was still entranced by her screen. Jodie tapped on the glass with her knuckle. The girl looked up from her phone. "Can I help you with something?"

"I need to use a rest room. Could you tell me where it is?"

The girl rolled her eyes and pointed to the right. "Just take that down."

"Thank you." Jodie made her way down the dark hallway. The hallway came to an end. There was no bathroom, just another hallway that ran in the opposite direction. Jodie turned from side to side, and then decided to make a right. The hallway opened into a large room filled with mirrors. She watched herself change sizes as she continued walking, finally finding a sign above the doorway that said exit and restrooms. As she walked through to the next room, the sounds of the ocean surrounded her and a bright light shone in the corner like the sun.

The room was set up like a maze. She entered it, running her hand along the wall as she walked. She turned into a dead end and saw a mean looking crab painted on the wall. She laughed; it was the most ridiculous painting she ever saw. She backtracked a little and made another turn. Her hand felt wet as it ran across the wall. She pulled her hand away and looked at it. A red, blood like substance dripped from her hand onto her foot and flip-flop. She kept walking, holding her hand out to her side.

The bright light in the corner of the room shut off. Jodie was surrounded by darkness. She stopped walking and tried to make out the shadows. The smell of vodka filled her nose when she turned around and saw the figure of a man walking a few rows next to her.

Her heart began to pound as she crept along the wall of the maze. A song the girls always listened to when they were at parties drowned out the sounds of the ocean. The bass of the song coincided with her accelerated heartrate. She turned another corner and saw Lisa standing before her, with an open bottle of vodka in her hand. She took a swig of it and said, "I'm so glad we are done with that hell hole! Bye-bye Bayshore High!" The voice echoed in her head. She remembered Lisa pouring the vodka into Jodie's mouth, and always making sure Jodie had a drink in her hands.

She closed her eyes for a moment, trying to shake the voice from her mind. After a deep breath, she opened her eyes and found herself in the family room of Joe Rappaport's mansion, dancing the night away with Amanda and Lisa, celebrating the end of their schooling, knowing that the three of them would be going to separate colleges. Jodie had consumed so much alcohol at that party. She remembered people leaving Joe's house, talking about making their way down the block to Gilbert Park and having a bonfire.

The short walk had done little to sober any of them up, the three girls walking arm and arm, the bottle of vodka in Lisa's hand. "This is the best night ever!" Lisa exclaimed, followed by a squeal as Joe ran up behind her a picked her up, then ran towards the fire.

Amanda and Jodie followed, sitting on a blanket someone put by the fire. Amanda threw her arm around Jodie's shoulders and slurred, "This really is a great time. I'm so glad you finally decided to cut loose with us for once!"

Jodie smiled and started to reply when someone called Amanda over to a volleyball game starting a little further down the beach. "Oh! Be back in a bit!" She said as she jolted up, stumbled slightly, and ran off to the net.

Jodie remained on the blanket, observing her classmates enjoying their last moments together. Most of the people she grew up with, knowing for twelve of her eighteen years on earth, and she would never see most of them again after this night. It was a bitter sweet thought, and she focused on the flickering of the flames. In her peripheral vision, she watched as Lisa walk away arm in arm with Joe Rappaport. Something did not feel right, and Jodie called out to her, as the sudden sense of panic rose. She tried to stand up, but the sky started to spin, causing her to lay back and close her eyes.

She had awoken on the beach, still laying on the blanket from the night before. There were others around her, all passed out. She walked around looking for Amanda and Lisa, holding her head and shielding her eyes from the morning sun. She searched the volleyball area and the rest of the park, but no luck. She pulled her phone from her pocket to find the battery dead. Sighing, she made her way up the block to the Rappaport's house.

Relieved to see Amanda's car parked down the block, she entered the house, finding people passed out on furniture and on the floor. She found Amanda in the kitchen, hunched over the island with her head in her hands.

"You look like how I feel," Jodie said as she approached her. Amanda strained to look up without moving her position. "I feel like shit," she responded.

"I'm so ready to go home." Jodie said as she sat on the stool next to Amanda.

"Yea, let's get Lisa and get the fuck out of here."

Amanda and Jodie searched the house for her but could not locate her. Amanda called her cell, but it went straight to her voicemail. She opened the Find My Friends App, but Lisa was not appearing. Jodie looked at the phone, "She disabled that app, she didn't want her parents tracking her when she was having her rendezvous with Joe."

The made their way to Joe's room, figuring she was in there with him. Amanda knocked gently, but there was no response. She tried a few more times, the knocks growing in volume. Joe finally threw the door open, standing in his underwear, with one eye opened. "What the fuck do you want?"

"Lisa, we're leaving. Is she in there?" Amanda asked. Jodie looked past Joe, seeing a blonde girl laying in his bed, completely naked. Jodie looked back at Joe and yelled, "Are you serious?"

"What?" He asked, shrugging his shoulders. "Lisa took off last night. She was pissed about something and left me on the beach."

"And she is?" Jodie asked, gesturing to his bed.

"None of your business."

Jodie crossed her arms and stepped closer to Joe. She sized him up and said, "What about Lisa?"

He scoffed and looked to the side, "We're not exclusive. She knows she's just a booty call."

"You're a real piece of shit," Jodie said in a quiet but stern voice. "You've always been a piece of shit, and you'll always be a piece of shit."

"And you'll always be alone, you prude bitch. Get the fuck out of my house." He responded. He began to close the door and shouted to them as the descended the stairs, "and let Lisa know that her services are no longer needed."

"What an unbelievable asshole!" Amanda shouted as they approached her car. They entered the car, Amanda slamming her door shut as she continued to rant about Joe. Jodie sat there in silence, buckling her seatbelt, and looking down at her lap. His words cut her deeper than anyone would know. They drove in this manner to Lisa's house, Amanda oblivious to Jodie's silence.

"Hey girls," Lisa's mother said as answered the front door. "What are you doing here?"

"Is Lisa here?" Amanda asked, Jodie still repeating Joe's words in her head.

"No, Lisa said she was sleeping at your house, Amanda." Her mother responded. She turned back to her husband, who was standing in the hall, "honey, can you check Lisa's room and see if she is here?"

He nodded and retreated down the hall, returning moments later, shaking his head.

"Did something happen?" Lisa's mother asked.

"Oh, no, she probably ran out to surprise us with bagels," Amanda said with a smile. "We'll have her call you later."

The girls retreated to the car, a puzzled look on their faces.

***

Jodie moved further through the maze, blinking the memory away. She turned another corner, the light dimly pulsating as she progressed down the corridor. She moved closer to the light, her body pulling her as if she was in a trance.

She stumbled onto sand. She looked up and saw stars shining down on her with a full moon in the sky. She heard blood-curdling screams coming from the end of the beach. Jodie picked herself off the ground and ran to source of the screams. She found Lisa yelling at Joe, pushing him away from her. He dove on top of her, pinning her down with his body as he tore her panties from under her dress. She was crying and screaming as he thrusted himself into her. She writhed beneath him, trying to get away. He smacked her over the head with a bottle of vodka until she stopped screaming. She laid still underneath him. He kept thrusting into her until he was finished. Jodie watched him tighten up and yell. He collapsed on top of Lisa and took another drink of the vodka.

Jodie watched Joe stand up and zip up his pants. He looked down at nudged her with his foot, but she was unresponsive. He picked up the used condom and wrapper and threw into the water. He watched the waves pull it out to sea as he took another swig from the bottle. He then walked back over to Lisa and grabbed her ankles. He dragged her limp, unconscious body to the edge of the water. Jodie tried to run after him, push him over, and knock him out. Jodie ran, but they stayed the same distance from her. She ran harder, pushing herself as far as she could go, but she did not gain any distance.

Joe looked around, making sure nothing was left behind. He walked away from the secluded area of the park to rejoin the party, leaving Lisa lying there. Jodie watched the whole night and following day go by in a matter of seconds. It was late the following evening. An older couple walking along the beach discovered Lisa's body lying on the beach. Jodie saw the police lights flashing in the distance. She tried to run to Lisa. She was finally able to run towards her. She ran up to her. Just as she was about to reach Lisa's body, something hit into her. She felt like someone knocked her into. She flew onto her back and the wind was knocked out of her. Just as her eyes began to fall into unconsciousness, she saw Lisa standing above her saying, "Help me, Jodie."

Eleven

Jodie slowly opened her eyes to find herself staring at a white ceiling. She blinked a few times, expecting to see the stars or the black of the night sky. She moved her head a little and felt a sharp pain in her forehead. She parted her lips and let out a soft moan.

Amanda ran to her side. "Pete, she's up." She grabbed a hold of Jodie's hand. "Jode? Jode, can you hear me?"

Jodie looked over at Amanda. "Jodie?"

"Yeah. I hear you." She sat up on her elbows. "What happened?" She asked as she winced in pain.

"They said that you ran into a wall. That you were yelling and hit into a wall."

Jodie shifted her eyes from Amanda to Pete. "Where did this happen?"

"The girl said you were right outside the bathroom. She said you were out cold, and you were holding your head." Pete explained.

Did I imagine everything? Jodie thought to herself as Amanda and Pete watched her. *I can't tell them what I saw. That I might actually know what happened to Lisa that night?* "Yeah, I got one of those headaches again and I must have tried to run into the rest room and hit the wall."

Pete looked suspiciously at Jodie as Amanda hugged her. "We were so worried, Jodie. We had no idea what happened to you. The guys said that you went to the bathroom and we waited for like twenty minutes. Then the girl came out yelling for help."

"Where are Ben and Doris?" Jodie asked as she looked around the room.

"They went to get you water and some food, just in case you felt sick" Pete said as he reached his hand down to Jodie. She took it and slowly stood up from the floor of the funhouse. "Are you ok, can you stand?"

"Yeah, I'm good," she said as she straightened herself, Amanda's hands on her waist to steady her. He looked at his phone said, "I texted Ben and let him know that you are up. They are going to meet us at the hotel."

***

Ben ran down the boardwalk, searching for a place that sold something edible. All he could find were places that deep-fried or battered everything. He found a small store that sold sandwiches. Doris chased after him, her chest heaving as she sucked in her breath.

They entered the small shop. It was overcrowded with people yelling over one another to place an order. A short, stocky man with a bald spot in the middle of his bushy black hair stood behind the counter. Ben pushed his way through the crowd as Doris clung to the back of his shirt.

Ben shouted out his order of turkey and lettuce on whole wheat to the lanky kid with bad acne behind the counter, then turned back and asked Doris if she wanted anything. She shook her head and tightened her grip on his shirt. Ben took the order ticket given to him and studied the pink piece of paper with a thirty-two printed on it as he moved down the counter, waiting for his order. Doris looked over at him and saw the worry shadowing his face. She grabbed his hand and squeezed it. Ben hardly noticed.

"I wonder how Jodie is doing." She said into his ear.

Ben looked over at her and shrugged. He shook his head and looked down at the floor. Doris' heart broke for him. He was so worried about her. She could see the love he had for Jodie in his eyes. She felt warm inside, knowing that someone could care for another person in such a way. But then the warmth slowly dissipated as she realized that no one felt that way about her. She wanted someone to look that way and worry about her. She wanted someone to love her the way that Ben loved Jodie. Then she admitted to herself, she did not want anyone to love her that way, she wanted Ben to.

***

It was dumb luck that Ben spoke to Jodie before he spoke to her, Doris thought, reminiscing about the night they met. She was dancing with Jodie at the party, feeling eyes on her, as she usually did. She looked to the door and saw this incredibly attractive guy standing there, watching as they danced. His over six-foot-tall, lean but muscular body looked as though it was supporting the door frame, his eyes not moving away. Doris smiled at him, pulling Jodie closer to her as she swayed their hips together.

By the time the song ended, Doris was hypnotized, her eyes not moving as Jodie went to leave. Thinking that kissing Jodie might get this guy interested in her, she grabbed her face and went into kiss her on the lips but caught Jodie's cheek. Jodie laughed and left the room. Doris gave herself a onceover and headed over to introduce herself, but the guy had left. She went to look for him, but was caught by Robert, her casual fling.

Days later, Doris spotted Jodie sitting in the lounge, in her typical position of headphones in and starring at her phone, absentmindedly chewing on an apple. She sat across from her, waiting for Jodie to acknowledge her presence. A few moments later Susan, one of their sorority sisters, approached them, and plopped herself down next to Jodie on the couch. Jodie finally looked up from her phone and noticed them.

"I've legit been here waiting for you to disengage from your book. It took Susan basically assaulting you to notice." Doris complained with a smile on her face. Jodie was a huge nerd, and usually a bit of a downer, but she was always a designated driver, and she was a sweetheart, so Doris was ok with associating with her. Jodie was also attractive, but not as attractive as her, so she helped with attracting men to their group when they were together. And Jodie never posed a threat of taking one of the guys since she was never interested, which helped Doris get first pick for the night.

Jodie looked up and smiled, "oh, sorry... you know me... head, book." She said as she pointed to her head and then down to the phone.

"Nah-uh, she ain't reading... she's messaging someone named... Ben!" Susan shouted as she looked over Jodie's shoulder.

"What?! Is Jodie interested in a boy?!" Doris squealed.

Jodie rolled her eyes and smiled. "No, it's just someone I spoke with at the party the other night. He found me on Facebook the next day and we've just been chatting. No big deal."

"Oh my god, does my little Jodie finally have an interest in the opposite sex?!" Doris teased, pushing Jodie's foot with her own.

"Stop," Jodie said with a blush creeping over her cheeks.

"Let's meet up with him! Tell him to bring some friends. A few of us can go! Jodie, hook a sister up!" Susan suggested, wagging her eyebrows.

Jodie shook her head, but Doris jumped up and pulled the phone out of her hands. "Hey!" Jodie yelled as she reached for her phone.

Doris sat back down as Susan threw herself on top of Jodie.

Doris: Hey, would you wanna meet up with a me and a few of my friends? Maybe bring some of yours?

"Send!" Doris announced, smiling as she watched Jodie throw her hand over her face in embarrassment.

"What the fuck, Doris. He isn't going to want to, he's busy with school and..." Jodie was saying as she was cut off by the sound of her phone.

Ben: I'd love to. My schedule is a little hectic. I'm in the city MWF for class. Working @ nite WTFS.

Doris: Ok, how is Fri nite, after work?

Ben: Um… I won't be out until 11pm.

Doris: We can come to you?

Ben: K, the restaurant is pretty upscale. Let's meet @ another bar, Maxwell's in Islip? 11:30?

Doris: can't wait!

"Done. Friday night, 11:30, in Islip. You're welcome." Doris said with a smile as she tossed the phone back to Jodie. Jodie shook her head and smiled as Susan squealed and hugged her.

Three nights later, Doris and Susan busted into Jodie's room to help her get ready to meet Ben. Susan curled and brushed out Jodie's hair as Doris ransacked the closet, trying to find something "un-Jodie-like" for her to wear. Jodie's roommate grunted, grabbed her stuff, and left the room.

"What's up her ass?" Doris asked as she re-entered the room. "You have nothing appropriate for tonight, so you're wearing one of my shirts."

"Oh, no, Dor, you know I'm not super comfortable with the whole cleavage thing," Jodie said as she was applying her makeup.

"I don't know why, you have great tits, they are bigger than mine, you should use them to your advantage. But I know how reserved you are, Sister Jodie, but your holy habits are not gonna work tonight. When are you scheduled to join the convent?" Doris teased as she held up a dark green long-sleeved semi cropped top.

Jodie rolled her eyes and took the shirt. "Hurry up!" Doris smacked her in the ass as she walked by. Susan and Doris were adjusting themselves in the mirror when Jodie came back. She wore black skinny jeans, Doris' green crop top, black ballet shoes, and a black zip-up hoodie.

"Nah-uh, lose the sweatshirt," Susan said, shaking her head. Jodie shook her head tightly. "Cut Sister Jodie a break, Sue, I'm shocked she actually has the shirt on, and we can see some skin. Bless her, father, for Jodie has sinned!" Doris exclaimed as she did the sign of the cross in front of Jodie.

Jodie turned red and zipped the sweatshirt. "We are busting your balls, girl. Come on, you can see a little bit of your waist. Susan's ass is basically hanging out of her dress, and you know I have to let the girls out. You look beautiful, and I'm sure Ben will be drooling." Doris said as she adjusted her cleavage once more, her shirt barely covering anything else. She smoothed her jeans and headed out of the room, the clicking of her heels echoing down the hallway.

Susan smiled at Jodie while shaking her ass in her short black bodycon dress. Jodie rolled her eyes as she grabbed her bag and her keys, following the sounds of clicking heels out to the car.

Doris and Susan chatted the entire forty-five-minute drive, with Jodie barely listening to them. She occasionally nodded or grunted a slight response to the girls, but her nerves were overtaking her. She was completely ok with chatting online, but the face-to-face thing was too overwhelming.

They pulled up to the bar on Main Street, the street crowded with cars and patrons. She took a deep, shaky breath, and unlocked the doors for the girls. Susan jumped out of the back seat as Doris looked at Jodie. "Breathe Jodie, he's just a guy, and we are just a group of people who are going to socialize and have a good time. And if you get super uncomfortable, there are a few other bars in this area that we can easily walk to."

Jodie nodded her head, forcing a smile with her lips pressed together in a tight line. Doris rubbed her back and smiled. "You look hot, just not as hot as me, you've got this! Go, park the car, we'll meet you inside." Doris said with a wink as she hopped out of the car to join Susan. Jodie watched as her friends sashayed their way into the bar, purposefully exaggerating the sway of their hips as they passed a group of men outside. She watched the guys' heads follow the girls, a few arm taps between them, and saw them follow her friends in. She shook her head and pulled away, searching for a spot in the parking lots behind the buildings.

Doris and Susan entered the bar and looked around, trying to find Jodie's man. Susan looked to Doris with an eyebrow raised, "So, do we even know what this Ben guy looks like?"

Doris smiled and laughed, "Nope. His picture on her chat was food."

Susan nodded and headed to the back of the large bar, near the back entrance. They found a four-seater bar top and claimed it, their heads swiveling in search of both Jodie and some cute guys. "I have a pretty good view of both entrances from here," Susan reported as she sat down. Doris gave her a thumbs up and headed to the bar to get them drinks.

She squeezed herself between a group of guys at the end of the bar, smiling sweetly as she parted the group. The four guys who were standing behind their two friends sitting at the bar laughed as she tossed her hair and leaned against the bar. She waved at the bartender and winked to get his attention. She placed her drink orders and turned to face the group standing around her. "Hey fellas, thanks for letting me through."

"Sure thing, you're lucky you're so pretty," one of the guys said with a smile. She winked at him and returned the smile. "I'm Doris."

"Fred," the guy responded as he moved a little closer. His friends nudging each other and laughing, egging him on. The two in the chairs turned their heads to see what their friends were laughing at. Doris recognized the one in the seat furthest from her. "Hey, I know you!" She said excitedly, recognizing him from the party at the dorm.

He looked at her with a confused face. "Was I your server or something?"

"No! You were at a party at LIU like a week or so ago. You were supporting the doorway to my room." He returned a blank stare, unsure of who she was. He thought back to the party and finally realized she looked slightly familiar.

"Were you dancing with a brunette?"

"Yeah, you looked like you were enjoying the show," she responded with a smile as she nodded at the bartender when he returned with her drinks.

"Hm, yeah, I guess you could say that," he said with a distant smile. The younger guy sitting in the other chair turned to her and smiled, "You go to LIU too? I just started there this year!"

"That's nice," she said dismissively as she turned her attention back to the hottie from the party. "So, what brings you all of the way out here," she inquired.

The younger guy answered, "My brother works down the block. We're meeting someone here. Well, this one over here is," he said as he nudged his neighbor with his elbow. "We're all here to embarrass the shit out of him."

Doris nodded as she looked back to Susan, who was waving her back over to the table. She rolled her eyes in response, turning her attention back to the group of guys. "My friends and I have a table over there; you are more than welcome to join us."

Ben was getting a little annoyed with this girl but realized that she is probably there with Jodie. He looked at his friends and his brother and said, "sure, why not."

Doris' smile brightened as she headed back to Susan, with the six guys following her. Susan watched in astonishment as they approached the table. She could not understand the power Doris had over men. They were there less than fifteen minutes and she already reeled in more men than they could handle.

Doris turned back to her target for the night, "I have to confess, I have been thinking about you since I saw you at the party. You are really fucking hot."

Jodie finally found a spot down the block and turned the car off. She looked in the mirror, checking her hair and make-up. *She's right... I've got this,* she thought as she got out of the car. She looked down at herself and decided to step out of her comfort zone. She took off the hoodie and draped it over her arm as she headed to the back patio of the bar.

She made her way through the smokers and entered the crowded bar. Her nerves were starting to take over, and she was thinking about turning around and heading back out to the car when she saw Ben smile at her. Her nerves started to melt away as a smile overtook her face as he waved at her.

Doris placed her hand on his chest and leaned in. He looked up over her head, distracted by something. She turned and followed his gaze to the back door. She was about to suggest that they go outside so they could talk when she saw Jodie make her way through the crowd.

She waved her over, seeing Jodie smile and wave back. Doris started to say, "Oh good, my girl is finally here," as she turned back to the guy standing behind her but saw him smiling and waving. "Hey Jodie," he said quietly as he stepped closer to her. She said hi back as he hugged her and gave her a quick kiss on the cheek. Jodie returned the hug and blushed, looking over at Doris and the rest of the people. "Doris, Susan, this is Ben."

Doris' face faltered as her heart slightly broke, a feeling of jealousy flowing through her veins. She caught herself and quickly plastered a bright smile on her face. "Wow, no way! What are the chances that we found the right guy?"

Jodie smiled and walked over to the table, sitting in the chair that Ben pulled out for her. Doris watched as she continued, "So, how did you two even meet?"

Ben smiled at Jodie before turning his attention to Doris. "Funny enough, at the party. I was watching you two dancing."

Doris cocked an eyebrow at his response. "Really?"

"Yeah, you guys are really good dancers," he said with a smile. Susan smiled at Ben and asked, "Yeah, but *how* did you meet? Our girl here hasn't really spilled much about you."

"Well, to be honest, I followed her. I just thought she was so beautiful, I had to know her."

Jodie looked down and blushed as Susan exclaimed, "Awwww!!! That is so incredibly sweet. He sounds like a keeper, Jodie."

Doris shook her head slightly in disbelief. *He chose her over me? He saw us at the same time… I'm the hot one,* she thought to herself as she sipped on her drink. Ben's brother watched Doris' reaction, taking note of the attitude change.

Ben laughed and cleared his throat, "Ok, enough of that. So, introductions. This is Steven, Fred, and Kevin, my friends from back in the day. This is my brother, Jimmy, and his friend Chris. They both go to LIU."

The girls introduced themselves to the group. Susan, being the giant outgoing flirt that she is announces to the group, "I've gotta say, I am *in* with Stev*en* and Kev*in*," annunciating the "in" in their names. Everyone got quiet and exchanged looks. "Come on guys, I'm a lyrical genius. And I'm hysterical." Ben broke the silence with a loud laugh. "If these are the kind of jokes I am going to be hearing tonight, I think I'm gonna need another drink! You want anything, Jodie?"

"Just a water is fine, thanks." She responded with a smile. She watched Ben walk to the bar and turned to Susan shaking her head with a laugh. "That was a terrible joke."

Steven and Kevin laughed, "I don't know," Kevin said with a smile, "I'm flattered."

Doris watched as the group slightly split up into smaller segments. Jimmy and Chris went off to find girls closer to their age. Susan spent most of the night flirting with Steven and Kevin. Fred placed himself next to Doris, trying to continue their small flirtation in the beginning of the night, but Doris spent most of the night watching and listening to Jodie and Ben.

***

Doris' eyes began to well up with tears as she stood there, holding onto Ben's hand. Her body began to shake. Ben felt little quivers in his hand, and had no idea Doris was holding it. He looked over and saw her crying. "Aw, Doris. It's ok. She is going to be alright." Ben said as she hugged her.

Doris let her body be enveloped in Ben's arms, enjoying the heat of his body. She pressed into him and sobbed more. "Oh, now I feel horrible. I wasn't crying over Jodie."

Ben pulled back a little and looked her in the face. Doris' big blue eyes were floating in her tears. She sniffled and continued. "Oh, I am a horrible friend."

"Why are you crying?" Ben asked as he patted her on the back. His thoughts drifted back to Jodie as he waited for her answer.

"Well, I don't know how to say this, but." She said as her voice trailed off. Ben took his phone out of his pocket, reading the text aloud, "oh, thank god, she up." She knew that Ben was not listening to her. She subtly jolted him, so his gaze returned to hers as he slid the phone back into his pocket. She held it in a mesmerizing stare and said, "Ben, I was raped last night."

Ben's eyes widened at her words. "Number thirty-two, order up."

***

Ben walked along side Doris, while Jodie's food swung in the bag as they walked. With thoughts of Jodie in the back of his mind, he listened to Doris' story of the night before.

"Well, it happened after you left the casino. I was sitting at the bar you left me at, you know the one in the poker room?" She asked as Ben nodded his head.

"The bartender back there, the bald guy, well he kept giving me these martinis. I didn't have many; I didn't want to get drunk. Well, he must have slipped something into it. Well, I don't really remember what happened next, he must have dragged me into the bathroom, because when I woke up." She paused, fresh tears began to fall down her face as she looked down and shook her head.

Ben put his hand on her shoulder. She put her hand on his and looked up. "I was laying on the floor, and he came on my face."

Ben's face fell into a look of shock and disgust. "That is horrible Doris. I don't know how anyone could do that."

She buried herself into his chest and began to weep. He hugged her. He was horrified that someone could do this to another person. "I wish you would have stayed last night. If you stayed, this wouldn't have happened." Doris said, her voice muffled by Ben's shirt.

Guilt shot through Ben's heart as Doris' words came out. She was right. If he had stayed there, she would not have been attacked. "Don't worry Doris," he said as he kissed her head, "We'll find him and make him pay. We should go to the police and report this."

Doris smiled up at Ben and nodded her head. Ben smiled back but was taken by surprise. He could have sworn that Doris' blue eyes flashed green for a moment.

***

Ben tapped on the door as he opened it, Jodie's food in his other hand. Pete walked over to the door and took the waters from Doris. "Is she okay?" Ben asked as Pete turned to put the waters in the refrigerator. Pete nodded his head and moved out of the way.

Ben saw Jodie sitting on the bed with Amanda behind her braiding Jodie's hair into a thick single braid falling on her spine. Ben could see the cut above her left eye was swelling a little. When he walked over to the bed, Amanda got up from behind Jodie. She patted Ben on the arm and said, "I'll let the two of you be alone for a bit." She joined Doris and Pete in the other room and closed the door behind her.

Ben looked down at Jodie and smiled. Jodie looked up at him, and then shifted her gaze to the bed. She did not want Ben to ask her any questions, and she did not want him to look at her like she was crazy.

"Here, I bought you food. Just in case you didn't feel good."

"Thank you. I'm not hungry right now." Jodie answered, still looking at the foot of bed.

Ben sat on the bed, placing himself in her gaze. He touched her cheek with his hand and smiled a little. Her eyes focused on his. "God Jode, you are going to make me crazy."

She smiled a little. *Must be contagious.* He moved next to her and wrapped his arms around her. She let herself sink into him. "Maybe we should leave tonight." Ben suggested as he wrapped his leg around hers. She felt like a helpless little worm, protected by her cocoon. She inhaled his scent and closed her eyes.

She nodded her head in agreement. The sooner she went home, the safer she would feel in her own house. She looked up at him and kissed his chin. "Thank you."

He kissed her on the forehead. "For what?"

"For everything." She pushed her fingers up through the back of his hair. She lightly pulled on it and repeated the cycle. He felt himself melt from her touch and stared into her eyes as she continued to play with his hair. He took the end of her braid and tickled the end of her nose with it, which made he smiled.

"God, Jodie. That smile is going to be the end of me."

Jodie smiled again as she wrapped her arms around his waist. She laid in his arms until she drifted off to sleep. Ben stroked her hair as she slept, staring at her reflection in the mirror. He smiled, realizing how good this trip had been for the two of them. He knew that he wanted her to be his again. She was a part of him, no other girl had gotten under his skin before. No one drove him crazy and made him happy like she did. She was it for him, and he promised himself that he was going to marry her one day.

After a few hours, the adjoining door opened, and Doris poked her head in. Ben looked up at her. "Are you ready to go?"

He looked down at Jodie, her breath slow and steady. "You think it's ok to leave her?"

Amanda entered the room, looking through Jodie's bag. "Yeah, she just needs to rest. I'll let her know what's going on."

Twelve

Amanda, Pete, Doris, and Ben walked down the boardwalk to the Tropicana. They decided that tonight would be there night to go to the casino and enjoy themselves. Amanda texted Jodie, letting her know where they would be. Doris walked into the casino first, making her grand entrance. She wore a short white skirt with a laced up black tank top. Her strappy black sandals made her almost five inches taller than she really was. She tossed her long blonde hair and looked back at Ben.

Ben held the door open for Amanda and Pete. Ben's khaki pants covered part of his brown shoes. His green button-down shirt was slightly open at the top, revealing his white tee shirt. He pushed his unruly brown hair out of his face before closing the door.

Amanda stood next to Doris and waited for Pete to get a map of the casino from the main desk. Amanda was three inches shorter than Doris in her kitten heels. She pinned half of her hair back with clips that matched her lavender tank top. Her black skirt was short, but not nearly as short as Doris'. Amanda rolled up the sleeves to her cropped cardigan and walked over to Ben.

"Do you think she will be okay in the room?" Ben asked as Amanda approached him.

Amanda nodded. "I told you that she'll be fine. I texted her to let her know where we will be, so if she wants to meet up with us, she can. I told her to dress nice too, so she won't show up in jeans."

Pete came back over with the map, his blue shirt clung to his muscles as he walked over to the rest of them. His dark denim jeans folded over his black shoes. He pushed the front of his hair to a point and wore his glasses. Amanda thought he looked so handsome.

The foursome took to the casino like ducks to water. Amanda and Pete headed over to the slot machines. "Twenty dollars." Amanda stated when she sat down at the slot machine.

Pete looked over at her from the other side of the machine. "What?"

"That's all I'm spending. Twenty."

Pete started laughing and pulled the lever on the machine. Amanda scowled and pulled the lever on hers.

She stared as the wheels spun different pictures. She watched the colorful dollar signs come to a sudden halt in the center of the plexiglass, one after another. A blue dollar sign, a yellow dollar sign, and a green stared back at her. She looked to the side of the machine, looking for the color key. Her eyes raked over the key, then back at the dollar signs. She won nothing.

"Alright!" Pete exclaimed with a smile. Amanda looked at him between the machines. He looked up at her and rubbed his hands together. "I just doubled my money!"

"How the hell did you do that?" She asked looking around her machine for a trick button.

"I guess I'm just lucky." He said with a brilliant smile, pulling on the lever. "All right! I just won another five bucks."

Amanda rolled her eyes and pulled down on the lever, harder this time, hoping that it would give her a different outcome. Within five minutes, Amanda lost her twenty dollars. "Son of a bitch." She said as she opened her pocket book.

Pete looked over when he heard her curse. She looked up at him and held up another twenty dollars. "Forty."

***

Ben rubbed his hands together as he sat down at the poker table, it was why he came on the trip. He looked around the table, studying his opponents. There was an older gentleman with a blue polo shirt and a cane to his left. Then there was a man with mousey brown hair with a comb over and thick glasses sitting to the left of the old man. The dealer, dressed in his uniform, shuffled the cards. A woman with red hair and bright green eyes sat herself next to the dealer. Ben studied the man next to him, knowing that he would be his competition at the table. The man's slicked jet-black hair reflected the lights of the casino. He adjusted his black shirt and looked over at Ben, sized him up, and then looked over at the woman on the other side. He smoothed his black moustache and sucked at his teeth. Ben did not like him, and he could not wait to beat the cocky man next to him.

Doris stood behind him, staying as close to him as possible. Her eyes shifted around the casino, searching for the large man with the bald head. She wondered if Charlie would be there, working at the bars. She was in another casino from the previous night, but she could not help but feel nervous. She pulled a stool up to the table but positioned herself as close to Ben as possible. Ben was oblivious to her as he became further involved with the cards in his hands.

Forty-five minutes into the poker game, Doris became restless. Deciding to doge the stares coming from the redhead at the table that she had be receiving the entire time, she stood up and stretched her legs for a moment. Seeing that Ben was still engulfed by the game, she walked around a few of the card tables. She kept Ben in her sight as she walked over to an open bench against the far wall. She fell back against the wall, letting her back press against the cold wall. She smiled from the sensation.

Doris watched as couples of all ages walked around the casino. She studied the people walking around. Some were dressed in everyday clothes; jeans and a tee shirt with sneakers. Others overdressed for the casino, wearing glittery dresses and suits. The older crowd seemed to dress that way. She watched people walk to the cashier with giant smiles of triumph as they cashed in their winnings. Others ran to the dozens of ATMs located throughout the casino, searching frantically for their debit cards, resembling a person on crack looking for their next hit.

She suddenly felt uneasy, a feeling that someone was studying her washed over. She looked over at Ben, hoping it was him, but he was still focused on the game. The redheaded woman was no longer at the table. She slowly scanned around the room, trying to find the source of the uneasy feeling. At the corner of the room, Doris saw someone staring at her. She did not recognize the person, though she could tell it was a male. Her heart began to race, thinking it was Charlie, but the man had black hair. She sucked in her breath he waved black gloved hand at her.

***

Jodie woke up after a two-hour nap, surprised that the room was empty. She sat up and checked her phone, seeing a text from Amanda.

A: @ the Tropicana. Meet us there. Left u an outfit. Lemme know when ur here. Dinner???

Jodie stretched as she tossed her phone on the bed. She turned around and found an outfit laid out on the bed for her. She studied the outfit. Her black skirt was there, along with a tight, bright blue top. The neckline plunged open into a sheer lace pattern. Black heeled sandals were placed on the floor. Jodie smiled to herself. Amanda, the little athlete, sure could put together a sexy outfit.

After twenty minutes, Jodie grabbed a cab and headed to the Tropicana. She slipped a white flower above her left ear that she picked from a planter outside of the street entrance and texted Amanda when she entered the casino.

J: Here. Gonna look 4 u guys.

Jodie walked over to one of the slot sections, knowing that it would be the first place Amanda would go. She walked around but could not find anyone. She left the slot section and walked over to the poker area. She wandered the room, trying to find Ben. She had no luck, so she returned to the main entrance and texted Amanda again.

J: Where r u? Going back to main area.

Ben counted the twenty-eight hundred dollars he won from his poker game. He turned from the cashier counter and headed over to the lobby. He checked his watch, seeing he had a half an hour before he had to meet everyone for dinner. He somehow lost his way, and wound up on the upper level of the casino. He walked past the comedy club and a few bars, making his way to the staircase of the main entrance. He nodded his head and said hello to everyone that passed him on the stairs. He was in a great mood; it had been a while since he won big in poker. It had been even longer since he could wipe the smirk off a cocky jerk who had been winning almost every hand.

He made it to the first landing of the spiraling staircase and stopped for a moment to look around the central hub of the casino. He loved the Havana theme of the hotel, the feel of victory, and the winnings in his pocket. He inhaled the air and slowly released it back into the atmosphere. He looked over to the left and saw Jodie smiling up at him. His chest tightened at the sight of her. He made his way down the rest of the stairs, walked over to her, and stared, looking dumbfounded. Jodie touched her hand to the flower in her hair and smiled.

"You look stupid. What's with the face?" Jodie asked with a laugh.

Ben smiled wider. "You look stunning."

"Oh. Well, thanks." Jodie said as she blushed. She pushed his shoulder and asked, "Why did you go say something nice like that? Now I sound like a bitch."

"Because you are one," Ben said with a smile as he playfully pushed her shoulder back, "but I think I'll keep you around anyway."

Jodie laughed and saw Doris walking down the stairs. She looked like a scared deer, trying to escape a hunter. Her head swung from left to right as she watched her surroundings. She reached for Ben and threw her arms around his waist.

"Are you okay Doris?" Ben asked as he lifted his arms and tried to look behind him. He felt Doris' head nod into his back.

"What's wrong Doris?" Jodie asked as she touched Doris' arm. Doris pulled away from Ben as if she had been hit with scalding water. Her face flashed from fear to anger and then to shock.

"Nothing, I'm fine. I just thought I lost everyone. When did you get here?" Doris asked, swinging her hair over her shoulder.

"Not too long ago. I kind of wandered around for a bit trying to find someone, but then I luckily ran into this one." Jodie said as she nudged her head over at Ben.

He smiled at her as Doris rolled her eyes. "Yeah, me too. I guess we were both lucky to find him in this crowd." Doris rubbed his arm while she smiled flirtatiously.

A wave of jealousy crashed over Jodie as she watched Doris deliberately flirt with Ben in front of her. Jodie's intuition perked up as she began to realize that it had been a mistake to bring Doris on this trip. She knew that Doris stopped at nothing to get whatever, or whomever she wanted. She narrowed her eyes and furrowed her brows.

"Too bad I found him first." Jodie said as she stared at Doris. Doris smiled, acknowledging Jodie's silent challenge.

"I think I will try to find Amanda and Pete." Doris said as she began to walk away, still touching Ben's arm until her fingertips could not reach. "I'll meet you at the restaurant at seven."

Jodie looked over at Ben. Ben stared back and stepped in front of her. He wrapped his arms around her and softly kissed her on the neck, "What the hell was that about?"

"What?" Ben asked softly as he continued to place kisses on her neck and shoulder.

"Did something happen between you two?"

Ben put his hands on Jodie's arms and stepped back. "Are you kidding me?"

Jodie shook her head. Her eyes widened. "No. She is a slut, Ben. She has no loyalty to anything but herself. She's done this to so many of the girls at school. And I honestly think that she has always had a thing for you."

Ben rolled his eyes. "Jodie. Nothing is going on between us. She is freaked out because," he said and then drastically lowered his voice, "because she said she was raped last night."

"Oh, that's cute." Jodie said looked around. She leaned in and lowered her voice in the same manner Ben did. "I call bullshit. She's pathological and desperate.

She probably wanted it and passed out drunk or something in the middle of it because that is what she does. Trust me, I've seen the act before."

Ben shook his head, shocked by her reaction. "That's out of line Jodie. I don't know the whole story, but whatever happened last night, she is freaked out about and I promised that I would help her."

Jodie's face contorted as if she sucked on a lemon. Ben knew that she was getting jealous, although she had nothing to be jealous about. Ben admitted to himself that he did find Doris attractive, but he would never do anything about it. Doris was harmless, she had been doing her whole flirting routine with him since the first day he met both her and Jodie. Jodie was the one he wanted to be with. He touched her chin with a hooked finger. "Besides Jode, why would you care? It's not like we are together." He said, trying to flirtatiously joke with her. He thought it could be a good segue into a discussion about their relationship.

Jodie's eyes grew as her mouth opened. She felt like she was struck by a two-by-four as she jerked her head away from his touch. "You're right, Ben. We aren't. Go fuck her."

Jodie turned and started to walk away as Ben followed her. *Whoops, read that wrong,* he thought. He knew that he was in trouble, but he smiled because he loved arguing with her. It kept their relationship interesting. He quickened his pace and stopped in front of her. Jodie furiously dodged him and continued walking. He kept stride with her and said, "Because, I mean, it's not like you love me or anything."

Jodie stopped in her tracks and turned her head to face him. His face was mere inches away from hers. She pointed her finger in his face and said between gritted teeth, "Don't you ever say that to me. Like I just make love to anyone." Her voice began to shake from the overwhelming hurt she was feeling. To stop herself from crying, she stopped her quivering chin by spitting out, "Fuck you."

She turned to walk away as Ben grabbed her wrist. She turned back to him and tried to pull her wrist away. He kept a firm grasp and smiled. "Say it."

"Say what?"

"Say you love me."

"Let go."

"Say it."

"No."

"Say it."

"Ben seriously, let go of my wrist. You are making a scene." Jodie looked around her to see people starting to stare. She stopped pulling her arm.

"Tell me."

"Ben," she warned.

"I'm not letting go until you say it." Ben's smile did not falter. He knew that she loved him, but he knew that she was too proud to admit it to him. She would think it made her weak. He also enjoyed pushing her buttons and watching her getting flustered.

"Ben," her voice fell into a whisper, "People are watching."

"Tell me Jodie. Tell me what you felt last night. Tell me what you have been feeling this whole weekend. Tell me what you have felt for years."

Jodie looked down. *Tell you that I'm scared, that I've been seeing my dead best friend everywhere? Tell you that I don't want to go back to therapy?* She shook her head and looked up at him blankly. Ben could usually read her eyes, figure out what she was thinking or what she was going to say next. Jodie swallowed a lump in her throat as she looked the other way.

His smile began to falter as he loosened his grip on her wrist. He watched a beautiful waltz of emotions dance across her face. His heart began to feel that familiar ache, and he realized that he needed to hear her answer. Her reaction was making him rethink their relationship. *What if she doesn't love me? What if I have messed up too many times?* He thought, feeling vulnerable.

She saw him blink back a tear as she stared into his hypnotizing green eyes and felt her heart swell. No matter how much of a jerk he was from time to time, he somehow hand dug himself a home in her heart. She sighed and slightly nodded her head.

Ben smiled and nodded his head as well. He hugged her tightly, as if she would float away if he let go.

Thirteen

"You totally have a gambling problem." Pete said as he stepped outside, holding the door open. Amanda walked through it, staring over at him.

"I do not." She said as she crossed her arms and walked across the boardwalk to a vacant bench. She sat down, tucking her skit behind her legs.

Pete followed behind her letting out a hearty laugh. "Are you serious?"

"Are you?" She asked, digging through her bag.

"Absolutely. How much did you spend in there?" He asked as he sat down next to her, pointing over at the casino.

"About fifty." She said, pulling her lip-gloss from her bag. She unscrewed the top and removed the wand, spreading the gloss over her bottom lip.

"And how much did you lose?" Pete asked, watching her paint her lip. Amanda paused mid-glossing and looked over at him. He smiled back at her, knowing that she was being pushed. "Well?"

She pressed her lips together as she screwed the top back onto the tube and dropped it in her bag. "A lot, but it wasn't my money."

He shook his head as he laughed. "You should have stopped when I told you." Amanda looked up at the top of the Tropicana and said, "Don't ruin my night."

Pete laughed and looked at his watch. "It's almost seven, should we go in and get a table?"

Amanda nodded and remembered to check her phone. She saw missed texts from Jodie and quickly responded.

A: Sorry, didn't see this. Heading back in now. Meet you by Carmine's.

Amanda put her phone away and stood up. Pete stood next to her, waiting for her to start walking. "Don't be annoying," she said laughing.

Pete walked over and opened the door for Amanda. She looked up to thank Pete when they heard, "Erickson? Is that you?"

Pete turned to see Sean, one of his shipmates, walking down the boardwalk. "I thought that was you." Sean said as he shook Pete's hand. "Hey, what's going on?" Pete asked Sean.

"Nothing, just enjoying the time off. What day do you go back to the ship?"

"Monday afternoon, what about you?"

"Same." Sean said as he looked over at Amanda. "Hello, I'm Sean, I am on the same ship as Pete."

Amanda shook his hand. "I'm Amanda. I knew Pete back in college."

"We used to date." Pete said, smiling at Amanda.

"Oh, that's nice." Sean said, turning his attention to Pete. "I'm glad I bumped into you, I wanted to ask you about the next deployment."

Pete nodded his head and looked over at Amanda. "Can I meet you inside?" Amanda nodded and smiled. "It was nice to meet you, Sean."

Amanda walked into the marketplace of the casino, standing near the entrance. She watched him as he spoke with Sean, his white teeth shining as he laughed. She leaned her head against the wall and smiled as her heart ached, she was still in love with him. She had forced herself to believe many years ago that she did something wrong, driving him away from her. Now she learned that she was wrong; everything that had happened to his family pulled him away. His mother's drinking, his sister's pregnancy, the loss of money; none of it had to do with her.

She still believed that somewhere, deep in his heart, he still loved her. Not the sisterly way that he has been showing this weekend, but the passionate way he used to love her. She wanted his strong and full-of-lust love. She wiped a tear from the corner of her eye. She was a mess. This weekend had been a sweet torture. She knew that she could not have him the way she wanted, but she knew that she could not let him go.

Pete walked into the door after shaking Sean's hand. He offered his arm to Amanda, and they headed up the escalator to meet their friends at the Italian restaurant. Doris spotted Amanda from their table and waved her hand to catch her attention. Pete saw Doris' wave and waved back. He nudged Amanda's shoulder and pointed in Doris' direction. Amanda jumped from the intrusion of her thoughts and walked over with him.

Amanda looked down at the table and inspected it. "Why are there only four chairs?"

"You, me, Pete, and Ben." Doris said as she took a sip of her water.

"And Jodie. She texted me that she's coming too." Amanda said as she sat across from Doris. Pete sat down next to Amanda and placed the linen napkin on his lap.

"Oh," Doris said in a surprised tone, "I didn't know. Well, I was lucky to get this table. The wait is over and hour."

"It's ok." Pete said as he caught the attention of a waiter. "I'm terribly sorry to bother you. We have a fifth joining us for dinner. Could we possibly move to a larger table?"

"I'm sorry sir, the dining area is full. If you do not mind the squeeze, we can place an extra chair at the end of the table." The waiter suggested.

"That would be wonderful." Pete answered.

The waiter nodded his head. "Very good sir, we will set that up for you in a moment."

The waiter walked away as Ben and Jodie walked into the restaurant. Pete waved his hand and caught Jodie's attention. She pointed over at the table and then followed Ben over to it. Their fingers were laced together as they approached the table. Doris' eyebrow raised as her eyes focused on their hands. Amanda watched Doris' reaction and then looked over at Jodie.

Knowing what Amanda was looking at, Jodie rolled her eyes and mouthed "I'll tell you later."

"Hey everyone." Ben said with a grin. "How is everyone's night so far?" Amanda grunted as she looked over at Ben. "I lost about fifty dollars."

Ben laughed as he pulled out the chair next to Doris. He started to sit when he stopped and looked at Jodie. "Um, were we supposed to get our own table or something?"

"No, Doris asked for a four-person table. She didn't know Jodie was coming. Don't worry, the waiter is coming over with another chair and place setting." Pete said as he slightly shook his head.

Jodie looked over at Doris, watching her smile into her glass of water. Jodie could feel her blood begin to boil at the confirmation that Doris was trying to get to Ben. Although Jodie and Doris were not the closest of friend, they were more party friends, Jodie had confided in her about her relationship with Ben on more than one occasion. Doris knew their history, about how they fought and then got back together and how much she cared about him. Hell, she was there the first night they met.

Ben offered the chair to Jodie. She shook her head. "No, Ben. I'm the fifth wheel here. I guess my presence in the lobby wasn't enough of a hint that I would be joining everyone for dinner."

Doris shrugged her shoulders as she took another sip of her water. Amanda and Pete looked at each other, searching for a clue as to what was going on. Just as Amanda was going to ask, the waiter came over with the extra chair and place setting. Jodie sat down at the head of the table and opened a menu.

"Hello, my name is Bradley, I will be your server tonight. Would you like to hear tonight's specials?"

***

"So now Andrew is in this stage of running around without his pants or underwear on. Poor Andrea calls me up every time, so I can yell at him to put everything on. It's hysterical." Pete said with a smile. "I can pretend over the phone to scold him, but when it's facetime, forget it!"

Jodie looked over at Pete with her chin in her palm. "Do you want kids someday?"

Amanda choked a little as Pete smiled and looked over at Jodie. "Someday." Amanda patted herself in the chest as she calmed herself. *I guess adoption or surrogacy is an option* she thought, looking over at him.

Pete picked up the wine glass by the stem. He swirled it around and stated, "This is really good wine."

Ben looked up and smiled. "No seriously, it is really an excellent choice." Pete said as he took another sip of his wine.

Ben nodded as he placed his glass on the table. "Thanks. I've spent the past decade of my life in the food industry."

"That is one thing you can always count on Ben for, his knowledge of good wine." Amanda said as she poured herself another glass. "That and his excellent taste of food."

"Of food?" Pete asked as he looked at Amanda. "What are you a food critic or something?"

"Something like that." Ben said as he chewed on a piece of steak.

"He is a chef. He graduated from culinary school a few years ago. Now he's a chef at the restaurant he used to waiter at." Jodie elaborated. Ben smiled at her and squeezed her thigh.

"How many glasses of this have I had?" Pete asked as he finished off another glass of wine.

"I think it was four." Amanda said as she poured him another glass. Her eyelids were heavy as she smiled at him.

"You are being awfully quiet over there, Doris." Pete commented as he twirled his spaghetti.

"I'm just thinking." Doris said as she popped a piece of bread in her mouth, her gaze drifting back to Ben.

"Or plotting." Jodie said, taking a long drink of her wine. She held the empty glass out to Amanda and made it dance. Amanda took it and filled it up. She examined the bottle and realized that they were almost done with a third bottle.

Pete choked on his wine at Jodie's comment. Doris looked over at Jodie. "If you have something to say, Jode, say it."

Ben rubbed Jodie's thigh, trying to calm her down. Jodie looked over and smiled as she felt a tingling sensation at the top of her spine. "Just commenting. You always seem to have a hidden agenda."

Doris nodded her head. She slid her foot up the side of Ben's leg and smiled. Ben's head swiveled like a snapped rubber band. "I'm just a thoughtful person, Jode."

"Yeah, extremely thoughtful. And not a boyfriend-stealing slut at all." Jodie said, looking at Doris.

"Now Jodie, just because men flock to me and not to you is no need to call me a slut. Besides, who's boyfriend am I supposedly stealing?" Doris said, sliding her foot higher up on Ben's leg, waving her hand at the notion.

Ben slid closer to Jodie and smiled. He placed a kiss on her cheek and finished the wine in his glass. He caught the waiter's attention and said, "We will be needing another bottle."

"Well, if I sat around with my legs spread open, I'm sure I'd have men flocking to me too. And you know damn well you've been all over Ben since we've been here."

Pete choked on his wine as Amanda covered her mouth, her eyes wide with excitement. Ben stared down at the table, pausing all movement, as Doris' mouth dropped.

Ben sat there, his brother's words coming to the forefront of his mind. Jimmy had pulled him aside after they first hung out with the girls. Ben could not stop talking about Jodie, and his brother had been happy for him, but he stopped him, and his face turned serious. "Listen bro, I'm happy for you. Jodie seems like a really great girl. But watch out for that friend of hers. I get a bad vibe. She's trouble and she's into you." His attention returned to the conversation when he heard Jodie's next comment.

"Oh Doris, close your mouth. I know you are used to it in that position, but please, we are eating dinner."

"Jodie, stop. This is very unlike you." Ben whispered as he looked around, making sure no one was hearing the conversation.

"I need to use the bathroom. Jodie, come with me." Amanda said as she stood up from the table.

***

"Jodie, what has gotten into you?" Amanda asked as she washed her hands. "Ben." Jodie said with a sly smile as she twirled her hair.

Amanda looked at Jodie through the mirror and smiled. "So, you two?"

Jodie nodded her head. Amanda smiled and shook her head. Jodie leaned against the bathroom counter, like she could not support herself. "It was really good too. I came... twice."

Amanda busted into giggles, feeling the wine go to her head. "Pete's gay."

"What?" Jodie asked as her eyes grew wider. She went to walk to Amanda, but almost fell when she let go of the counter. "Yeah. Crazy." Amanda said as she walked over to Jodie.

Jodie held onto Amanda's shoulders and looked her in the eyes. "I am going to beat the shit out of Doris if she doesn't back off."

Amanda nodded. "I know. But nothing is going to happen. Ben loves you."

"Really?" Jodie asked with a hopeful smile.

"Really. Have I ever been wrong before?" Amanda asked as she hugged Jodie. "Yes." Jodie said as she hugged Amanda back.

"Shut up. I'm right."

"So, what about you and Pete?"

Amanda shrugged her shoulders. "He's gay. That's it. The love of my life is gay." Jodie started to giggle. "It's not funny." Amanda said, trying to hold back her giggles.

"Oh god, how pathetic." Amanda said as she laughed. Jodie shrugged her shoulders and kissed Amanda on the cheek. "Don't worry, we'll find you a straight man," Jodie said as she began to open the bathroom door. She paused, looked back over her shoulder to Amanda and continued, "Hopefully one that Doris won't try to screw?"

Amanda rolled her eyes and laughed as she exited the bathroom.

***

Amanda and Jodie joined the rest of them at the table to drink the tension away. They sat there, giggling like children who shared a secret. The waiter walked over with the desserts. The girls clapped as their desserts were placed in front of them. Jodie took a bite of her chocolate mousse cake and moaned. "This is the best thing ever."

Ben looked over at her and smiled slyly. He moved his kneading hand higher up on her thigh, underneath her skirt. Her eyes grew wider at him as he teased her with his fingers. She leaned over with a piece of cake and put it in his mouth. "Mmm. This is really good."

"You know what I want to do?" She asked as she squeezed her thighs together. "What's that Jode?" Amanda asked as she licked her French vanilla ice cream off the spoon.

"I want to go dancing."

"That is an awesome idea." Pete said as he took the spoon away from Amanda. "And this is how you lick ice cream off a spoon." He said as he held the spoon straight up and seductively licked the dripping ice cream off the handle.

Amanda burst into giggles as she watched. "I think you just gave Doris a run for her money!"

Doris nodded, swallowing a piece of her warm apple pie. "There's a club on the beach not far down the boardwalk."

"I hate dancing." Ben said. Jodie unclenched her legs a little and winked at him. She licked her lips and smiled at him as she leaned over and kissed him. "Dancing it is!"

Amanda waved at the waiter. "Can we get the check please?"

The waiter placed the check on the table as everyone grabbed for their wallets. Ben put his hand on the check and shook his head. "It's ok, tonight it's on me."

"What, why?" Amanda asked as she closed her bag.

"Because I won big tonight." Ben said with a smile as he stuffed the money in the checkbook.

Amanda rolled her eyes as Pete laughed and said, "Well, at least one of us did."

Fourteen

Doris stumbled to the Beach Bar with Amanda and Pete close behind her. "I think it's right over here." Doris said as she pointed across the boardwalk.

Amanda turned to talk to Jodie, but found her a few feet behind them, pressing herself against Ben as they kissed. "Oh, sweet lord! That is not what I needed to see." Pete and Doris turned to see what Amanda was talking about. Ben grabbed at Jodie's skirt and almost fell over from trying to grind into her. Amanda walked over and grabbed Jodie's arm, dragging her to the club's entrance. The bouncers stopped them for their IDs and let them in.

The music was pumping though the air as they made their way to the bar. Pete went up to the bartender. "We need a round of tequila shots. And keep them coming until one of us hit the ground." He yelled over the music. The bartender nodded and set up five shot glasses. They all put salt on their hands. Pete held up his shot and yelled, "To Atlantic City!"

They all took their shots. The bartender filled them up again. Amanda held hers up and yelled, "To old friends." The five of them took their shot. Jodie put the glass down and threw her arms up in defeat. "I give up. I can't take another shot." She yelled over the music. Amanda, Doris, and Pete booed her. She opened her mouth is protest, but Ben put a lime slice in her mouth.

She looked over at him as he licked his finger and ran it from the base of her neck to the middle of her chest. He poured some salt on the saliva trail. He raised the glass and said, "to love." He licked the salt off her from the chest up, took the shot of tequila and took the lime from her mouth. A crowd of people around them began to cheer as Jodie turned bright red.

Amanda took another tequila shot and then ordered a Long Island Iced Tea. She stared at Pete as he danced next to the bar. His muscles moved like a well-oiled machine, in one smooth, hypnotizing movement. Her body reacted to his, the way it used to when they were together. She could not stand just being next to him. She grabbed him by the hand and dragged him to the dance floor. Amanda pushed herself against him as they danced. Pete put on hand on her behind and held her closer to him as he grinded into her. Amanda began to unbutton his blue shirt as they danced. His stare bore into her as she completely opened his shirt. Some of the surrounding people cheered as his carved marble stomach was exposed.

Amanda's drink sloshed around, some spilling on Pete's chest. She went to wipe if off with her hand, but then decided that her tongue made a more exceptional sponge. She felt his body react to her touch, so she traced her tongue to his chin. She looked at him only for a moment before he pressed his mouth against her, thrusting his tongue into her mouth.

Pete could not explain the reaction he was having. He had not felt this way since the last time he was with Amanda. Pat did not make him feel this way. Maybe it was the alcohol making him behave in the manner he was, or maybe it was just Amanda.

Suddenly being on the dance floor was not enough for him. He pushed them to the fence. Amanda smiled as he took her hand and ran down the beach. He looked around for a private place and dragged them over to a group of barrels by the side deck of the club. Amanda fell on top of him as he looked at her and laughed. She started to giggle, and she nibbled on his neck.

"Mandy, I don't know what is happening." He said as she pulled her underwear down. Amanda shut her eyes for a moment, praying that this was not her imagination playing a trick on her. She swallowed hard when he entered her. She felt like no time passed between them. She was taken back to the nights in her dorm room, afternoons behind the bleachers of the football field, mornings in the library. Ecstasy flooded through her as her past and her present collided.

Amanda snapped out of her daydream when she felt Pete convulsing with pleasure underneath her. "Oh Mandy." It was all he could say.

***

Doris, Ben, and Jodie watched Amanda and Pete out on the dance floor while they stood at the bar with their drinks. Jodie leaned against the bar, swaying to the music as she sang along. A tall man with tanned skin and black wavy hair walked over to Jodie. He stood there, watching her, and licking his lips. "Hey there sweetie."

Jodie looked up at him with a drunken smile. "Hello there."

"You look like you are having a good time. My name is Dan, what's yours?" He held out his hand and went to shake hers. Ben intercepted hand and shook it. "She's taken."

Doris poked her head around Ben to look at whom he was talking to. Dan looked over at Doris and smiled. "Is she taken too?" Doris flipped her hair and swayed her hips as she walked over to him.

Ben was going to respond for the guy to leave when Doris said, "No. I'm Doris."

Dan smiled. "Well Doris, would you be interested in moving that fine body of yours with me on the dance floor?"

He'll do, Doris thought as she took him by the hand and walked out onto the floor. She wrapped her arms around his neck as she rubbed herself into his hips. She kept a smile on her face, but her eyes looked over at Ben. She saw him watching her dance and purposely moved seductively on Dan. Dan was straining against her as his hands wandered all over her body. Doris kept her eyes on Ben as she kissed Dan.

Ben stood there, shaking his head as Doris made out with the random guy on the dance floor. "I don't understand her, she cries that she was taken advantage of, but then she acts like this," he shouted over to Jodie. When she did not respond, he turned his head to find Jodie in front of him, dancing like no one was watching. She looked over at Doris and started laughing. "What?" Ben asked as he pushed his forehead against hers.

"I bet I could dance like that." She said as she wiggled in front of him like a stripper giving a lap dance. He watched her body move as she licked the tip of his chin. *She is adorable when she is trying to be sexy,* he thought to himself, knowing it would not be what she would want to hear.

She laughed as she pushed off him and turned to head to the dance floor. He pulled her against her and began to dance. She pushed herself into him until she felt him react against her. He sniffed the flower in her hair as he nibbled on her earlobe. She began to moan a little as she wriggled is his arms. He licked her earlobe and whispered, "Want to go somewhere?"

She nodded her head in response as she turned. She plunged in for a kiss, looking like someone who was starved, and he was the food. She pushed him against the bar, and she continued her consumption of his mouth. The bartender leaned over and yelled, "Can you two please leave the bar area? People are complaining."

Ben led them down to the beach and sat her down on a lounge chair. There was a drunken couple a few chairs down from them. They paid little attention to Jodie swaying back and forth on the chair. He laid her down and pushed a chair next to her. He lay down on the other chair and held her hand. They stared up at the stars together. Ben rubbed her hand with his thumb.

She felt tingly all over, and was not sure if it was from the alcohol or the gentle caress of his thumb. "The stars are beautiful." Ben said after he slowly exhaled.

Jodie looked the stars, never fully understanding the astrological signs or meanings. She did not know why, but they all seemed to fall into place tonight. "I love you."

Ben blinked and looked over at Jodie. She did not remove her gaze from the stars. He was positive that he heard her say I love you.

Jodie smiled. She could see him staring at her as he said it back. He propped himself up on one elbow and leaned over her. He gently kissed her and brushed her hair back past the flower.

"Hey Jodie," Ben asked quietly, "Meet me at the hotel room in half an hour."

She raised an eyebrow and looked at him quizzically. He smiled and responded quietly, "It's going to be a really nice surprise." He kissed her softly on the cheeks and nose, emphasizing the last three words. She smiled, her eyes closed, and nodded quietly, pulling him in for a long kiss. He whispered, "I love you," into her ear and then walked away.

Jodie laid on the chair for another five minutes, repeating the three words in her head until she shook herself out of her trance. She slowly stood up, stretching every love filled muscle in her body. She looked over her shoulder and saw the drunken couple sloppily kissing one another in the heat of the moment. She laughed, appreciating their desire, and left the lovers alone.

She started to walk up the bar, having to walk through dance floor. She made her way across the floor, searching for the rest of her friends. She got lost in the crowd, being knocked into by the dancers. When she finally made it through the ocean of people, she fixed her hair and smoothed her skirt when she was free enough to do so. She sent out a group message to everyone, trying to find where they were. She waited for a few moments, seeing that she was left on read. She surveyed the area one last time and began to walk to the exit walkway when a deep voice stopped her.

"Well, well, well. I can't believe my eyes. Jodie Rogers. It's been a long time."

Fifteen

Ben rushed into the hotel room, throwing the plastic bag from the general store onto the bed. He turned on the light and pulled out a few candles from the bag and lined them across the dresser and on the nightstand. He turned down the bed and put flowers on the pillows then looked around the room, satisfied with what he did. He played his favorite playlist on his phone and walked into the shower.

Ben held himself up in the shower, bracing one hand against the wall as he washed. Between his declaration of love and the alcohol he consumed, the shower was doing little to sober him. Through the rhythm of the water, he heard the hotel door open and close. Shouted over the water, "Jodie, baby, I'm in here."

Silence was his answer. He heard her walking around the room, and adjoining bedroom door being closed as he turned off the water. He grabbed a towel and wrapped it around his waist as he opened the door and walked into complete darkness. The room darkening curtains pulled closed over the window. "Jodie?"

"Mmh?" she mumbled in response.

"Oh, you kind of freaked me out. Why did you blow out the candles?"

He heard a small giggle and felt the towel torn from his body, a hand griping his member. He was pushed down on the bed. "Jodie, damn!"

She climbed on top of him naked and ready to go, sliding herself on top of him. "Jesus, Jode, wait, can we turn on a light or something? This isn't what I had planned."

There was no response, other than the bed rocking like a small ship being tossed in a hurricane. Ben gripped the sheets as he felt himself begin to climax.

"That's right, Ben. Fuck me like you've never fucked her before."

Ben sucked in his breath; his hazy mind cleared in a sharp second. That was a very un-Jodie thing to say. He tried to push it out of his mind, blaming the alcohol, but then he realized the feel of her was not right. He shoved her off him, reached over to the light and turned it on.

Blonde hair flung back, revealing Doris naked on the bed. She pouted at him and complained, "But I was so close to coming."

Ben jumped up from the bed. "What the fuck?" He screamed as put on a pair of shorts on. She spread out on the bed, staring up at him as she touched herself.

"Ben, you know you want me, you have ever since we first met. Always staring at me? Please, you wanted this, and you know it. Jodie is a prude."

"What the fuck did you just do?" He asked, running his hands through his hair. He looked around the room, the flowers crushed on the floor, the candles on their sides.

"Well Ben, the question is what the fuck did you do. Or rather, who did you just fuck?" She stood up, then bent over to pick up her panties, showing Ben a full view of herself.

"The way I see it, you seduced me. Playing with my mind this whole trip. Tisk-tisk Benny. You should have known better." She pulled on her skirt and shook her head. "Jodie will be crushed."

"Wha—how…what…" he mumbled, still in shock. He looked at her, full of hatred and dread. "What do you want from me you bitch? She won't believe you." He said as he threw the rest of her clothes at her. She caught them and answered, "Oh, she will. Or at least it will ruin her perfect little image of you. Look, I don't want to ruin your newfound love with Jodie, so I won't say anything. But the next time I come to fuck your brains out, you better enjoy it."

Ben sat down on the bed shaking his head. "You're fucking psychotic. What makes you think I would let that happen?"

She took out her cell phone and said, "What is Jodie's number? 555-275…"

"Okay, enough. Just get the fuck out of here."

"Good night, Ben," she said as she blew him a kiss and walked out of the door. She looked back at him as she closed to the door and said, "By the way, nice dick. Does Jodie realize what she has been missing out on for so many years?"

***

Jodie spun around, stunned to hear her name. There was a man standing behind her with a black baseball cap. His icy blue eyes sparkled at her as he smiled. His build was intimidating. He wore a black tee shirt and jeans with flip-flops.

"I'm sorry, do I know you?"

"Come on Jodie, it hasn't been that long." He said as he looked around. He leaned closer to her face and asked in a hushed, but amused tone, "are you that drunk?"

Jodie shook her head and focused on the stranger. She knew this face; his eyes were frighteningly familiar. She suddenly felt like the wind was knocked out of her. She tried to catch her breath as she whispered his name. "Joe Rappaport."

***

"That was amazing Mandy." Pete said as he struggled buckle his belt closed.

Amanda stood up and smoothed her skirt. She took her cardigan and tied it around her shoulders. She went over and helped him with his buckle. He almost fell back as he stumbled to stay standing. He looked down at Amanda and smiled. She smiled back at him and watched his eyes roll up.

"Pete?"

"I'm gonna vomit." He said as he turned around. He threw up on the spot they just made love. She grimaced at the sound and shut her eyes. He stood back up and looked over at her. "Let's go back to my hotel room."

Amanda took Pete's arm and threw it around her neck, guiding him as they walked over to his hotel, which was much closer than the Burgundy. His sister answered the door in an oversized tank top. Her hair was in curlers and covered with a shower cap. "Hey sexy." Pete said as he stumbled into the room.

"Pete, have you been drinking?" Andrea asked as she watched him fall onto the couch. He smiled up at her.

"Sorry Andrea." Amanda said as she shut the door behind her. "Is the baby sleeping?"

"Yeah, but he's in the bedroom. He'll sleep through anything."

"Shit! I forgot something in my car. Be right back." Pete said, stumbling to the door. He sloppily kissed Amanda and smacked her in the behind. "Ow!" He yelled as he walked into the hallway.

Andrea shook her head as she shut the door. "Sit down."

Amanda took a seat at one end of the couch. Andrea sat down on the other, then jumped over and hugged Amanda. "I'm really happy to see you again."

"Me too. I can't believe it's been so long." Amanda said as Andrea sat back down. "I know. So much has happened too." Andrea said as she glanced back at the bedroom.

"How old are you now?" Amanda asked, following her gaze. "I'll be twenty in March."

"Wow. It really has been a long time. That's insane."

"Yeah. It really has." Andrea said as she looked down at her hands.

"So, I got pregnant with Andrew when I was sixteen." Andrea said after a long pause. Amanda looked at Andrea in shock. Andrea was still studying her hands as she continued. "I was at a friend's party. Well, actually, it was a friend of a friend. It was a lame sweet sixteen party, you know, the spoiled brat party thrown at a country club. Well, it was boring. I was sitting there, listening to the music when a worker walked over to me. He was beautiful; jet-black hair, bright blue eyes, and a gorgeous smile.

"He started talking to me, asking me my name and everything. I was shocked that he was paying attention to me, the one with the braces and frizzy blonde hair. He asked me if I wanted to go outside with him while he took a cigarette break. I said sure, it was only outside." She paused for a moment and swallowed. "So, we were talking, and he said that I was beautiful and then said he was going to get a drink. He came back with one for me, and we both drank it. I don't know what was in it, but after a few minutes I felt funny. He asked me if he could kiss me, and I said yes."

She started to cry. "It was my first kiss, Amanda."

Amanda moved next to Andrea and put her arms around her. Amanda sniffed and swallowed hard.

"Well, the next thing I remember, we were down on the beach. He kept kissing me, and his hands were everywhere. I kept telling him to stop, but he wouldn't. He got mad at me and hit me in the face. I lost count of how many times I was hit. I remember feeling an immense pain and that was it. The next thing I knew I was laying on the beach with blood dripping down my legs. I went to the public bathroom and cleaned up. My friend found me in a heap on the bathroom floor. She called the police, and they took me to the hospital. I passed out after I spoke to the police. Winds up he didn't even work at the country club."

"Andrea, that is horrible." Amanda said as she rubbed her arm. Andrea wiped the tears that escaped from her eyes.

"Well, a few months went by, and I hadn't gotten my period. I just thought it was because of trauma and stress. My friend wanted me to take a test, and then I found out I was pregnant. I didn't want the baby, but I couldn't tell my parents. Then it was too late, they got divorced, mom was an alcoholic, and Pete was away. The baby was the only thing I could take comfort in."

"Wow, Andrea."

Andrea nodded her head and smiled. "Well, I heard that they caught the bastard. Arrested for statutory rape. It's sick Amanda, he was twenty-two."

***

"How've you been Jodie?" Joe asked as he surveyed their surroundings.

"Um, fine. You?" Jodie asked, her heart still thumping in her chest. She never felt comfortable around him, not when they were children, not when he was with Lisa, and especially not now since she had been drinking. *Oh my god, Lisa,* she thought, the visions from when she passed out flashing in her mind. That odd, tingly sensation creeping up her spine.

"Ok. A lot has happened in the past few years. You have a minute? I'd love to catch up."

"Um, actually, no. I'm supposed to meet my boyfriend back at our room."

"Nice try, Jodie. Come on. We were close once." He said as he grabbed her arm and walked over towards the ocean.

"Okay, but five minutes. I really have to get back." She yelled out above the music, hoping that someone would hear her.

He nodded as they walked over to the beach chairs that just moments before she professed her love to Ben. Joe sat down across from her; a smile sat uncomfortably across his classically good-looking face.

The couple at the other end was getting up to leave. The girl looked over at Jodie and said to her boyfriend, "What a slut, she was just here with another guy."

Jodie gave them a pleading look, praying that they would not leave, but she had no luck. "So, it's been a while. When was the last time I saw you?" Joe asked, pulling her attention back to him.

"Um, probably back when we graduated." She said, looking back towards the club. She returned her glare to him, "You know, when Lisa died."

He did not flinch at her name, just casually responded, "Oh yeah, that's right. To think I was the last person to see her alive."

"How would you even know that?" Josie said, cocking an eyebrow and crossing her arms.

He studied her; his stare intense. "According to police records, no one really remembers that party too well."

In her peripheral vision, Jodie could see Lisa, a look of fear and accusation in her eyes as she stared at Joe. *This is crazy,* Jodie thought.

"Convenient for you, huh?"

Joe raised an eyebrow. "Wow Jodie. It's like I told the police, I left to get her a blanket, she kept complaining she was cold. When I came back with one, she was gone. I heard what happened the same time you all did, the day after the party when the cops found her."

Jodie nodded her head, not believing a word that came out of his mouth. "Yeah right. So why did you disappear after? It was like a few days later and your house was just vacated."

"My dad got transferred to Connecticut. We still cooperated with the authorities."

"Right." Jodie said as she looked out to the water. A chill ran up her spine, as she heard a whisper in her ear, "he's guilty". She shivered, knowing who's voice she heard.

"You got hot Jodie. I must say. You weren't much to look at back in high school, but you definitely filled out in all the right places." He said as he licked his lips.

Jodie crossed her arms to cover herself, as if she was suddenly naked. She scowled at him and said, "Get over yourself Joe. Never going to happen."

Joe sat next to her on the chair and slid his hand up her arm. Jodie went to stand up, but he grabbed her arm and turned her head to face his. "I kind of wish it was you that night."

"What?" She said, as her eyes grew huge. "What night?"

"That party back in tenth grade. I totally would have taken your virginity. Are you still one?" He asked as he ran his hand over her thighs, his eyes raking over her body.

She smacked him in face and hissed, "Listen you fuck rag, I know what you did to my best friend. Let go of me right now and don't you ever touch me or speak to me again, you dirty, murdering, motherfucker."

"I didn't do anything to her except what she wanted." He said as he tightened his grip on her arm.

"Oh, she wanted to be used by you for years, nothing more than your booty call? She wanted to be smacked in the head with the vodka bottle? She wanted to be dragged to the water? You sick fuck!" Jodie said, spitting in his face.

"You are a sick bitch. Who did you hear that from?" He asked as he stood up. "Who?" He yelled as he violently shook her. Jodie kept her lips sealed, watching him with accusing eyes. He yelled in frustration, hitting her in the face.

Jodie fell back on the chair. He hit her over and over, screaming "Who, you fucking freakish bitch, who?"

Joe heard a commotion from behind, and saw people coming down from the club, heading towards the beach. He grabbed her shoulders and threw her back down on the chair. "I'm not done with you, bitch. I have something more pressing to take care of. But this isn't over." He spat on her face and ran down the beach.

Jodie laid there, fading in and out of consciousness, her eyes involuntarily closing, the red and blue lights of police cars filling the darkness.

Sixteen

The morning after the graduation party was spent looking for Lisa. Jodie and Amanda searched all her favorite places, checked social media, and called her constantly. By the late afternoon, the girls were worried. They decided to return to Lisa's house and tell her parents.

Lisa's father answered the door, his face dropping when he saw the look of worry on their faces. He let them in, calling out to his wife to join them. They sat in the living room silently, as Lisa's mother entered the room.

"Where is Lisa?" She asked, observing their body language.

"Mrs. Parker…" Amanda trailed off, her voice beginning to tremble. She looked off to a picture of Lisa on the end table and clammed up.

"We haven't seen Lisa since last night. We couldn't find her this morning, and we have searched everywhere. Her phone is off, going straight to voicemail." Jodie stated the facts, devoid of emotion. She was empty, her gut telling her that something bad had happened to her friend.

The Parkers exchanged glances, Mr. Parker calling the police to file a missing person report. He was notified that they could not process the claim until she was gone for 24 hours.

The girls notified their parents, who in response came to Lisa's house. They decided to split up and look for her, Lisa's parents staying home in case she called or returned.

Time passed excruciatingly slow, but also passed too quickly. Around eight in the evening, they all returned to the Parker's home, to share their lack of information. Hope was fading fast, until a knock on the door snapped them all out of their trance.

Mr. Parker opened the door to find two police offers standing there. He looked back at his wife, who collapsed into Jodie's mother's arms. They informed them that Lisa was found at Walker Bay, west of where the party was. She was found by an older couple going for their nightly stroll.

The Parkers were escorted to the beach by the officers, the rest of them followed in their cars. They arrived to find the road blocked by police cars, their lights filling the night sky. They approached the crime scene; caution tape kept them back from the body bag on the gurney. The detectives finishing up their investigation by the time they arrived.

The dread and loss of losing a piece of yourself is unbearable and indescribable. Amanda and Jodie clung to each other in despair, the knowledge that nothing would ever be the same crashing over them.

***

Jodie sat up, her right eye swelling as she licked her lip and tasted blood. Her head throbbed as she wiped the blood off with the back of her hand. She looked around for assailant, but she was alone. She wandered down to the beach in a bit of a haze, approaching a group of people sitting around a fire. She circled them, searching for those ice-cold blue eyes.

The group of older hippies sat there with guitars, singing, and laughing. They did not pay attention to her circling them, but passed a brown paper bag around, taking swigs of it as it passed from hand to hand. Jodie searched their faces; each blurred a little more than the next. She could not make out their features. Her head spun as she finally looked at a face that was clear to her. Lisa was sitting there, staring up at Jodie, waiting for her recognition.

Jodie's eyes widened as Lisa stood up. "Jodie don't run away from me."

Jodie stumbled backwards, then turned and began to run. She ran up to the club and into the crowd of people. The dancers moved in slow motion as she pushed through them. She emerged from them like a breeching whale, throwing her arms out from her sides. She looked back, knowing she lost Lisa in the crowd. She turned to leave and came nose to nose with Lisa.

"Jodie, stop running." Lisa said as she put her arms around Jodie, the icy arms chilled Jodie to the bone. She closed her eyes and held her breath.

"Jodie, you need to stop him. He will do it again."

Jodie pushed through the icy grip and ran down the walkway to the boardwalk. She stood on the mostly empty boardwalk and turned her head from left to right, trying to remember which way the hotel was. She turned to the right and ran as fast as she possibly could without falling over. She eventually reached the Burgundy Inn and ran inside.

The lobby was dark, and no one was there. The light from the bar spilled onto the dark floor like a glass of tipped milk. Jodie followed the light, her hands on the frame of the doorway. She stepped in, finding Lisa sitting behind the bar, pouring two shots of whiskey. Jodie shook her head as Lisa looked up at her.

"Sit, Jodie. We need to talk."

Jodie put her hands over her ears and ran out of the room. Lisa yelled after her as she ran up the stairs. "Don't go up there Jodie, you'll find no comfort there."

Jodie made her way to the bedrooms and banged on her door. She screamed out and cried as she slid to the floor. She buried her head in her knees, with her arms hugging her kneecaps. She cried until she felt something in her hand. She peeked her head up and saw a room key dangling from her finger. She studied it and felt the etching of 324 on the red plastic key chain. It was the key to Ben's room.

She looked up at the door next to her and then back at the key, then picked herself off the floor and placed her hand on the bright blue wall. She slid the key into the door and turned it. She heard the soft click of the lock and she removed the key. She slowly opened the door, seeing nothing but darkness. She heard low moaning as opened the door a little more. Suddenly the bed came into perfect view as Jodie searched the room with her eyes. She stood there in horror as she saw Doris on top of Ben, grinding her hips into his. Ben's face was twisted with pleasure as Doris looked over at Jodie. Doris licked her lips as her face morphed into demon-like features.

Doris let out a low maniacal laugh as Jodie ran from the room. She tripped down the steps and stumbled over herself as she ran back to the lobby. She found herself back in the bar and stared at Lisa.

Without looking up, Lisa shook her head. "I warned you. Why don't you listen to me?"

Jodie hugged the doorframe as she stared at Lisa in fear. "Why are you so scared of me Jodie? I was your best friend."

"Because you are dead." Jodie whispered. She slowly let go of the doorframe and moved into the room. "Because you are dead!" She screamed at the top of her lungs.

Lisa looked up at her and nodded her head. "Hmm, well, you're right. I am dead." Jodie slowly moved her way to the bar stool across from Lisa. She slid onto the stool, not talking her eyes off Lisa.

"I want you to know that what you saw was not Ben's fault. That bitch seduced him." Lisa said as she placed the bottle of whiskey back on the wall. Josie stared at the whiskey bottle, the tan label curling away from the green bottle, looking like a weathered pirate's map. Lisa turned around and looked Jodie. "And you know what to do about that."

Jodie's eyes shifted back to Lisa as she shook her head, then averting her eyes down at the shot glass. The brown liquid sat in the glass, waiting to be consumed. Lisa lifted her shot glass and raised it to Jodie. Jodie watched as her hand involuntarily lifted the shot glass and met Lisa's. "To us." Lisa said as she downed the shot.

Jodie lifted the shot glass to her mouth and emptied it, feeling the warm liquid coat her throat like tar on pavement. She coughed a little and returned the glass to the bar top. She looked down at the glass, and what once was filled with alcohol now had a little puddle at the bottom of it. The puddle was darker than the alcohol. She dipped her finger into the puddle and studied her finger. Blood covered her fingertip and slowly dripped down her finger. A coppery aftertaste filled her mouth as she looked up at Lisa.

Lisa smiled, exposing bloodstained teeth. Jodie jumped back from the bar as Lisa laughed. "You can't escape me Jodie, I'm a part of you."

Jodie awoke with a jolt, looking up at the sky. She heard voices next to her as she slowly sat up. Her head was pounding, and her right eye was swollen. She reflexively raised her hand to her lip, then looked down to find blood on her fingers. She looked over to her left and saw a few hippies sitting on the chairs next to her. A voice from behind her startled her.

"Are you okay dear? You had us worried." Jodie looked back to find an older woman with large glasses looking down at her. Her brown hair was frizzy and streaked with gray. She wore a scarf tied in her hair and a large beaded necklace. Her long-sleeved purple shirt fell over her long multicolored skirt. Brown sandals hugged the white socks on her feet.

"What? I'm fine, I think."

"We ran over as soon as that man ran away. You've been out for about a half an hour." She explained as she helped Jodie stand up. "You were screaming so loud, we heard you all the way from down there," she explained as she gestured towards the fire.

Jodie watched as a police officer walked across the beach, holding a flashlight. He put his hand on the hippie's shoulder. "Hey Mel, is this the girl?"

Mel nodded her head and stepped to the side. "Hello, miss, I am Officer Jensen. I have to ask you a few questions about what happened to you tonight."

***

Amanda fell asleep on the couch of Pete and Andrea's hotel suite. She laid on her stomach, with one arm hanging over the side. Her face was buried between the cushion and the pillow. The padding on the couch muffled her light snoring.

Amanda felt something brush against her hand. She ignored it, snuggling deeper into the couch. A chill ran up her spine as something pulled on her hair. She slowly opened her eyes, staring at the back of the off-white and pink-stripped couch. She turned her head and blinked her eyes.

Lisa sat on the floor, next to the couch. She looked up at Amanda and waved shyly. Amanda smiled and sleepily waved back. "Hey Lee."

Lisa looked up at Amanda with guilt all over her face. Amanda ruffled her eyebrows in concern. "Lee, what's wrong?"

Lisa lifted her hands to show Amanda her blood-covered palms. "What happened Lisa?"

Lisa shook her head and put her finger to her mouth, silencing herself. She stood up leaving a slight line of blood bisecting her lips and walked over to the window of the room, opened it up, and jumped out.

Amanda sat up on the couch, rubbing her eyes. Shaken from the dream, she walked into the bedroom and climbed into bed with Pete.

***

Officer Jensen drove Jodie back to the Burgundy. She sat in the back seat, staring out of the window, the copper taste lingering in her mouth. She sucked on her lip, investigating the cut with her tongue. She closed her eyes as they pulled up to the hotel, the exhaustion of the night consuming her. Officer Jensen put the car in park and stepped out, then opened Jodie's door and offered his hand to help her out and shut the door.

"Jodie, if you need anything or remember anything, please call me. You have my personal number on the back of the card."

Jodie took the business card and nodded her head, then walked to the hotel door. Jensen did not pull away until he saw Jodie walk into the elevator.

She stepped out in the motel section and stared at Ben's bedroom door, shaking involuntarily as she walked over to the door. She entered her room, finding it dark and cold, the air conditioner on full blast. She turned it off, making her way to the adjoining room. She peeked in, finding Ben sleeping under the covers.

Jodie climbed into the bed and snuggled herself into him. She pulled the blankets over them both and closed her eyes. Ben woke up from the feel of her body against his. He pulled away from her, unsure of who was next to him. He smelled her perfume and relaxed a little, knowing it was the right girl.

"Jodie?"

"Yea?"

"I need to tell you something."

"I'm sorry I wasn't here sooner."

"Jodie, we have to talk."

"Please, not now."

Jodie kissed Ben on the cheek and snuggled into him again. He put his arm around her and hugged her tight. He kissed her shoulder, guilt overwhelming him. He kept her close through the remainder of the night, cherishing the moment because he did not know what the morning would bring.

None of them could have known what the morning brought.

Seventeen

Amanda walked into her hotel room, followed by Pete, holding a bag of bagels and a large coffee. Amanda set the orange juice on the dresser then took the bag of bagels from Pete. He kept his sunglasses on as he nursed his hangover with a cup of coffee.

Amanda walked into the bathroom, looking for Jodie. She walked out and looked at Pete, who was sitting on the edge of a bed with his head hanging between his legs. "It's funny, this is the earliest we've all been up this trip." Jodie said, looking at her watch.

"Six o'clock is an ungodly hour." He said as he took a large sip of coffee, "Especially when you don't get in until two am." Amanda walked over to the adjoining door and knocked as she peeked her head in. "Wakey wakey, eggs and bakey." Amanda said as she opened the curtains in the bedroom.

Light flooded the room like a dam busted open by a rush of water. Ben raised his arm, blocking the light from his eyes. Amanda laughed as she walked over and pulled the covers off them. She looked down at Jodie's back and shook her shoulder. "Let's go woman, up and at 'em." Jodie slowly turned her head to face Amanda and was greeted with a scream when Amanda saw her face.

Pete ran into the room as Ben sat up and looked down at Jodie. "What the fuck happened?" Amanda asked Ben.

Jodie opened her eyes; the right one was a dark purple color. She looked up at Amanda, watching her yell at Ben.

"I swear to God, Ben, if you did this." Amanda yelled as she started to lunge at Ben. Pete ran over and grabbed her arms to prevent her from pouncing.

"He didn't do it." Jodie said as she sat up. She looked out of her swollen eye at everyone and touched her lip. She looked down at her fingers, realizing that her lip stopped bleeding. "Joe did it."

"Who the fuck is Joe?" Ben yelled as he sat up. He grabbed Jodie's chin and moved her head as he examined her. Jodie jerked her head back and smacked his hand away.

"He used to date Lisa." She said, as she stood up and walked into the bathroom. She turned on the cold water and filled up her cupped hands. She put her face into it and let the water drip down. Jodie enjoyed the peaceful sound of the running water for a moment before hearing Amanda at the door.

"Joe Rappaport? What the hell is he doing here, and why would he do that?" Amanda asked as she followed Jodie to the bathroom.

Jodie looked over the towel at Amanda and shrugged her shoulders. "I don't know why he is here. And he did this," she said, circling her finger around her face, "because he tried to hit on me and I turned him down, and then told him exactly what I thought of him." Jodie pushed past Amanda and walked to the center of the room.

"Which was what?" Pete asked as he returned from the other room with the bag of bagels. "It had to have been something for him to do whatever he did to you."

Jodie grabbed an egg bagel from the bag and ripped a piece of it off. "That he is a murder."

Amanda's eyes widened as she looked at Jodie. "What? Jodie, he was at the party."

"He murdered her. I know he did." Jodie said as she put the bagel in her mouth, wincing at the stinging in her lip. She turned and walked over to the window and closed the curtain to block out the rising sun.

"How?" Amanda challengingly asked.

Jodie put her back against the wall and looked over at Amanda. "I just do. Don't tell me that you don't feel it in your gut either."

Amanda thought back to that night when the they sat at Lisa's house, the swell of hope when they heard the knock on the door, the moment is deflated when it was the police. She remembered Joe walking down to the beach with his letterman jacket on, and Lisa's denim jacket in his hands. She looked over at Jodie and shook her head, about to respond when there was a knock at the door. Pete walked to the door and opened it. The little man from the counter was standing there with two police officers towering behind him.

"This is them. The girl is in this room." The owner said, pointing into the room. Jodie walked over to the door and looked at the officers. Jensen was standing next to a larger man. He removed his hat and tipped his head, "Good morning, Miss Rogers."

Jodie smiled at Jensen, thinking that he had information on Joe. "Officer Jensen, did you find him?" Jodie asked as the little man walked away.

"Unfortunately, Jodie, that is not why we are here. May we?" He said as he gestured his hat towards the door.

Jodie nodded at him and allowed the officers in the room. Jensen addressed the others in the room. "Good morning, I am Officer Jensen, this is my partner, Officer Wilder. We unfortunately have some bad news for all of you."

Amanda and Jodie sat down on a bed, holding each other's hands tightly. The two of them sat together on the couch in the same way when they heard about Lisa. The officers back then approached them in the same way when they were questioned about their whereabouts when Lisa disappeared. Pete sat on the other bed with Ben, looking up at the officers.

"When is the last time you saw Miss Doris Sullivan?" Officer Wilder asked as he took out a notepad.

Jodie's eyes grew as she almost jumped off the bed. "Doris? What happened to Doris?" Jodie asked as her heart jumped into her throat. She looked frantically around the room, as she realized that Doris was missing.

"We found Ms. Sullivan on the beach this morning." Officer Wilder said.

"She is okay, right?" Pete asked, assuming they would say that she was drunk or passed out and needed to be picked up.

"No. She was found unresponsive with a bottle of whiskey in her hands. The bottle was empty, and it seems that she received a blow to her head." Jensen said, looking over at the girls.

Jodie began to cry as Amanda shook uncontrollably. The girls shared a glance, noticing the eerie similarity to Lisa's death. Jensen shifted his eyes to the men and continued. "We are going to have to run through where you all were last night."

Everyone looked around at one another as the officers pulled the two chairs on either side of the dresser together. They sat down on the chairs and looked from person to person. Jodie began to speak as she kept her head down and her eyes shut.

"The last time I saw Doris was at the bar. She started talking with this guy, and they went off and started dancing together. Then I went down to the beach with Ben. Then Ben left, and I went to leave about five minutes later, and that's when I saw Joe Rappaport. He led me back down to the beach, and we fought, and then he hit me, and then that woman Mel was with me until I came to. Then I spoke with you, then you dropped me off here, and I went to sleep."

Jensen nodded his head as Wilder continued writing. "Did Ms. Sullivan say anything to you before she walked away with that man?"

Jodie shook her head. Amanda squeezed her hand and looked over at the officers. "I was with Pete all night. We separated from everyone soon after we got to the club. We went off dancing and then after a few hours we went back to his hotel room. I sat up with his sister and spoke with her until I fell asleep on the couch. Then we walked to the bagel place up the road and came here."

"A few hours? Can you be more specific?" Wilder said, looking up at Amanda. "Well, we walked away after we took some shots, then we went dancing for a while, and um." She said, looking up at Pete.

"We walked down to the beach and we had sex. Then she walked me back to my room." Pete finished.

"Was there any point that the two of you weren't together?" Jensen asked. "Yes, Pete went to his car shortly after we got to the hotel. I stayed with his sister." Amanda said.

"And what were you doing at your car?" Wilder asked Pete. "Getting my medication." Pete answered, looking down at the floor. "Which is?" Wilder asked, looking up from his notepad.

"Paxil." Pete answered. Amanda looked up at him.

"And how long ago were you put on the anti-depressants?"

"About three years ago."

Jensen nodded and turned to Ben. Ben stared straight ahead of himself, feeling eyes on him, and knowing it was his turn to speak. He did not want to speak in front of Jodie, knowing that he had to say what happened the other night. He inhaled as a name popped into his head.

"Dan." Ben said, still looking at the wall. "Excuse me?" Jensen asked.

Ben looked up at the officers. "The guy's name was Dan. Tall guy with a tan and wavy black hair. That's who she went off with.

"Doris, Jodie, and I were standing at the bar when this sleaze bag walked over and tried hitting on the girls. I tried to get him to leave, but she went to dance with him. She was all over him; they were practically having sex on the dance floor.

"Jodie and I walked onto the beach and stared at the stars. Then I had an idea to create a romantic night for us and I told her to meet me in half an hour. I ran to the convenience store and bought some flowers and candles. I came back here and set it up, and then I took a shower."

He paused for a moment and looked at Jodie, who was staring at him. Guilt filled him as he turned to face her. "I'm sorry Jodie."

The officers looked up at Ben, who was staring at Jodie. Jodie closed her eyes, remembering what she saw in her dream. She sucked in her breath and tried not to sob. "Excuse me?" Wilder asked as Ben broke his gaze away from Jodie and looked back at the officers.

"I heard someone walk in, and when I came out it was completely dark. My towel was ripped off and I was pushed onto the bed. I thought it was Jodie, but I turned on the light and it was Doris. I told her to get out. She said that she would tell Jodie, unless I promised that the next time, I would enjoy it. She left and I fell asleep, then Jodie came in about a half an hour later, and we fell asleep again."

"So, in other words, you had sexual relations with Ms. Sullivan last night." Jensen said, confirming and clearing up Ben's story.

Ben opened his mouth to protest but nodded his head instead. "But it wasn't consensual," he added.

Jodie's eyes were wide as her mouth opened in horror. "It really happened."

Ben looked over at her. "Jodie, I swear it was that one time. Not back when you asked me. I didn't even know it was going on and when I did, I tried to stop it. It was like..." he stumbled to find the words, "It was like she raped me."

"She was right, it really did happen." She said to herself as she shook her head in disbelief and walked into the bathroom. She threw up into the toilet and continued to dry heave for another two minutes. She flushed and walked out to the officers collecting personal information.

"I am very sorry for your loss. However, we are going to have to ask you to stay here until further notice." Jensen said as he headed for the door.

Pete jumped up. "That's not possible sir, my boat leaves tomorrow afternoon."

"We'll handle it. In the meantime, please keep in contact with us." Wilder said as he put his hat on and closed the door.

Pete walked over to Amanda and put his arms around her. She inhaled deeply and fell into him. She sat there, watching Jodie sit on the edge of the bed. Ben sat on the other bed, unsure of what to do.

***

Jodie was lost in her thoughts as she sat there, studying the pattern of the carpet. She watched the green intertwine with the pink as they danced across the carpet. Ben walked outside for a moment. The sunlight flashed into her sight, and her thoughts focused on her memories from the bar last night.

She said that she was a part of me, she thought, trying to fit pieces together. *There was the alcohol ... it was the same kind that Doris had. She kept warning me about Doris and Ben.* Jodie raked through her memories until finally something flooded her mind.

"Would you kill her?"

"Who, Anna Kendricks?"

"No, the seductress, would you kill her?"

Jodie's eyes flew open as she heard Lisa's voice echo in her head. *'I am a part of you."*

Eighteen

Jodie jumped up from the bed and ran into the adjoining room, closing the doors behind her. The pounding in her head was deafening. She pulled at her hair and started screaming.

"What did you do Lisa? What the fuck did you do?"

She turned around is circles, sobbing, her hands pulling at her roots. She looked to the ceiling and kept screaming. "Where are you, Lisa? Huh? Where the fuck are you?"

Amanda and Pete jumped from the sound of Jodie's screaming. "What the hell is she doing? Lisa... what is she talking about?" Amanda asked as she got up from the bed. She tried to open the adjoining door, but it was locked.

"Lisa?" Pete asked as he watched the horror dance across Amanda's face. "Dead Lisa?"

Amanda nodded her head as she began to pound on the door. "Jodie? Jodie what are you doing?"

Jodie ignored her cries and kept screaming. "Lisa, I swear to God if you did this. Why did you do this? Why?"

She screamed so loud that she began to gag. She grabbed the edge of the bed cover and threw it across the room. The cover knocked over the chair, blocking the adjoining door. She threw the pillow in her fit of rage, knocking over the lamp. She knocked the phone off the table and threw another pillow against the mirror.

"Jodie, stop!" Amanda pleaded as she tried to open the door. Pete rammed his shoulder into the door, but it did not budge. Amanda fell to the floor sobbing. "Not again, please lord, not again."

Pete looked down at her. "Again?"

Ben walked into the room, finding Amanda crying on the floor. "What is going on?"

Jodie screamed at the top of her lungs again, causing Ben to jerk his head up at the door. He ran outside, trying to open the front door to Jodie's bedroom. It would not budge. He slammed his fist against the door. "Jodie, open the door." He yelled as he tried to kick the door open.

Jodie fell silent for a moment and landed in a heap in between the two beds. She quietly whispered as she stared at the dresser across from her. "Lisa, what is wrong with you?"

Ben pressed his ear against the door and heard nothing. He ran into his room. "Where is your key Amanda?"

Pete looked over at him. "We left it in there."

"Shit." Ben said as he slammed his hands against the wall. He paced back and forth, trying to think of what to do.

Amanda sat there and trembled, staring at her feet. Pete sat down next to her. "What do you mean not again?"

Ben stopped pacing, as he asked, "Not again what?"

Amanda looked up at Ben and started to cry again. "After Lisa died, Jodie started having dreams about her. She would explain the dreams to me, and they were so vivid. Like Lisa was trying to communicate with her."

Ben sat down at the edge of the bed as Amanda continued, his hands under his chin. "So, they wanted her to go for a psychiatric evaluation. They made me go too, loss of a close friend."

"Who are they?" Ben asked quietly.

"Our parents, the police, Lisa's parents. They didn't know about her dreams though. So, we went. They said that I made quicker progress then Jodie. I was done within a month. They made Jodie go through her second year of college. It's one of the reasons she stayed close to home for school.

"They had her on medication, saying that it would calm her nerves. They said that she couldn't deal with Lisa's death. They made her write about it and talk about it and relive it almost every day. How do you expect someone to get over a death if you make them keep talking about it?"

Pete looked at Ben as he shook his head. Tears slipped down Ben's face as he sat with his hands folded around his mouth. His brain going a mile a minute, flashing through memories of her from college. He remembered how closed off and quiet she was at times, other times she was full of laughter and life. He wondered if it was the medication she was on.

"She hasn't had a dream since she stopped the medicine." Amanda choked out. Ben closed his eyes as he inhaled.

"Yes, she has."

Amanda looked up at Ben, waiting for his explanation. "She told me that she thought she saw Lisa on the beach Friday night. I watched her sitting at the edge of the water. She was staring at something, and then she suddenly jerked and looked another way, just staring again. I asked her what was going on, and she said that she thought she saw Lisa, but then she shooed the idea away and changed the subject."

Pete chimed in, "Wait a minute, but she wasn't sleeping? And she said she saw her?"

Ben nodded his head. Amanda looked up at the them, her eyes full of terror. "It's getting worse."

***

Jodie made her way to the bathroom, hugging the wall as she walked. She slipped in and turned on the light, then turned on the cold water and stuck her face under the faucet. She let it flow over her face, welcoming the ice-cold daggers stabbing her flesh. She turned off the water and lifted her head to study her face in the mirror.

She looked up and saw Lisa standing behind her. She turned around quickly to find only the lime green tile and cotton candy pink walls staring back at her. She paused for a moment, and then faced the mirror again. Lisa's green eyes were staring at her, right over her left shoulder.

"What did you do Lisa?" Jodie asked the mirror. Lisa just stared back. "I said, what did you do Lisa?" She repeated herself sternly.

"Exactly what I said I would." Lisa answered, her voice calm and cool. "What are you talking about?" Jodie asked, her face scrunching together.

"I said I would come after you. Twenty-three." She said as she raised her hands, showing two fingers on one hand and three on the other.

"I am twenty-three. What does that have to do with anything?"

"You were taking too long. I pushed you along the way."

Jodie stood there, studying her dead friend. She thought for a few moments, remembering the dream she had of the scene in the bar. "The virginity thing? That's sick."

Lisa shrugged her shoulders as she smiled.

"What did you do to Doris?" Jodie asked, gripping the edge of the sink.

"She was a slut, Jodie."

"What did you do?"

"She seduced your man, Jodie."

"What did you do?"

"She had it coming to her."

"What did you do?"

"I asked you if you would murder her. You never answered me."

"What did you do?" Jodie screamed at the top of her lungs as she threw a glass cup against the mirror.

Lisa's face disappeared from the mirror as it cracked. The glass shattered and fell to the floor. Jodie ran out of the bathroom and sat down on the edge on the bed. Lisa's voice echoed in her head. "I killed her for you."

Jodie's eyes darted over to the dresser mirror, watching Lisa sit down on the other bed.

"I never asked you to do that. I never said that I would." Jodie said in a hushed tone.

"Please Jodie, I know you, I am a part of you." Lisa said as she laid on the bed. "How the hell did you have sex on this bed? It's so uncomfortable."

"Don't change the subject Lisa. Why did you do it?"

"Wasn't it eerily familiar? Friend, dead on the beach, alcohol in hand, bruises on head. And look who you bumped into on the beach last night."

Jodie's eyes widened. "Now you see what I'm getting at." Lisa said as she nodded her head. "Don't worry, the autopsy results will say that she had very high levels of alcohol in her blood, and she must have passed out and hit her head. Then she stopped breathing, a concussion or something."

"Why are you doing this. What do you want from me?" Jodie asked as she began to cry.

"Revenge, Jodie. I want revenge. I want him put away for life. I want him dead. I want revenge." She said as her eyes flashed a deeper green.

Jodie shook her head violently. "No. I won't do it."

"Come on Jodie, I killed for you."

***

Pete felt his heart jump into his throat when he heard the glass breaking. He jumped up from the floor and ran out of the room, down the flights of stairs, and into the lobby. The cupboard of keys was on the wall, behind the counter. The little man was nowhere in sight. He jumped over the counter and grabbed the spare key for Jodie's room. He hurdled himself back over the counter and dashed up the stairs.

He returned to the room to find Ben slamming his shoulder into the door as Amanda banged on the window, screaming Jodie's name. A few occupants in the other rooms peeked out of the windows, others brazen enough to walk onto the balcony.

Pete shoved Ben out of the way and inserted the key. He opened the door and rushed in, followed by Ben and Amanda. The three of them stopped in front of the two beds when they saw Jodie sitting in an upright fetal position, rocking herself back and forth. She looked up at them with tears streaming down her face. "She did it. She killed Doris."

Nineteen

Amanda sat in the corner of the waiting area of the police station. They received a phone call about twenty minutes after getting into Jodie's hotel room. Amanda slouched in the chair with her ankles crossed. Her foot shook uncontrollably as she waited for Officer Jensen to speak with them.

Amanda debated about what had previously happened. She was deciding if she should inform the police of Jodie's outburst. They had all agreed to keep it quiet until they got her home, then they would take her to the hospital. She looked over at Jodie and studied her as if it was the first time she had ever seen her.

Jodie's usually tanned face was drawn of color, except for the purple bruise surrounding her right eye and the redness of her lip. Her dark brown hair hung about her face, almost like a veil to keep out the light. She leaned into Ben like she needed him to breathe for her. His arms wrapped around her like ivy on a wall.

Pete was standing at the desk, trying to get information on his leave. His boat was scheduled to set sail tomorrow at noon. His orders were to report to the ship at nine in the morning to prepare for the trip. The officer at the desk shook her head, telling him that he needed to wait for Officer Jensen.

He walked back over to Amanda, his hair flat, hanging over his forehead. He still wore the sunglasses he had on in the morning. Pete sunk down into the seat across from her and put the toe of his sandal to the top of her foot to stop it from shaking. She looked up at him.

"Are you okay?" He asked, tipping his sunglasses.

Amanda shook her head slightly. *Is Jodie really crazy? Could she be right, did Lisa really do it?* She pondered as she remembered her dream of Lisa's bloody hands. She looked back over at Jodie as the officer at the desk walked over to them.

"Jensen is ready to see you all. Follow me." She said as she walked to the door behind the desk and held it open for them.

Amanda followed the officer down the gray cinderblock hallway. She looked back at Jodie, who stared at the floor as she walked, still leaning against Ben for support. Amanda's gaze shifted to Ben, who stared straight ahead of himself, his face unreadable and emotionless. His left hand was clenched as he walked, as if he was ready for a fight at any moment.

The officer led them into a large, empty white room with florescent lighting. A large white rectangular table surrounded by folding chairs stood in the middle of the room. A two-way mirror lined one wall; the others painted plain white.

They all sat on one side of the table, facing the mirror. A light flickered overhead as the humming of the bulbs filled the room. Jensen walked into the room, holding a folder and a cup of coffee.

He shut the door behind him and placed the folder on the table. He took a drink of his coffee and stretched his back before addressing the group. "Thanks for coming here. We have some news about Ms. Sullivan."

Jodie's eyes grew wide as she looked up at Jensen. She grabbed Ben's hand and squeezed it. Ben hardly noticed the pressure on his hand as he listened intently.

Pete sat up in the chair as Amanda put her hands to her mouth with her elbows on the table.

"Ms. Sullivan's cause of death was asphyxiation. We believe that around two fifty-one a.m., Ms. Sullivan took a bottle of whiskey from the Burgundy Motor Inn's abandoned bar. She then proceeded to the beach where she drank the bottle of alcohol. The deceased then tried to walk away, causing her to fall, where she hit her head on a rock. The head trauma caused a concussion, which prevented her from vomiting up the alcohol. We are ruling murder out of this case, it was clearly an unfortunate series of events that lead to an unnecessary loss of life. You are all free to leave as planned for tomorrow afternoon."

Amanda closed her eyes and saw Lisa's bloody hands from her dream, disbelief dancing across her face. She opened her eyes to find Pete and Ben standing by the door. Jodie stayed seated, staring at Amanda. *She saw something,* Jodie thought as Amanda quickly stood up, avoiding Jodie's stare.

***

Jodie laid in the bed with a cold washcloth over her right eye. She stared up at the ceiling, trying to let all the memories of the past flush from her mind. She studied the cracks in the plaster, trying to make out little designs, like she used to do while staring up at the clouds.

Amanda stood in the doorway of the adjoining doors with her arms wrapped around herself, watching Jodie stare at the ceiling with tears in her eyes. She did not know if she could handle losing her other best friend; she could see Jodie was slowly slipping away.

She walked over to the bed and aligned herself next to Jodie. Jodie did not break her gaze from the ceiling as the bed shifted from Amanda's weight. She put her head next to Jodie's and looked up at the cracks with her. They lay there for a few minutes before Jodie broke the silence.

"That looks like a teddy bear." She said, pointing above her head. Amanda looked over and smiled. "Yeah. It looks like there is a duck next to it."

Jodie nodded and put her arm down. They laid there in silence again for a few moments. Jodie turned her head towards Amanda. "Doris' death wasn't an accident."

Amanda looked over at Jodie. "What?"

"Lisa did it."

"Lisa is dead."

"Lisa told me she did it."

Amanda sat up on the bed. This is what she was afraid of. "So, you talk to her now?"

Jodie shook her head and looked over to the window. "I'm having the dreams again. I saw it... Joe killed her. He hit her in the head with a bottle of alcohol, raped her, and dragged her out to the water."

"Jodie, she was with him, remember? They were basically dating. And the police told us she drowned."

Jodie shook her head. "No, no, no. That's what they thought, but they were wrong. I know. I know what really happened that night. Now Lisa wants revenge. She did to Doris what was done to her."

Amanda stood up from the bed and looked down at Jodie. "I love you Jodie, but when we get home, you need to go to the doctor." A tear escaped her eye, and she quickly wiped it away with the back of her hand. She looked away from Jodie and continued, "I am afraid for you. I'm afraid that you are going to be too far gone this time."

"She hasn't shown you anything? You haven't had any dreams at all? I find it hard to believe that I'm the only one she shows things to, you were her best friend too." Jodie said as she called after Amanda.

Amanda walked into the other room and shut the door behind her. She leaned against the door and put her head against it. Ben looked up at her from the bed, the light of the television dancing across his face. He nudged his head toward the television. "Coverage on Doris."

Amanda sat down on the other bed and watched as a reporter stood feet away from where the police found her. "A twenty-four-year-old woman was found dead early this morning when police came to investigate an earlier crime scene. A twenty-three-year-old woman was assaulted by a man just feet away, outside of the popular beach nightclub on the boardwalk. The man is described as mid-twenties with a large build wearing a black tee shirt and a black hat with dark denim jeans, about six foot five." The reporter said into the camera.

"Un-fucking-believable." Ben said as he covered his face with his hands.

Amanda shook her head, as she walked over to the television and turned it off, then leaned against the dresser. "Where did Pete go?"

"He went back to his hotel to talk to his sister. He wanted to let her know what happened before she heard about it on the news. He said that he would be back later."

Amanda nodded and put on her shoes. "I'm going to go over there. I will be back in about an hour. Do me a favor and don't let Jodie leave. She is freaking out in there and I don't want her disappearing."

Ben nodded his head and watched Amanda leave the room. He walked over to the adjoining door and opened it a crack. He looked at Jodie as she laid comatose on the bed, her eyes fixated on the ceiling.

"Don't just stand there, creeper." She said, not moving.

Ben smirked as he walked in and stood next to her bed. He crossed his arms and looked up at the ceiling. "That looks like a teddy bear." He said as he pointed above her head.

She smiled and looked over at him. He looked down at her and took her hand, rubbed it for a moment and then kissed it. She moved over and let him sit down next to her. He sat there for a bit, brushing her hair back from her forehead.

"Jodie, I am really sorry about last night." He said as he paused, resting his hand on her head.

"It wasn't your fault. I know." She said, trying to comfort him.

"You know that I love you." He said, kissing her forehead.

"Yes, but I don't know how much longer it will last." She said, not looking at him.

He kept his lips pressed against her forehead as he asked, "What are you talking about?"

"How can anyone love a crazy person?" She asked, closing her eyes.

Ben sat up and looked down at her. "Hey," he said, lifting her chin and causing her to open her eyes, "what are you talking about?"

She shook her head, Amanda's words echoing in her ears. "Ben, there are things about me that you don't know. I used to be a serious mess. Like on meds and seeing a shrink and everything."

He nodded his head, surprised that she was telling him. In all the time he had known her, she never mentioned it. Then again, it had never come up before.

"Well, it is happening again, and I don't know what to do and I'm scared and I know that no one could love a crazy person, and since it's happening again, I must really be crazy." She said without taking a breath.

"Jodie, you are crazy if you think I won't love you. You are not crazy. You went through a traumatizing experience when you were younger. So, your repressed feelings are resurfacing. No big deal, you got through it once. This time you have me to help." He said, then kissed the top of her head.

"Really?" She asked, grabbing his hand. He let her fingers fall in between his as he answered, "Really." He reclined back onto the bed, pulling her so her head rested on his shoulder.

She wanted to go into more details, tell him what she had been experiencing the entire time they were there, but she knew it would push him away. So, she let it go, just needing to enjoy the few happy moments she would have with him. She knew that the time would come, and he would see her true craziness, and he would walk away. They lay there for a few minutes in silence until Jodie sat up and looked down at Ben. "So, what were you planning last night?"

Ben looked up at her with a smile. "Well, I had this whole romantic set up with candles and flowers. And I was going to make love to you the way that I have always wanted."

She pushed her hair away from her face and kissed his cheek. "That is the most romantic thing ever."

He raised his eyebrows and smiled. "Thanks."

"Ben?" Jodie asked as she leaned over him a little.

"Yeah, baby?" He asked as he rubbed her arm.

"I feel so empty. Like my life was drained from me. I mean, jeez, Doris is dead."

Ben nodded as he wiped a tear from the corner of her eye. She looked at him and continued, "I just don't know what to do with myself. I feel like there is nothing to make things right. Nothing will bring Doris back, nothing will change what happened last night, and nothing will ever change what happened to Lisa."

Ben laid there, staring up into Jodie's eyes. She looked down and looked back into his eyes. He reached up and put his hand into her hair. She lowered her head to his and lightly pressed her lips against his. She rested them there until Ben gently lined her bottom lip with the tip of his tongue. She pulled her face away slightly until Ben touched the tip of his nose to hers.

She gently kissed him again, lightly brushing her tongue against his. He kissed the cut on her lip, then the corner of her bruised eye. He brought her hand to his face and kissed the inside of her wrist. "I'm here for you, Jodie. I won't let anything happen to you."

She sighed as her eyes fluttered, then turned over on her side, her back facing Ben. Curling up into a ball, she shook as the past twenty-four hours flashed in her mind.

Ben ran his fingers through her hair, a habit of his that always relaxed the two of them. He sighed and leaned into the back of her head and pressed his lips into her hair. He slowly inhaled her scent as he quietly said, "I really do love you. So much."

The words pierced her heart and took comfort in them, but knew deep down that it would not last. A tear slipped from her closed eyes and traveled down to land in the pillow underneath her head. She whispered her response back, unable to trust the quivering in her voice. "I know. I always will love you too."

Twenty

Andrea sat in the park, watching Andrew run around the sandbox. He ran over to Andrea every few minutes when he found a rock to his liking. His little legs worked overtime to get him over to his mother faster each time. "Mommy, look," he said as he held up a black and white speckled rock.

"Wow Andrew, that is wonderful! It's so pretty." She said as his placed it in her hand. He looked up and smiled, "I know, mommy."

He went running back over to the sandbox and kept digging to see what other buried treasure he could find.

She rolled up her short sleeves as she baked in the sun, and noticed a person walk up next to the bench as she watched Andrew climb up the stairs to the slide.

"Is this seat taken?" She heard from the person standing next to the bench. She looked up and shook her head no.

The man sat down next to her and smiled. "Thank you."

She nodded and held her arms out as Andrew came running in for a hug. She picked him up and put him on her lap.

"He's cute. Is he yours?" The man asked, looking at Andrew.

"Yeah, this is my little bundle of joy, aren't you?" She said as she poked Andrew.

He giggled and wiggled around in Andrea's lap. The man removed his sunglasses and placed them on top of his head. "How old is he?"

"He'll be three." She answered as Andrew took her sunglasses off her face and placed them on his head, imitating the man. Andrea laughed as she turned to meet two icy blue eyes staring at her under black eyebrows.

She sucked in her breath as he said to her, "Well, holy shit."

***

Amanda walked down the stairs of the hotel and into the lobby. The old man behind the counter glanced at her when she walked in but turned his attention back to the newspaper he was reading. She headed to the door, noticing the yellow caution tape over the abandoned bar door.

She walked over to her car in the lot down the road and climbed in. She turned to look at the back seat and saw the nail file that Doris was using on the drive down. She stared at it, unable to comprehend that Doris was gone. She hugged the back of her seat and cried into the headrest. She could not pinpoint the exact reason for her crying, so many horrible events happened that she was emotionally drained, and she took pleasure in the cry.

She thought of Doris, wondering what had really happened to her last night. Did she really die from alcohol like the police said? Did someone attack her? Could it have been Joe Rappaport? Or maybe, just maybe, Jodie wasn't crazy. What if Lisa did do it? The image of Lisa's bloodied hands flashed into her mind. Was it a mere coincidence that Lisa came to her in her sleep the same night that Doris was killed? Maybe she was going crazy too... maybe Jodie's crazy was contagious.

Amanda shook her head, trying to push the thought out of her mind. She turned around in the seat and gripped the steering wheel. Her knuckles turned white as closed her eyes, trying to think of something else. Slowing her breathing, different subjects flashed through her head. Her thoughts turned to Pete and what had happened this weekend. The way he came back into her life, the way he fit in like no time had passed between them. It was as if it was meant to be.

Suddenly, as soon as the momentary comfort came, a chill ran up her spine. Her eyes flew open and she could not catch her breath. "Something isn't right," escaped from her lips. She suddenly felt uncomfortable in her own skin, wanting to run away. She threw the car in reverse and peeled out of the parking spot. She sped out of the parking lot and flew down North Carolina Boulevard. She did not know why, but her stomach flipped when she thought of Pete. It was not the butterfly feeling, but the kind that forced bile into the esophagus.

As fast as she drove, it seemed like an eternity before she reached his hotel. She circled the parking lot, unable to find a spot. She slammed her hands against the steering wheel and shook her body. Gritting her teeth, she drove around the block and parked on a side street. She slammed the door, ran to the front of the hotel and busted into the lobby. All the patrons turned to watch her dash up the stairs.

She ran up to the door and pounded with her open hands. She tried jiggling the handle, but the door was locked. "Fuck!" She yelled as she slammed against the door.

As she leaned against the door, she heard the click of the door unlocking. She waited a moment, thinking Pete would open the door. When he did not, she slowly turned the handle and pushed the door open carefully, making sure she would not hit whoever was behind the door. She was surprised to find no one standing there.

The living room area was empty, except for Andrew's toys on the floor. She stepped in and looked around, searching for someone. As she was about to step into the bathroom, she heard a soft moan come from the bedroom. She stopped and lightly stepped over to the door, seeing a light coming from underneath. She opened the door a crack, an uncomfortable feeling spreading throughout her body. She peeked in through the crack to find Pete standing there without his shirt on. His face was strained from what she could see of it. She heard another moan but saw it did not come from Pete. She opened the door a little more, seeing the rest of Pete's naked body thrusting into another man bent over on the bed.

"Oh, Pat," she heard Pete moan. She stumbled into the room, losing her balance from not being able to believe what she was witnessing.

Pete jumped back from Pat, startled to see Amanda on the floor of the room. Pat's bald head snapped up, his piercing blue eyes studying Amanda.

"Oh my God, Mandy, what are you doing here?" Pete asked as he struggled to wrap a sheet around his waist.

Amanda shook her head in disbelief and pushed herself against the wall. She wanted to scream and cry out, but she choked on everything that tried to find its way through her mouth. Tears blurred her vision, but she could see Pete reach out to her.

"Mandy, I-" he started to say. He was cut off by an animalistic shriek that finally emerged from the depths of Amanda's bowels. Like a skittish rabbit, Amanda dodged away from his hand and ran out of the room, hitting into the doorway as she ran.

Stumbling from bashing her arm into the doorframe, she held onto her upper arm, trying to hold in the throbbing. She approached the entrance of the room, but Pete was right behind her. He grabbed the back of her shirt and pulled her back into the room.

"Let me explain." He said as he tried to spin her around. He was met by Amanda's right hook straight to the mouth. Her impressive force caused him to lose his balance, and as he tried to straighten himself out, she was able to pull her shirt away from his grip and make her way to the staircase.

Pete stood there in shock, touching his fingertips to his lips. Wincing at his own touch, he looked down to see his blood staining his fingers. Pat walked out of the bedroom fully naked. He approached Pete and studied his swelling split lip as he placed his hands on his hips. He spread his legs apart slightly, and in the intimidating position said one command. "You know what has to be done."

He looked out of the hotel room, and then gave one brief disapproving look at Pete before retreating to the bedroom. Pete stood there in awe for a few moments until rage began to spread to every crevasse of his body. He knew exactly what had to be done.

***

Amanda ran as fast as she possibly could down the stairs. Once she emerged into the lobby, she hit into an older woman standing next to her large tan suitcase. The woman toppled over, her skirt flying above her head, exposing her white undergarments and pantyhose. The young bellboy saw the woman fall and ran over to assist her. The greeter at the front of the lobby moved out of the bellboy's path and was knocked into by Amanda, causing him to lose the pamphlets he was holding.

Amanda ignored the commotion behind her, as well as the hotel manager shouting after her. The pudgy middle-aged man with a horrible midnight black comb over chased her outside of the hotel, shouting after her as he continued his chase. She could not make out what the man was yelling, but she decided not to take a chance of him following her. She looked back to see what she had to run away from. After seeing the man huffing and puffing his life away, she decided to keep running rather than go to her car. She would come back for it later, when it was dark, and no one could see who she was.

She made her way to a small park at the opposite end of the block. Bursting through the metal chain linked fence, she hid behind the plastic jungle gym off to the side of the park. All at once, she fell apart. Sharp pains cut through her sides as she doubled over from the sudden marathon she had endured. She cried out in pain, the cry changing from a shriek to a sob. The emotional pain was overpowering the physical. Her mind raced; she was unable to control anything.

She sucked in for oxygen as if it was not there, a tightening in her chest becoming more persistent. She felt like she was dying. How could what she had seen been real? Suddenly, she was unable to breathe. Her eyes bulged as she tried to gasp for air. She tried to stand up but was too weak from the physical exhaustion. She laid there in a panic, believing she was not going to make it. Her eyes began to flutter as she slowly stopped resisting the choking. Pete's face came into view with Pat's, joined by a third. A hand reached down covering her face. Before her vision was gone, Lisa's face flashed before her eyes.

Suddenly air rushed into her lungs, causing her to gag. She sat up, staring at her surroundings. There was no one there, nor were there footprints surrounding her. *I'm going crazy* she thought to herself as she tried to control her breathing. She swallowed hard, still studying the park. Wearily, she reached up for the handle on the side of the jungle gym and slowly tried to hoist herself up. Making it a few inches off the ground, she slid onto the bottom of the yellow plastic twisty slide.

As if trying to literally hold herself together, she drew her knees into her chest and hugged them as tight as she could. Slightly rocking to calm herself down, she buried her face into her knees and tried to make sense of all that was going on. Nothing on this trip seemed normal. The way they planned the trip, the people who went, the hotel they wound up at, Jodie's hallucinations, Doris' death, none of it made sense. Amanda slowly looked over the horizon of her knees and whispered, "Jodie."

"Jodie would be able to explain what is going on," she explained out loud. "She's the one who has been seeing everything this week. She must have some inclination as to what is going on. I mean, if Lisa has been talking to her, she must know something."

Dusk was covering the park by the time Amanda pulled herself from the slide. She strode across the park with brisk steps, determined to discuss everything that had happened this weekend with Jodie. As she reached the gate, she looked over at a bench and noticed a woman sitting there, clutching a child as a man hovered over her. Amanda could tell the woman was upset and could hear the child wailing.

She slowly moved away from the gate and stepped closer to the bench, still maintaining her distance as she observed the situation. The threesome was unaware of her spying. She inched her way closer, trying to make out what was being said. She sucked in her breath when she recognized Andrea sitting there with Andrew choking on his cries. Amanda went to dash out and help, but she stopped in her tracks when she saw the man's face. She could not believe Joe Rappaport was standing just feet away from her. Jodie was not completely crazy. He was in Atlantic City, harassing Andrea.

***

Joe stared down at Andrea, clenching and unclenching his fist as the air rushed in and out of his nose. His face turned into a horrible sneer as he looked back at Andrew. "This should have never been," he said, pointing at the little boy.

"What do you want from us?" Andrea cried out, pressing her son against her chest.

Joe's head snapped up, staring up at the darkening sky. "I know what has to be done."

Without a second glance, he ran to the opposite side of the park and darted down the street to a small parking lot.

Amanda ran over to the bench where Andrea had collapsed over her son. Andrew still cried out, mucus dripping down his nose and his cherry red cheeks blotchy and tear stained. Amanda placed her hand on Andrea's shoulder, but pulled it back as though she scalded herself when Andrea shrieked out, "What do you want from me?"

"Shh, shh. Andrea, it's Amanda." She said in a soothing voice.

"Amanda?" She asked as she slowly looked up, still clutching Andrew for dear life.

"It's ok Andrea. I'm here." Amanda said as she started to sit down on the bench.

"Oh Amanda!" She exclaimed as she burst into tears. "I was so scared; I didn't know what to do."

"Andrea, it's ok. What happened?"

"I was sitting here with Andrew and a man approached me and started talking. The next thing I knew I was staring into his eyes. *His* eyes, Amanda." Andrea explained, a look of shock overtaking her face.

"Whose eyes? Who is that man Andrea? How do you know that man?" Amanda asked, grasping her shoulders and squatting in front of her.

Andrea closed her eyes, tears streaming down her face like waterfalls. She slowly nudged her head against Andrew's. She inhaled deeply through her nose and exhaled through her mouth, then kissed Andrew on the head.

Amanda braced herself for the answer, her stomach a mix of flips and knots. She gently rubbed Andrea's arms, encouraging her to speak.

Barely audible over Andrew's hiccups and heavy breathing, Andrea whispered the horrifying answer Amanda somehow knew was coming. "It's Andrew's father."

Twenty-One

Amanda's face scrunched up as if she was in pain, allowing the words to settle into her brain. Amanda must have misunderstood what she heard. There is no way that Joe is Andrew's father.

"I'm sorry, what did you just say?" Amanda asked in disbelief

"That's him. That's the guy who raped me. That is Andrew's father." She said, her voice shaking.

Amanda felt as though a semi-truck just hit her square in the chest. She started to mumble as she slowly stood up and turned around. She wrapped her arms around herself for heat, despite the eighty-five-degree weather. Andrea looked up to find Amanda's back facing her. A few silent moments passed as Andrea studied Amanda.

Amanda clasped her hands over her mouth and slowly exhaled. Closing her eyes, she spoke "I know him, Andrea. He's the man that killed my best friend."

***

Joe ran over to the black corvette parked not far from the park. He took out his phone and dialed a number. He rested against the car door as he waited for the other party to answer.

"What is it?" The voice on the other end asked as soon as the phone was answered.

"I found her. She has the child." Joe said, short of breath.

"You know what has to be done." The voice said, then hanging up the phone. Joe let the phone slide down the side of his face before looking down at the screen. He deeply inhaled and slipped the phone it into the front pocket of his jeans.

Digging his other hand into his pocket, he retrieved his keys and opened the door, staring back in the direction of park. Just as he was about to get into the car, another figure at the park caught his eye. He squinted, trying to focus his vision, but he was too far away to make out anything.

He climbed into the car, and started it up, making sure to keep the headlight off. Slowly, he made his way out of the parking lot and inched down the road as he approached the park. Rolling down the window, he stuck his head out and stared at the three people left in the park.

He stopped the car as he made eye contact with the person who was standing up in front of the bench.

Amanda watched the black corvette suspiciously make its way down the road and saw the look of shock and then recognition that danced across Joe's face as they made eye contact. She watched him peel down the road, swerving around cars that were preparing to stop at the traffic light.

Amanda quickly turned to Andrea and reached for Andrew. "Andrea, I think we need to get out of here."

***

Jodie's eyes suddenly opened, jolting her from the few hours she had passed out for. She felt strange, something was not right in the room. She was not tired, which was odd for her. When she usually woke up from a nap, she was drowsy and sluggish. She felt as though she had a intervenes dose of caffeine in her arm, and that strange tingly sensation on the back of her neck.

"What do you want?" Jodie asked as she stared straight ahead.

The only response to her question was Ben shifting next to her in the bed. His arm draped over her waist as he snuggled into her. Jodie ignored it and continued to stare into the darkness. "I know you're there." She continued.

"Jodie, we need to talk." Lisa's voice said, coming from deep within the darkness.

"I'm not doing this anymore. Leave me alone."

"You have to Jodie. You have no choice." Lisa replied, her voice growing with strength.

"What do you mean I don't have a choice? I do have a choice. I choose not to listen to you anymore. I choose to have a normal life. You are dead!" Jodie yelled as she sat up in the bed.

"That was bad Jodie. That was really bad." Lisa said as she approached Jodie. She looked her straight in the eyes and said, "You are going to listen to what I have to say."

***

Ben awoke, feeling a shift in the bed. He rolled over, lifting his arm to place it over Jodie. His arm touched nothing but air until it hit the mattress. He lifted his head from the pillow and looked over to find Jodie's side of the bed empty.

Flipping over onto his back, he supported himself on his elbows and strained his neck to look at the bathroom. The doorway was open and completely dark. He studied the room, trying to see where she was. "Jodie?"

Silence was the only response. He got out of the bed, feeling around for the light switch. Just as he was about to turn on the light, he heard the click of the door latching closed.

Ben ran to the door and opened it to find Jodie walking towards the steps of the motel. Her steps were slow and staggered, as her fingers dragged across the blue wall. Her pace was jagged and temperamental. She would pause, begin to lean back, but then jerk forward.

Ben stepped out of the room and watched her for a few more moments, wanting to see where she was going. He slowly emerged from the doorway and stepped closer, noticing that her fingers were not trailing against the wall; they were digging into it. Flakes of painted cement jumped from the face of the wall as her nails excavated the surface.

She descended the stairs in the same fashion, seeming to fight it the entire way down. Ben crept slowly behind her, making sure there was enough distance for her to not see him behind her, but close enough not to lose her.

She stumbled out onto North Carolina Boulevard and made right, passing the parking lot, and heading straight for the boardwalk. The people on the boardwalk ignored her, except for a few stares and head nods. She walked across the boardwalk and through the crowd of people as if no one was there, pushing in between people and cutting others off.

Her zombie-like walk finally slowed when she reached the sand. Continuing her journey, she walked to the area where the club was that they went to the other night. She seemed to fall to the ground behind a few barrels in front of an opening next to the boardwalk.

He went to run over and help her but stopped short when he saw her look around and begin to talk.

"Where am I?" Jodie asked in a hushed whisper.

Ben watched her look around again and try to get up. He saw her fall back down and strain against what seemed to be nothing. Intrigued by what he was witnessing, he hid himself from view and observed her actions.

***

"Lisa, what did you do?" Jodie asked, looking around. "How did I get here?"

"Are you ready to listen Jodie?" Lisa's voice asked, hovering by her left ear.

"Lisa, what are you doing?"

"You have to listen Jodie." Lisa demanded. "This is so much bigger than you realize."

Twenty-Two

Amanda waited until Joe was no longer in sight and pulled Andrea and Andrew away from the playground.

"Why are you going right? The hotel is back that way." Andrea asked in a hushed tone as she crept behind Amanda.

"Because we aren't going there."

"But I need to get to Pete. He can help me." She said as she started in the direction of their hotel.

"No!" Amanda said as she grabbed Andrea's arm and spun her around. "We can't go to him. He was occupied with something else."

"Stop it, he's my brother, he will help me." She said, pulling her arm away.

Amanda rolled her eyes in frustration. "Fine. Go to him. But you need to get out of here. I don't think it is safe for you. The way he was acting…" Amanda said, her thoughts returning to Joe. She could not understand how he of all people was Andrew's father. He was a disgusting human being. If he was capable of raping a fifteen-year-old girl, maybe Jodie's accusations had a possibility of being true.

"I can't go back there with you," Amanda explained, refocusing her attention on Andrea. "I'll walk you back there, but I can't see him."

Andrea cocked and eyebrow at Amanda, "Why?"

They headed towards the hotel, Amanda keeping a watchful eye on their surroundings. "Pete was busy with his boyfriend, and I walked in on them. It was terribly embarrassing and life changing, and I would much rather just not see him again."

Andrea chuckled, "Ha! Boyfriend... okay," she said sarcastically.

Amanda looked at Andrea, "Ben is gay. His boyfriend Pat is here."

Andrea shook her head. "Ben isn't gay. He's married."

Amanda stopped short. "What?!"

"Didn't he tell you? He got married right before he went into the military, to his high school girlfriend."

Amanda did not think her heart could take anymore. She was going to speak, but they were standing in front of the hotel. "Listen to me. You go up there, you tell your brother, and you leave. Get away from here. Don't let Joe find you." The women embraced, Amanda not wanting to let her go. "Text me when you are safe."

Andrea nodded and entered the hotel.

***

Amanda walked to her car; the tears unstoppable at this point. He lied to her, multiple times over this weekend. He cheated on his wife with both her and that Pat guy. She struggled to open the door, unable to see through the blurry tears.

Frustrated, she threw her keys onto the pavement and slid down the door of her car, planting herself on the ground.

She fished her phone out of her pocket and dialed Ben. She listened to the rings until his voicemail answered. "Hey, you've reached Ben. Text me." She sighed, trying to gather herself before speaking. "Ben, it's Amanda. Um... I just wanted to check in on Jodie. And I, ah, I could really use a friendly ear to talk to. Call me back."

She sat there a little longer with side of her phone pressed against her forehead. She could not focus on one thought in her head. Pete, Joe, Jodie, and Lisa swirled in her head so much she felt nauseous. She tried to calm her breathing, but it was interrupted by her hiccups.

Her phone rang, and she answered it without looking at the screen. "Hey Ben."

"Amanda, can you hear me?" A whisper asked. "It's Andrea. I need you to get me out of here."

***

Andrea walked up to her hotel room, soothing an emotionally drained Andrew. She pushed the room key into the lock, but the door was slightly open. She pushed it in with her hip and called out, "Hey Pete, I'm back. Listen, something crazy happened and we need to get out of here."

She made her way further into the room, hearing the water running in the bathroom. She was about to place Andrew down on the couch when she saw the bathroom door open. A man she did not know, bald with blue eyes in his early thirties walked out. His broad chest and muscular shoulders naked, a towel wrapped around his waist.

Amanda paused, lifting Andrew back to her chest. She looked at him, not sure what to say. He looked very familiar, but she knew that she had never met him before. She straightened herself and said, "Oh, you must be a friend of Pete's."

His eye contact was intense, but his focus was not on her, it was on Andrew. The man's chest heaved; his breath steady. His hands clenched a bit, his head moving quickly to the side, the sound of his neck cracking was audible across the room. She began to tense, not knowing if Pete was in the room.

"Is this the little shit?" He asked, angling his head to Andrew. "Pete's nephew?"

"Um…" She hesitated.

He started to come after them, advancing as he said, "I've been waiting for this for a long time."

Andrea screamed and ran out of the room. She headed to the staircase but noticed the elevator doors just about to close. She jumped in, seeing the door close on the man in the towel. The elevator rose to a few floors above her own. She cursed, not knowing what to do. She pushed a few floor numbers between hers and the top floor. She left the elevator at another floor and ran to the other side of the hotel, praying that the man was still climbing the stairs after her.

She made her way to a different bank of elevators and headed to the main floor, calling Amanda and praying that she did not get too far away.

***

"Get you out of where, what is going on?" Amanda asked, getting nervous from the sound of Andrea's breathing.

"A man just came after me. He was in the room. I'm in the elevator in the back of the hotel. He was..." She broke down crying, sucking in a deep breath.

"Ok, listen to me. I am getting in the car. I will meet you at the back entrance. Just run." Amanda said as she grabbed her keys from the pavement and got in the car.

She barely shut her door before she was pulling out of the spot on the street down from the hotel. She stayed on the phone with Amanda, listening to her silent sobs as she heard the elevator door ding. "I'm almost there. Run."

Andrea dashed out of the elevators, making her way to the back entrance, her son crying in tow. She stepped out of the hotel, seeing Amanda pulling up to the curb. As she lunged for the passenger door, she saw the bald man come around the side of the hotel, heading straight for her.

She screamed as Amanda stepped on the gas. The man almost reaching the open door as they pulled away. Andrea sobbed alongside her son as she pulled the door closed. Amanda peeled out of the parking lot and out onto Atlantic Avenue, heading towards the Burgundy.

"That was the fucking guy!" Amanda yelled, recognizing him from his rendezvous with Pete in the hotel room. "Your brother was fucking that guy this afternoon!"

"What?! Who is he?" She yelled over the cries of her son.

"Pat!" Amanda shouted back. Her heart racing, her throat tight with emotion.

"He looked so familiar. He was asking if Andrew was Pete's nephew. He had the look of murder in his eyes." Andrea calmed down, in partial shock.

Amanda turned onto Brighton Avenue. "Where are you going?" Andrea asked in a panic.

Amanda parked on the side of the road and pulled out her cell phone. "We can't go back to the Burgundy. Pete knows where it is."

"What does Pete have to do with this? He's my brother, he wouldn't hurt me."

"I don't believe that." She said as she texted Ben. '911. Call me. Get away from the Burgundy.'

She checked her surroundings and then exited the car, instructing Andrea to do the same. She locked the car and headed towards the boardwalk, her hand on the small of Andrea's back.

"Why are we going here?" she asked, fear lacing her voice.

"We need to stay away from Pete and Pat. We need to find Jodie and Ben and we need to get the hell out of here."

They walked onto the boardwalk and tried to blend in with the crowd. "If I tell you to move, head towards the closest casino lobby."

Andrea nodded her head, agreeing to the plan, and hugged her son as they kept walking.

Twenty-Three

Pete was furious. Pat had warned him that if anyone found out about the two of them, they would have to take care of it. Pete had agreed, he had too much to lose if anyone found out about their relationship. What were the chances that he would run into an old flame while he was here in Atlantic City?

He smiled to himself. The chances were pretty good. He knew that she would be here this weekend, he stalked Jodie's social media accounts to keep tabs on her. He blamed Amanda for the way his life turned out. Her constant need for attention made him lose his scholarship. She overpowered his life; she was involved with everything. He did not see it at the time, but she consumed him. His parents saw it, his ex-girlfriend saw it, it took them banning together and pulling him out of school to see it. She was ruining his life, her plans did not have his best interest at heart, so he had to leave her.

He remembered how much his parents hated her when they met her. She had come home with him to visit over a long weekend, about six months into their relationship. He was so in love with her, and they made each other happy. Pete finally felt at peace with his life, knowing he met his soulmate. He was so excited to introduce her to his family. His sister already loved her; they would video chat when he had to step away from the call.

They had arrived at his childhood home to find his mother and father waiting for them in the study. The distain on his mother's face was heartbreaking. Amanda, being the sweetheart that she was, tried to overlook the obvious disapproval, and made the best of the weekend.

Throughout that weekend, his mother kept reminding him that Amanda was beneath him. She did not come from money. She was not as good of a match for him as his ex. He needed to maintain the family's good name and cut ties with her, reunite with his ex. It was the right thing to do.

He left there disgusted. Not speaking to his mother for a few months.

He eventually forgave his mother; her poison slowly filled his ears. His ex-girlfriend reached out through Facebook, and they slowly reconnected. Pete was often on the phone with his mother or ex, and he would get extremely annoyed when Amanda interrupted his calls. She would bother him for dinner, or to study for an exam, but he would make an excuse to stay in.

His mother, unhappy that he was still associating himself with Amanda, threatened to disinherit him if he did not cut ties. She convinced him that his legacy was more important than some college fling. He struggled with the situation his mother put him in, until he was notified by the dean that he was on academic probation, and his scholarship was forfeited.

He made the decision to cut all ties and leave school. Once his parents learned of his academic failure, he joined the navy. It was not his choice to get married, but his mother convinced him that it was the best thing to do for his legacy. His ex did help him see the error of his ways and figured he could help her by providing her lodging and benefits while he was enlisted. A few weeks before he shipped out, they went to city hall and made it official.

His anger against Amanda fueled him to thrive. He excelled in basic training, climbed to top of his class. The animosity he had for her destroying his life was palpable. He constantly trained, and when he was not on duty, he was in the gym, trying to expel his anger. He did not understand how he was so blind to her true self for so long. He would say that he was grateful to his parents and wife for pulling back the curtain, but it only angered him more—for being weak, for losing himself to a woman, destroying the future he planned. His hatred spread to his parents and his wife for forcing him down the path he was on, all his choices stripped away.

He felt consumed, he lost himself, he no longer knew who he was or what he truly wanted. No one could understand his inner turmoil. No one knew the rage caged within him. That was, until he met Pat.

***

Pete's ship was docked at Norfolk, Virginia. His wife and family were still back in Connecticut. He had no desire to speak with them or think of them. He decided to drown his sorrows in booze and headed to a small bar near the docks.

He entered the dark dive bar, the smell of stale beer clung in the air. He sat at the end of the counter, ordering a shot of whiskey, and asked the bartender to leave the bottle. After an hour and about a dozen shots, the bartender approached Pete.

"I think you've had enough buddy," he said as he put the bottle of whiskey back behind the bar. Pete looked up, eyes unfocused at the bald man, and smirked, shrugging his shoulders.

"If you say so, boss." Pete responded, he was not looking for a fight, he just wanted to numb himself, which he succeeded in doing.

The bartender cocked his eyebrow, not expecting such compliance. "You good?"

Pete shrugged his shoulders again. "Meh."

The bartender chuckled. "You know, bartenders are a lot like medical professionals. We dispense medicine and listen to what ails 'ya. Looks like you're pretty well medicated, so what's ailing 'ya?"

Pete laughs, "How much time you got?"

"Bar closes at 2 am."

Pete unburdened himself to the bartender, unable to hold back everything that had been bottled up for years. It felt good to let it all out, finally talk about his family and his life and how much he hated all of it.

Pete and the bartender sat there after the bar closed, just talking. "I completely get the family legacy thing," the bartender said, "my family is big on that too."

Pete laughed, he was sobering at this point, drinking water. "It's not even a legacy thing, they just want to make sure they keep the wealth in the family."

"Yeah, that's my family too. My brother and I have put up with a lot of shit from my family over the years. Always holding the money over our heads, trying to keep us in line by threatening to disinherit us." The bartender explained. "I couldn't take it anymore, so my brother and I decided to leave, put some distance between us and the powers that be. But one day we will inherit it all."

Pete felt a kinship with the bartender, he felt more like himself than he ever had, and it was nice to speak to someone from the same background. "Hey, thanks for the talk, man. I really appreciated it. I was in a pretty dark place when I got here tonight."

The bartender shook his hand, "No problem, stop by whenever."

"Thanks, I will. Oh, I'm Pete, Pete Erickson."

"Pleasure to meet you Pete, I'm Pat Rappaport."

***

Pete frequented the bar while he was in port, the two men becoming fast friends. While out to sea, they would communicate through social media and texting, when Pete could. They had much in common, easily falling into a comfortable communication pattern. Their friendship evolved over the course of a year, subtle flirting and double ententes easily peppering itself into their conversations.

Pete opened up about his family life, telling Pat about his wife and his sister and her son. Pat shared the news with Pete about his grandfather passing away. Shortly after, Pat's father and mother passed away, leaving him without any family, except for his brother.

Pete eventually fell in love with Pat. He confessed his feelings to Pat one time during a text exchange. Pat explained to Pete that he wanted to be with him, but something happened at the will reading. He told Pete that there were some lose ends that he needed to tie up with his brother before he was free to pursue a relationship.

Pete said he understood, that he would wait for him. Pat asked if he would be willing to help him and his brother, so they could be together quicker. Pete agreed, he would do anything for the man who understood him more than anyone in the world.

***

Pete made his way to the Burgundy. He was exhilarated that it was Amanda who walked in on them. He finally had a reason to remove her from his life, permanently. He was angry with himself for falling back into old habits when he spent time with her. It proved how weak he was, and how much control she always had over him.

He pulled into the parking lot of the rundown motel and headed to the rooms, pulling a baseball hat down over his head to hide his face from anyone in the lobby. He knocked on the doors of the rooms, waiting for a response. The rooms looked dark from behind the closed curtains. After a few moments, he sent a text message to Amanda and Jodie, asking them where they were. He watched the screen, seeing the message sent, but he was left on read by Amanda.

The anger boiled within him, his face hardening into a scowl. He made his descent to the lobby, about to exit the hotel when he felt his phone vibrate. His heart raced slightly as he unlocked his screen but was disappointed to see a text from his sister.

A: Pete, where are you?

P: I'm out. What's up?

A: We need to leave ASAP.

P: ???

A: Some shady shit is going on

P: Are you ok?

A: For now. I'm with Amanda.

P: Where r u?

A: Boardwalk, near Bally's.

P: Stay there. I'll meet u.

Pete smiled and went back to the car. She was only a few blocks away from him. He called Pat to tell him the good news.

"What?" Pat answered angrily.

"I found her. She's on the boardwalk with my sister,"

"With your sister?"

"Yeah, I can keep tabs on her now. I'll handle it. No one will know what she saw."

"Yeah, come get me. I'm coming with you." He demanded and disconnected the phone.

Pete looked at the phone, insulted that Pat did not trust him to handle Amanda. He got started the car and headed back to Pat.

Twenty-Four

"You are all in danger," Lisa said, as Jodie struggled to sit up.

"You're a figment of my imagination." Jodie responded.

"Listen to me," Lisa repeated.

"Yup, I've officially lost my mind." Jodie continued, trying to ignore her dead friend. "Put me in a padded room, I've finally cracked."

Lisa sighed, releasing her hold on Jodie's shoulders. The pressure holding Jodie in place dissipated. "I'm trying to save you... I'm trying to save you all."

Jodie laughed and shook her head. "I really should have never stopped that medication. Who knew the relapse would have been this bad."

"Look, I don't want what happened to me, and what happened to Doris, happen to you... or Amanda, or Andrea."

Jodie's face puckered, turning her attention to Lisa. "Andrea?" she asked incredulously. "How the hell do you know about Andrea?"

"At least I finally got your attention." Lisa said, turning to face Jodie. "Everything is connected. There is a common thread here. All our stories intertwine."

"Andrea, as in Pete's sister Andrea?" Jodie asked, still unsure how Lisa knew her. Jodie had never even met his sister.

"There is a reason you are all here. Don't you think it's a bit of a coincidence that you are all here the same weekend?" Lisa asked.

"Well, I mean, yeah." Jodie stammered.

"Doris was just a casualty. She really had nothing to do with this. It was more of a case of being at the wrong place at the wrong time. But her fate is woven with the rest of you." Lisa explained.

"Why are you being so cryptic? I'm here, talking to my best friend who died five years ago. As much as I have tried to fight this, as much as I have tried to ignore you, I'm here, and I'm listening. So just tell me what is going on!" Jodie shouted.

Lisa looked longingly at her friend, distraught at the state she was in. Lisa was trying to save her, save all of them. She sighed, about to explain, when suddenly her head snapped up, staring down the beach.

"Shit. We may be too late." Lisa stated. Jodie stood, looking in the direction Lisa was staring. Jodie's heart began to pound as her adrenaline kicked in. Lisa looked back to Jodie, her face a twisted in fear. Jodie's hand instinctively went to her phone, ready to call someone for help.

"I think you need to call your police friend," Lisa said, her eyes drifting to the phone.

Jodie pulled out the business card from her pocket and keyed the number into the phone. She hit send and listened for the response on the other end. Just as she heard Jensen's voice, Lisa screamed.

"Officer Jensen I—" she was cut off by the scream.

"Jodie, it's Amanda... RUN!"

Jodie yelled out, "Amanda? What? Lisa?!" She watched Lisa dash down the beach. Jodie dropped the phone and took off to follow her friend.

Ben leaped forward when Jodie took out the phone, to let her know that he was there. He was startled when she ran off. He retrieved the phone, seeing that the call was still connected.

"Hello, Jodie?" Office Jensen asked.

"This is Ben," he responded.

"Ben? This is Officer Jensen, what is going on?"

Ben shook his head slightly, his eyes not leaving Jodie. He watched her get further down the beach, knowing that he was going to have to sprint after her. "I'm not sure, but something is wrong. You need to get down to the beach."

Ben took off after her, the phone still in his hands. Jensen could hear his heavy breathing "Ben, what is going on?"

"It's Jodie, I'm chasing after her. I don't know where she is going, but she is distraught, and she is acting erratic. I'm afraid she is going to hurt herself. There had to be a reason she called you."

"Ok, stay on the line with me, I'm going to meet you. Keep me posted on where you are."

***

Amanda and Andrea wove through the crowd on the boardwalk, keeping vigilant for anyone following them. They made their way to the more crowded section of the area, heading towards the pier. The summer crowd gathering in lines for rides or to play games made it a little easier to blend in.

While Amanda was ahead, trying to find other places to hide, Andrea was texting her brother, pleading for his help.

A: I'm scared.

P: Where are you now?

A: the pier. I just want to go home.

P: Is Amanda still with you?

A: Yes.

P: Good, stay with her. I'm walking onto the boardwalk now.

A: K. Please hurry.

Pete slipped the phone back into his pocket as he and Pat climbed the steps to the boardwalk. They had parked closer to Bally's casino, and made their way towards the pier. Pete watched as Pat answered his phone.

"Yeah, she's with her. At the pier. Meet us there. It ends tonight, brother."

"What ends tonight?" Pete asked as they stepped closer to their destination.

"Don't worry about it. Just handle what you have to." Pat responded, not removing his eyes from the pier.

"No, Pat, what the hell is going on?" Pete asked as he stopped and grabbed Pat's arm. Pat paused, his cold eyes focusing on Pete.

"I said don't worry about it. You need to take care of that bitch who saw us. She's the whole reason you are here, right? Revenge?"

Pete nodded. "Focus on that. My brother and I have other business to deal with."

They continued their walk when Pat's phone rang again. He rolled his eyes as he answered it, "What, Joe?"

Pat looked over slyly at Pete, and stepped away from him a bit, speaking in a lower tone. Pete noticed, but kept it casual as he listened into the conversation.

"Yeah, the kid is with them too." Pat hung up and continued the journey.

Pete's ears perked up at the mention of his nephew. His suspicion grew as they got to the edge of the pier. *What in the world did my nephew have to do with anything?* He thought. His focus now switching from Amanda to his sister.

"Maybe we should split up and find them," Pete suggested, trying to get some distance so he could call his sister.

"Not a bad idea. Keep your phone on you." Pat nodded and walked off.

Pete watched him walk away as he quickly called his sister.

"Pete?" She answered in a hush.

"Where are you?" He asked urgently.

"Near the Ferris Wheel, why?"

"You need to get out of here. Something is wrong. Get away from Amanda and run. Call me when you are a safe distance away. I'll come to you." He said quickly and hung up.

Andrea looked down at her phone, the fear doubling in her body. Andrew felt her arms tighten on him, and he looked nervously at her. "Momma?"

"Shh, baby, it's ok. Just stay quiet." She watched Amanda and waited until she was looking away to turn and run.

She made it a few feet before she felt a hand grab her arm. She looked back to seem Amanda's worried face; her eyes wide with questions. "What the hell are you doing?"

"Pete told me to get away from you."

"Pete? You've been in contact with him?" Panic filled her limbs as she looked around nervously. From the corner of her eye, she saw the bald head of Pat, and watched him scope the crowd.

"Fuck!" Amanda exclaimed as she pulled Andrea behind a game booth. Andrea tried to pull her arm away from Amanda. "Listen to me, your brother is with the bald guy. You cannot trust him."

"He's my brother, he is always going to protect me."

"I saw Pete, your brother, balls deep in the bald guy, Pat, no less than an hour before I found you in the park." Amanda explained in frustration, "I do not know what is going on, but your brother is romantically involved with him. And from what you said, that Pat guy is after you. So, we need to go, now!"

Andrea stood there for a moment, trying to process Amanda's words. Amanda shook her head and pulled Andrea and Andrew off the pier, running onto the sand, and going to hide beneath where they were previously standing.

Pete saw them run under the pier and smiled, knowing that his sister and nephew were away from Pat. His eyes narrowed at the sight of Amanda, but he knew he had to find out what Pat was up to before he could finish what needed to be done.

Pete's phone rang, "Yeah Pat?"

"Have you seen them?"

"I'm pretty positive I saw Amanda head towards the Hard Rock. I was just going to call you."

"Was your sister with her?"

Pete's face contorted from that question; his suspicion being confirmed that something was going on that he did not know about. Something involving his family.

"Yeah. Meet me at the entrance of the pier." Pete said and hung up, his new mission for the time being was keeping his family safe.

Amanda watched Pete and Pat head towards the casinos, her breath finally normalizing. She turned to Andrea and smiled. "I think we are ok. Let's stay here for a bit. Then we will keep to the beach and head back to the car."

Andrea smiled weakly and nodded, finally able to put Andrew down. Her arms were on fire from holding him for so long. Andrew sat down in the sand and began to play. The girls followed his lead, sinking into the sand with their backs against a pillar.

Ten minutes past, and Amanda felt the urge to get up and run. She stood suddenly, startling Andrea. "We need to go, now."

Andrea slowly stood up, looking cautiously at Amanda, making her way to her son. "What happened?"

Amanda's fight or flight response kicked into high gear, a voice in her head yelling at her to get out of here. It was not her internal monologue; it was Lisa's voice. The yelling increasing in volume until it was deafening. Amanda chanted the cry out in sync with the voice in her head, "Go, now! Go, now! Go mow!"

Andrea panicked and grabbed Andrew's hand as Amanda grabbed his other hand. They turned to run, but they did not get far. A familiar voice filled their ears as his form focused into their vision, "There you are. I've been looking everywhere for you."

***

Jodie made her way down the beach, following Lisa. The running was challenging, the sand impeding her speed as her chest heaved for air. She was not a trained marathon runner, but she did all she could to follow Lisa, her voice was echoing in her head.

"Faster, Jodie, faster! You need to help them!"

"Help who?" Jodie yelled out through deep breaths.

"You have to save Amanda!"

"Amanda?!" Jodie yelled back. "What is wrong with Amanda?"

Jodie saw the pier getting closer as she continued running. Lisa was suddenly gone from her field of vision. She slowed her run, observing her surroundings, unsure of what to do next.

Ben kept his pursuit, explaining to Officer Jensen what was going on. "She's yelling something about helping Amanda. She looks like she's headed towards the pier."

"Ok Ben, I have some officers nearby and I am dispatching them to the pier. I am heading over now."

He witnessed Jodie slow down, almost coming to a complete stop. He continued to run to her, hoping to catch her.

"Don't stop! Go now!" Jodie heard Lisa yell. Jodie started to run again, the beach emptying the deeper into the night they got. The sun was gone at this point, making her sight of distance significantly shorter. As she approached the pier, the lights of the carnival above casted shadows below.

Ben paused, his eyes focusing on the silhouette of four people below the pier. He watched as the larger of the four pulled out what looked like a gun and pointed it towards the others. "Holy shit, he has a gun." Ben said into the phone, but more to himself. He heard the police siren through the phone in response.

Twenty-Five

Amanda, Andrea, and Andrew stopped at the sound of the voice. They saw Joe Rappaport standing there with a sinister smile stretched across his handsome face. Andrea pushed Andrew behind her, as Amanda stepped in front of them.

"Aww, that's cute." He said mockingly, stepping a little closer to the trio. "Amanda Walker, long time no see."

Amanda scowled at him in response. "What? Nothing to say to an old friend?" He laughed. "I will say, I was very surprised to see you and Jodie this weekend. I had no idea you two were involved in all of this. I thought my story with you had ended all those years ago." He continued as he slowly stalked his prey.

Andrea cowered behind Amanda, still shielding her son. "And you," he continued, "you have been very hard to track down. That," he said pointing at Andrew, "was a mistake that needs to be fixed."

Andrea sobbed and hugged her son, Amanda stepping forward. "Haven't you done enough to her? You're a real piece of work, Joe."

Joe laughed, raising his eyebrows and pretending to back away from Amanda. "Whoa, easy there, Amanda. You're not a part of this for me, so just walk away."

Amanda smirked and took another step towards him. "I'm thinking that is a no."

Joe laughed, looked around, and pulled a gun out of his pocket, aiming it at Amanda. "I'm thinking you should reconsider."

Amanda stopped in her tracks, looking back at Andrea. Joe pulled out his phone, his voice pulling Amanda's attention back to him. "Yeah, I got all three of them. Under the pier. Do what you want with him."

"Now, as I was saying." He said as he ended the call. Amanda backed up to shield Andrea and Andrew again. "This doesn't involve you, Amanda. Hell, it really doesn't even involve this bitch here. I'm here for him." He said, gesturing to Andrew with the gun.

Andrea cried out, "No!" Andrew crying in response to his mother's wail. "I don't think so!" Amanda yelled over the cries.

"What do you even care, she's nothing to you." Amanda went to respond when she was cut off. "Oh, finally, welcome to the party!"

She turned to find Pete and Pat walk up behind them. Pete went to approach his sister and nephew when Joe focused the gun on Pete. "Uh-uh, none of that."

Pete looked from Joe back to Pat, to find Pat pulling a gun out on him. "Pat, what the fuck?"

Joe laughed, unable to contain his amusement of his brother's betrayal. "Oh Pete, you gullible asshole. It's been a long road, but at least we are finally here."

Pete focused on Pat, whose response was just a shoulder shrug and a side smile. "Sorry, babe. It's nothing personal."

"Now," Joe announced, pulling everyone's attention back to him. "The kid. I need him, here," he gestured with the gun from Andrew to the spot next to him.

Pete shouted out in unison with Andrea and Amanda, their cries almost drowning out the wails of the police sirens. The flashing of red and blue lights from beyond the boardwalk were filing the sky, pulling their attention away for the briefest of moments.

***

Jodie saw the gun come out of the pocket as she realized who she was staring at. Lisa's voice in her head confirming her worst fears. "It's Joe. He has Amanda."

Jodie focused on the gun, scared to death for her best friend. The thought of losing another person she loved tore through her mind. The lights in the distance barely registered, only the sirens. She heard her name being screamed from behind her.

Ben continuously called out for her as he chased after her. His heart was in his throat, seeing her not turning away from the assailant. For the briefest of moments, she looked back at him, a sad smile on her face as she returned her attention and sprinted forward. He continued his pursuit, but somehow, he could not catch up to her.

The sound of Ben screaming her name almost broke her. She did not know why he was there, or how he knew where she was, but she could not chance him being hurt by any of this. Her resolution was strong, she knew what she had to do. She had to save the people she loved from this psychopath. She failed once already, maybe twice if he had anything to do with Doris. A sense of calm came over her as she felt Lisa agree with her thoughts. She looked back at Ben, for one final look at him. His face was distraught, his voice strained from calling her name.

More than anything in the world, she wanted to turn around and run straight into his arms, but she knew she could not.

"Are you ready for this?" Lisa's voice echoed in her head. She nodded slightly and took off towards Joe.

The moments passed by quickly, but in Jodie's point of view, it lasted a lifetime. She could see from her peripheral that Pete slammed his elbow into Pat's nose, making him fall to the ground. He dove for the gun in Pat's possession, turning to focus it on Joe. She heard Amanda scream out her name as Joe turned slightly, seeing Jodie approach at an almost super-human speed. Jodie lunged forward and tackled him to the ground as the sound of two gunshots rang out in the summer air.

Joe fell on the ground with Jodie on top of him, both not moving. Ben screamed out Jodie's name as if his heart was ripped from his chest. He finally caught up with her, falling to the ground next to her as Amanda joined him. The police flooded the scene, surrounding the group.

Pete dropped the gun and fell to his knees with his hands in the air as the police approached, cuffing him behind his back. Pat was lifted by two officers, a third cuffing him behind his back. Andrea ran to her brother with her son in her arms, sobbing to the officers that he was innocent and not to harm him.

A few officers ran over to Joe and Jodie. They removed the gun from Joe's hand and cuffed him as Ben lifted Jodie from Joe.

Jodie opened her eyes and smiled. She took the outstretched hand and stood up, brushing the sand from her shorts and accepting the warmth of the hug presented to her. She smiled sweetly and said, "We did good, huh?"

"Yeah Jodie, we did good." Lisa responded, tightly hugging her friend again. Jodie looked over Lisa's shoulder, watching the rest of the scene unfold.

Ben held Jodie in his arms with Amanda next to him in the sand. "Hey baby, baby, come on, you're ok." He said smiling down at her, brushing the hair away from her face. Amanda looked down at Jodie and sobbed, drawing Ben's attention away from her face. The blood poured from the bullet wound in her chest, saturating her shirt, and spreading from the center of the wound.

Officer Jensen came running over, moving Ben and Amanda away from the body. He checked for a pulse, but there was none to be found. The gunshot killed her instantly from the close range. He looked over at the pair kneeling in the sand and somberly shook his head slightly. Ben and Amanda broke down, Ben grabbing onto Jodie again as Amanda sobbed into Ben's shoulder.

"No, no, no, no." Ben chanted through gut wrenching cries. "Jodie, no! Come back to me, baby. Please." He sobbed; his face buried in her neck. Never in his life had he ever felt something so strong. His life felt like it shattered into pieces so minuscule, the wind could take them away. The empty, cold permanence of the absence of Jodie from his life was unbearable. The past two years of his life felt like a cruel joke.

Office Jensen watched, a tear falling from his eye. This group of kids had gone through so much in such a short amount of time, he worried for them. He placed his hand on Ben's shoulder; Ben tried to shrug it off, screaming, "No!"

"Son, I'm sorry, but we need to remove you from the scene. We need to take her." Amanda then let out an animalistic screech. "No, you can't take her. She needs to come home with us. She belongs with us!"

Jensen motioned to two officers, and they slowly approached the grieving duo. Gently, they coaxed them away from Jodie's body. The two hardly moved, not taking their eyes away from her. The coroner appeared with some detectives, and they began their process of taking photos. The sight of the body bag being laid next to Jodie was too much for Amanda. She clung onto Ben and buried her face in his chest. "Ben, they can't..." she started to choke out, but the words were stopped by her cries.

Ben nodded slightly and held onto Amanda, the two of them supporting one another both physically and emotionally. Aside from her parents, Amanda and Ben were the closest people in her life. They knew her better than they knew themselves. And now they had to cope with her not being there at all.

The officers escorted everyone to the corral of police cars parked on the boardwalk near South Pennsylvania Avenue. Pete was taken in one car, Pat in the other. Joe was taken away in an ambulance, his status unknown. Andrea and Andrew were taken to the police station separately from Ben and Amanda. Jensen took them back, and watched them in the rearview mirror as he made a left down Atlantic Avenue toward the precinct.

The tears did not stop on the short drive to the station, nor as they sat in a room waiting for Officer Jensen to speak with them. They four of them sat around a table, Andrew in Andrea's lap, Amanda and Ben still clinging onto one another.

Andrea was the first to say something. "I can't understand what happened. My brother and that guy, and the…" her voice trailed off, realizing that she was talking to herself. "Can I ask you guys something?"

Amanda and Ben shifted their bloodshot, watery eyes across the table to Andrea. "Who was that? Who was the girl who saved us?"

Amanda could not hold back her sobs, unable to answer. Ben looked at Andrea for a moment, unable to string the words together. He started to speak a few times, but stopped himself. He looked down at his lap, staring down at his left hand. Quietly, he responded, "She was supposed to be my wife."

Amanda's cries caught in her throat as she heard Ben's words. He looked at her and nodded, the tears pouring out faster. "I wanted to marry her, Amanda. I wanted to spend my life with her. She's gone."

Ben's head fell onto Amanda's shoulder. They could not do anything but cry and mourn. Andrea joined them, unable to stop herself. A girl, who she had never met before, someone that she had only heard of, sacrificed her life for her son.

***

Jodie sat on the beach, Lisa sitting next to her, watching the police document and clean up the crime scene. It was strange to watch herself be placed into a body bag, and then lifted onto a gurney and taken away. The hardest part was to watch Ben and Amanda. She was heartbroken for them. There was nothing she could do. All she wanted to do was protect them and keep them safe. They may never forgive her for what she did, but she had no choice; she could not let Joe hurt anyone else.

"This is surreal." She said to Lisa, processing what she was watching. "I know, trust me." She responded as she put her arm around me.

"I've really missed you." Jodie said to Lisa, not moving her eyes from what was going on in front of her.

"I'm sorry, Jodie. I'm sorry for all of it. I just didn't know what to do. I knew what Joe was planning and it made me sick to my stomach. You were the only one I could contact. I tried with Amanda, but she never saw me like you did."

"It's ok, I get it. I just don't understand what Joe's deal was."

Lisa was about to explain when they were interrupted.

"That was pretty fucking badass, Jodie."

Jodie turned around to see Doris standing behind her. She jumped up from the ground and ran to her friend, throwing her arms around her.

"Oh my god, Doris!" Jodie exclaimed. A feeling of peace settled in Jodie's chest, not realizing how much she had been worrying about Doris.

"I watched the whole thing, can you believe that bald fucker fucked me in a bathroom and left me there? The guy nutted on my face and abandoned me. What a piece of shit."

"That's Joe's brother, Pat, his partner in crime," Lisa offered as an explanation.

"He told me his name was Charlie and he worked at the casino." Doris said with a scoff and a roll of her eyes. She then turned to Jodie and smiled. "I can't begin to apologize to you, Jodie. I mean, some of it was out of my control," Doris paused, giving Lisa a stern look, "but I never meant to hurt you. And I know how much Ben loves you, and I am just so sorry."

Jodie pulled Doris in for a large hug. "It doesn't even matter anymore. I would love to hear the whole story eventually, but I'm just so glad that the two of you are here with me. This is like, beyond hard, and I'm just grateful that I'm not alone."

The three girls turned, watching Amanda and Ben walk away with the officers. "I'm scared for them." Jodie said quietly.

Twenty-Six

A few hours had passed. Andrea and Andrew were asleep in the chairs. Amanda sat there, staring at the table, her whole body was numb. Ben paced the room, pausing occasionally to breathe deep and regain his composure.

The door to the room finally opened, and Officer Jensen walked in. He gently placed his hand on Andrea's arm to wake her up. Ben returned to his chair as Amanda looked at the new occupant. "So, we have been questioning the men for a while. There is going to be a murder investigation. The Rappaport brothers are not saying a word, but Mr. Erickson spoke with us."

Andrea sat up straighter, bracing herself for what her brother did.

"It seems as though Mr. Erickson met Pat Rappaport a few years back in Norfolk. They became friends, eventually lovers. He admitted that the trip to AC was planned not only as a weekend away with Pat, but apparently to come after you, Miss Walker."

Amanda's face contorted with confusion and disbelief. "What? Why... how?"

"Apparently, he blames you for him dropping out of college. He said that you ruined his life, and that he wanted to make you pay."

A sob escaped from Amanda's mouth, her shoulders collapsing. Ben placed his arm around her and supported her, his other hand gently rubbing her arm.

"He claims that he discovered you were coming on this trip through Jodie's social media account. He reached out to Mr. Rappaport, inviting him to help him with his plans."

Andrea shook her head in disbelief. "My brother would never do that. He loved Amanda."

"It also seems that your brother was neglecting to take medication for his depression. We had a psych evaluation done on him, along with some lab work. The doctor informed us that not only was he not taking his medication, he also has bipolar disorder. I just wanted to notify you that the three of them will be standing trial, saying that all of them survive."

"Survive?" Ben asked, watching Jensen stand up.

"The main suspect is in critical condition. It seems that a bullet lodged near his spine. We won't know his condition for a few days." Officer Jensen headed to the door. He placed his hand on the handle and sighed, turning back to face the others.

"I really am so incredibly sorry for your losses. There is really no need for you to stay in AC. We will be in touch for the trial. Jodie, ah, Miss Rogers seemed like a really good kid. I'm sorry things went the way they did." He looked at Ben and Amanda with a halfhearted smile, tuned and left the room.

Andrea picked up her son and followed behind the officer but paused briefly to look at Amanda. Amanda returned her stare her, but neither had any words to say. They had been through so much together but were separated by where their loyalties laid. They silently nodded at each other, and Andrea left the room.

"I need to call Jodie's mother. She needs to hear about it from me before she sees it on the news." Amanda said, her eyes still focused on the open door.

Ben nodded and stood up, holding his hand out for Amanda. She took it, letting him help her up. She squeezed his hand and let go, leading the way out of the building. They slowly made their way back to where Amanda had parked her car and headed back to the hotel.

She put the car in park and looked over at the hotel, her head shaking. "I can't go back in there, Ben." He nodded, took the keys to both hotel rooms, and went to retrieve their belongings.

He made his way through the lobby, taking the stairs to avoid the memories the tiny elevator gave him. He closed his eyes and took a deep breath before opening the door to his room. He walked in threw all his stuff in his bag and grabbed Doris' bag. He went back outside and unlocked the door to Amanda's room, the adjoining door still closed from earlier in the day.

He put the bags down by the door and froze, staring at the bed he shared with Jodie. Had he had any tears left in his body, they would have fallen, but he was beyond the point of crying. All he felt was emptiness. He went into the bathroom carefully stepping over the broken glass of the mirror, picking up her toothbrush and makeup, glancing at the shower and thinking of their shared time in there.

He mixed everything of Jodie's and Amanda's in the bags, not wanting to sort through their belongings. Sadly, he zipped up her overnight bag, lifting it into his arms and hugging it. It was the only thing close enough to her that he could hold. He carefully put the bags over his shoulders, leaving one hand free to close the doors and carry the keys.

As he turned back one last time to look at the place where he rekindled and then lost his love, he stepped back over to the bed and picked up her pillow. He raised it to his face, her scent still lingering. Feeling his heart ache at the memory of her, he tucked the pillow under his arm and left the room.

Without a word, he left the keys on the counter in the lobby. He opened the back door of Amanda's car and loaded the luggage but kept the pillow with him as he sat in the passenger seat. Amanda glanced at the pillow, understanding why he had it. She nodded her head and pulled out her phone. Ben held her hand as Amanda dialed Jodie's parents' house. It was a quarter after four in the morning, and Amanda could hear the sleep in Mr. Rogers' voice as he answered the phone.

"Mr. Rogers, it's Amanda."

"Amanda? Is everything ok?" Amanda could hear Mrs. Rogers in the background asking what was going on.

Amanda tried not to cry as she answered, "No, Mr. Rogers nothing is ok. Last night I was attacked, and Jodie…" she said as she started to sob, "Jodie saved me. Jodie risked her life to save me. Jodie died saving me."

***

Amanda and Ben returned to Long Island in silence, Ben driving after Amanda broke down on the phone. There was nothing to say anymore. They pulled up to Jodie's house, Ben's and Doris' cars parked in front waiting for their owners to return. The front door flung open, and Mrs. Rogers came running out to the car, throwing her arms around Ben and Amanda. They supported her as she collapsed into them, the three of them sharing their grief.

They walked back into the house where they found Mr. Rogers sitting in front of the television, a picture of Jodie appearing on the screen with news coverage about her death. It was a photo that Ben took before they went to dinner with everyone at the Italian restaurant. She was sitting in front of the fountain in the main lobby, a beautiful smile on her face with the white flower tucked behind her ear. There was another picture of the group of them at dinner that night, which Jodie had asked the waiter to take of them. That picture appeared when the reporter mentioned Doris' death. The reporter must have pulled the photos from Jodie's social medial page.

***

Jodie's funeral was a few days later. People from all stages of her life came to pay their respects. Her sorority sisters came together, still reeling from Doris' funeral the day before. Jodie's parents sat in the front of the room, Amanda and Ben not leaving their sides the entire time.

Jodie sat in the back of the room, observing the parade of people. She almost found amusement that she was able to do what most people joked about; she was able to see who showed up to her funeral. She eventually made her way to the front of the room. She did not want to look at herself in the casket, it was too weird. She kneeled in front of her parents and just cried. She wanted to take away their pain. Their only child was taken from them. She never considered what she would leave behind when she made the choice to stop Joe. She knew her parents would understand her decision, they knew she did not do it for selfish reasons.

She eventually looked to Amanda and Ben. She never thought of the repercussions her actions would have on them either. She just knew that she needed to save them. She looked in their eyes and saw the same desolation that she had felt when Lisa had died. She worried about all of them, but she was concerned about Amanda the most. This was the second time she had to go through this. Amanda was so strong for her when Lisa was taken from them. But this time she was not so sure.

She knew that from this moment on, she could only observe. She did not want to interfere like Lisa had done to her. It was not fair to put someone through that. Life was hard enough to live without the ghosts of your past appearing.

Jodie eventually found herself in the intensive care unit of Good Samaratin Hospital. She knew Joe was in there, placed in a medically induced coma. The bullet that Pete shot tore through Joe's lower right abdomen, ripping through his intestines, and embedding itself near his spinal column. The doctors repaired his bowels, removing much of the damaged organ and rerouting it, but they put him in the coma to stop him from moving, the swelling around his spine making the doctors reevaluate the possibility of removing the bullet.

She sat at the edge of the bed, staring down her killer. She felt her rage boil over, thinking about what he stole from her. She had so much life ahead of her. She was making her way to becoming an editor for a publisher, transitioning from her entry-level job as an assistant to the editors. All her time studying and writing essays and dissertations was for naught. Her plans of raising a family alongside her best friend, so their children could be best friends was gone. The joy of her parents growing old and spending time with their grandchildren vanished. And most heartbreakingly, the realization that she could never say yes to Ben asking her to marry him.

She stared down at his pale, unmoving face, studying his breathing patterns. She would love to smother him with a pillow, take him out for what he did to her and Lisa. She relished the thought of getting revenge for her friend, whose life was snuffed out even earlier than her own. The desire to block his breathing was overwhelming, and she needed to walk away.

She left the hospital, drifting east on Main Street. She knew she was not the type of person to seek revenge. Even in death, she could not lose sight of who she was. Lost in her thoughts, she found herself in front of Maxwell's, the bar she first met Ben in. She wandered in; the bar not nearly as crowded on a Wednesday night as it was on the weekends. She sat there and reminisced about that night. She thought about how nervous she was to meet Ben, and how Doris had encouraged her to get over her fears. She never gave Doris the credit that she deserved. They were never the best of friends, but Doris really helped her out of her shell. Doris did not know the details of what happened to Lisa, but she knew that something traumatic happened, that Jodie closed herself off to social situations.

She sat in a dark corner of the bar long after it closed. Time did not matter much to Jodie anymore. It no longer had the same significance as it did days ago. As much as she wanted to sit there and replay that night they met over and over again, her thoughts continued to drift to Joe, laying in that hospital bed.

She decided that he needed to survive, because he needed to spend the rest of his life paying for his actions. Justice needed to be served for Lisa and Doris. Andrea and her son deserved safety and peace of mind. Jodie needed to know that she made the right decision to risk her life that night on the beach.

Twenty-Seven

It was a somber, humid day in early September. Rather than spending her time on campus, beginning her master's program in education, Amanda sat in the quiet court room surround by many strangers. She took comfort knowing that her parents were sitting a few rows behind her, along with Jodie's parents. She chewed nervously on her lower lip as she heard the court door open, watching an officer walk in and speak with the stenographer. Her leg bounced in anticipation, her body a raw bundle of nerves.

Ben reached his hand out and placed it on Amanda's bouncing knee, trying to calm her down. The two of them had become quite the dynamic duo, leading the charge to get justice for Jodie. They spent many long nights with the Rogers family, prepping statements and gathering information.

Amanda smiled slightly as a thank you, acknowledging Ben's gesture. Her breath caught in her throat as she saw Pete's family enter the courtroom, filling in the row directly across from them. Amanda's hand clenched onto Ben's arm, causing him to look up and follow the direction of her stare. Andrea kept her eyes forward, not acknowledging the other side of the courtroom. Pete's mother, and a woman who Amanda assumed was Pete's wife, were whispering to one another, their eyes not moving from Amanda.

Amanda could not look away from them, until she saw Pete enter the courtroom. He causally glanced back at his family, smoothing the tie he paired with his designer suit, his mother nodding at him in approval. His eyes wandered over to her side of the courtroom, but he did not pause to look at any of them, he just slightly smiled and sat down.

Ben quietly whispered to Amanda, "he thinks mommy and daddy can save him with their bank roll. I can't wait to see what he does when he gets what is coming to him."

The officer announced for the courtroom to rise as the Judge approached the bench. Everyone settled as the Judge took his seat, beginning the proceedings.

"Today's proceeding is Erickson versus the state of New Jersey," the judge began, "I understand that a plea deal has been offered."

"It has, your honor," the prosecutor responded. "In exchange for testimony against the Rappaport brothers, the State has agreed to lower the sentence from accomplice to attempted first-degree murder to attempted malicious wounding."

"And does the defendant accept?" The judge asked.

"We are motioning for a lesser sentence of accessory to attempted manslaughter. In exchange, my client has agreed to go on record about what conspired between himself and the Rappaport brothers."

The judge looked to the District Attorney, and back to the defense lawyer. "I would advise the defendant to reconsider the DA's generous offer. You, sir, are in no position to haggle for a lesser sentence."

Amanda watched intently as Pete and his lawyer whispered back and forth, the look on Pete's face getting angrier by the moment. Amanda tried to read their lips, making out the words they spoke. She excitedly whispered to Ben, "they just said life in prison!"

Ben gave her side eye and responded, "there is no way he's getting that."

"Counsel, your response?" the judge asked impatiently.

Amanda watched as Pete looked back as his family, and slightly nodded his head to his lawyer, accepting the deal.

"You honor, my client has agreed to the terms presented by the DA."

"Fine, in return for your testimony, you are charged with attempted malicious wounding, carrying a sentence of ten years in prison. How do you plea?"

Amanda held her breath, her nails embedding themselves in Ben's forearm. Pete sighed and responded, "Guilty, your honor."

The court was adjourned with instructions that the case of Rappaport and Rappaport versus the state was to commence in two weeks' time.

Amanda jumped up and hugged Ben, sobbing into his shoulder. "Those sons of bitches are going to pay for what they did to you, and to Jodie." Ben said, watching Pete being taken away in handcuffs.

***

Pete sat in his orange jumpsuit; his hands clenched together as his knee bounced uncontrollably under the table. He studied his surroundings, watching the other inmates meeting with visitors, the sounds of the room a combination of joy and sadness. He focused his attention on the table in front of him, looking at the reflection of the florescent lights in the rough steel. His mind was racing, his feelings a mixed bag of emotions. It had been a week since he was in the courtroom, a week into his 521-week sentence.

He still had not processed the events that led up to his arrest. He nibbled on his lip as he thought about Pat, and how he had been betrayed by him. He could not understand how it happened. They met by chance; they slowly fell in love. Pete would have gladly left his wife and his family for him, not that it would have been too hard, he hated them. Between his family and Amanda, he completely lost sight of himself.

His blood started to boil as the thought of Amanda entered his head. His eyes narrowed as he scolded himself for falling back into old habits. Amanda was a witch, a sorceress, she was able to hypnotize him and control him. He expected more of himself, he thought his training in the military would have strengthened his resolve, and kept his head straight around her.

"Mr. Erickson?" He was called out of his trance, his thoughts of Amanda falling aside, the red in his vision subsiding as he looked up at his lawyer.

"Yes, hello sir," he responded as he stood up and shook the hand of the stout man standing on the other side of the table.

The lawyer gestured to the seat, as he set up shop on his side of the table. He looked through some file folders, nodding to himself as Pete watched on. The lawyer shook his head slightly and pulled out his cell phone, turning on the voice memo, and waving over a man in his late twenties. The second man approached the table with steno pad.

"Mr. Erickson, I am Rick Goldbaum, I was hired by your parents to take over your case. It is their hope that with your testimony, and hopefully character profile and good behavior, we will be able to reduce your sentence."

Pete nodded as the lawyer continued. "This is Josh Statinzwicki, he is my assistant and will be taking notes for me during our meetings."

The two men nodded at each other as Rick continued. "So, Mr. Erickson, we need to know everything. How you got involved with the Rappaports, how you ended up in Atlantic City the week of June 28th. We need to know your relationships to Ms. Sullivan, Ms. Walker, Ms. Rogers, and Mr. Thatcher."

Pete inhaled deeply, unsure of how much truth to tell. He still did not want to betray Pat; he still loved him. But he was well aware that his future depended on his testimony, and he did not want to rot in prison for ten years. He felt that he rotted his whole life, that was until he became his true self with Pat.

The lawyer watched the tango of emotion on Pete's face, and he knew that his client was not going to be completely forthcoming with the truth. He had represented clients like this in the past, and he knew that his work was cut out for him.

"Mr. Erickson-uh-Pete, I understand that you are in a difficult position," he said, catching Pete's eyesight. "I know you want to protect your friends, but I am telling you this from experience, the charges against your friends are serious… life in prison serious. I am here to protect you."

Pete broke eye contact with his lawyer, and scanned the room. His heart breaking in his chest as he thought of never seeing Pat again. He took a deep breath, the exhale shaky in its release. "Pete, need I remind you; your friend held your sister and nephew at gunpoint."

Pete's attention was brought back to the man sitting across from him. "I don't believe that."

"You were there, Pete. You wrestled the gun away from Pat to save your sister and your nephew. His brother tried to kill your family," the lawyer emphasized.

Pete shook his head as tears formed in his eyes.

"I'm going to play something for you, Pete." His lawyer said as he pulled his phone out and played an audio recording of Andrea's statement. Her voice filled the room as she tearily retold the story of what happened that night under the pier. Her broken sobs made Pete's chest ache as the pain and terror of that night flooded his mind.

"I met Pat at a bar in Norfolk. We began a friendship through texting and it eventually became more than a friendship. We were together for two years. He never once brought up my sister or my nephew. I was shocked when they went after them at the boardwalk."

"And what about Ms. Walker?"

"I dated Amanda in college. She ruined my life; I lost my scholarship because of her. She manipulated me and brainwashed me. My mother and wife showed me how horrible of a person she was. I almost sullied my good name because of her, had to join the navy because of her. I wanted revenge for her ruining my life.

"I told Pat about this, and he helped me plan my revenge. He said he would help me because he loved me, and that once I took care of her, I would be free to get divorced and we would be together. When I saw that Jodie posted on social media that they were planning a trip for their dead friend's five year passing, and it coincided with my leave, it was the perfect opportunity to do it."

"And how did your sister get involved with the plan?"

"She wasn't involved with the plan. I mentioned that I was on leave and it would be nice to see her. I said I thought it would be fun to go to AC and go to the boardwalk with Andrew."

"It was your idea to bring your sister and nephew down when you were planning on seeking revenge on Ms. Walker?"

"I... well... I remember Pat suggested that I should see my sister and nephew while I had some free time."

The lawyer nodded. "Mr. Erickson, I hate to say this to you, but I think Mr. Rappaport manipulated you by using your quest for vengeance to feed his own nefarious intentions. I don't think he ever intended to help you with Ms. Walker, I think he used you to get to your sister and nephew. If you love your family as much as you say you do, you need to cooperate with us. If you don't do it for yourself to lessen your sentence, do it for your nephew, get him the justice and protection he needs. If we aren't able to prosecute the Rappaport brothers to the fullest extent of the law, I fear that your nephew's life may be in danger."

Twenty-Eight

Jodie sat vigilant in Joe's hospital room, watching his progress, and making sure he did not die. She never moved from her perch at the end of his hospital bed, and watched countless hours of doctors and nurses checking up on him. No one ever came to visit, as his only family member was in prison awaiting trial.

Pat was unable to post bail because his assets were frozen due to the suspicious nature of the crimes he and his brother were charged for.

One afternoon when the leaves were beginning to bud on the trees outside of the hospital window, Jodie noticed movement from Joe's bed. His finger twitched a few times before she noticed his shoulders begin to move as he pushed himself up in the bed. He blinked a few times as he looked around the room, then sat up and looked down at his body that remained in the bed.

Jodie's eyes grew wide as he watched him staring down at himself.

"What a fucking waste," he commented.

"No," she breathed out quietly, which captured his attention and made him swivel his head and look at Jodie as she stood up from the bed.

"What are you doing here?" He asked as he looked up at her.

"Shit. No, this can't be happening," she mumbled.

"How are you even talking to me right now?" Joe asked.

"Because you killed me, you fucking asshole. You shot me at close range in the chest," Jodie yelled.

Joe sat for a moment and looked down at his body again, then looked up at Jodie. "Oh yeah, I forgot about that. Ha! I guess that's what you get when you mess with my plan. Shit, I guess that means it didn't work. That fucking sucks, we were so close."

Jodie started at him with her mouth agape at his words. His callousness should not have surprised her, he seemed like he lost any semblance of humanity years ago. "So close? You were trying to kill a child."

"That child should never have been born."

"Maybe you shouldn't have raped her mother."

"How would you even know that?"

Jodie smiled as she said, "oh, I know all of it. Every sick, twisted thing you did. And your brother. I know all about how you would beat and rape your girlfriends, I know that your brother was equally as sick and brutal as you, and I know that your grandfather found out about it and paid off your victims and tried to punish you himself.

"I know that the clause he put in his will that prevented you two from collecting your inheritance until all living members of the family had passed on. You and your brother conspired to kill your parents."

Joe smirked and shrugged his shoulders. "They really should have taken better care of their car; brakes are so important and need proper maintenance."

"Too bad for you that your grandfather knew about your son. Weren't you just shocked to shit when the lawyers told you that you couldn't collect because there was still a family member?"

His face turned a shade of red with anger. "That child should have never been born. My grandfather thought he was so smart, paying off the mother to get the DNA test and keep everything under wraps."

"Didn't stop you from tracking her down. You really were going to kill a three-year-old for money? You're a sick fuck."

"That money was rightfully mine."

"Have you ever heard of earning a living? Murder? Seriously?"

"I'm used to a certain level of comfort. That money is my birthright."

"And you were going to just share it with your brother?"

Joe shrugged his shoulders. "That remained to be seen. I needed his help to get to the kid. He long-conned her brother. Did his research and found where the guy was stationed, got a job at the local dive bar. Convinced him that he was in love with him, then got him to meet with his sister during his leave. It took a few years to get to that point, but it would have been worth it."

"He wanted to kill Amanda," Jodie said.

"Not my problem. Thanks, by the way, for sharing your plans on social. It finally gave us the opportunity we were looking for."

Jodie started at Joe as she processed his words. "You're telling me it's my fault that all of this happened?"

"It was going to happen eventually, but yes, your trip was the catalyst that finally made it a reality."

"That trip was planned because it was the fifth anniversary of Lisa's death."

"Oh, Lisa, I remember her. That first victim always holds a special place in your heart." He said with a wistful smile, then hit his hands on his lap. "Whelp, I'm done here. It's been real, Jodie." He said as he stood up, the machines his body was connected to started to beep wildly. He looked back at his body with a smile, then turned and began to walk away. "Oh, I have to ask, since you died, did you become all knowing?"

"No, Lisa has been watching you, learning all of your dirty secrets."

"Wow, some good that did her. See ya."

"No, this isn't fair, you can't just get to die and not pay for anything," Jodie cried out.

"I was never a loser, Jodie, you know that. What makes you think this would be any different?"

An animalist scream came from behind Jodie as Lisa rushed into the room behind the nurses and doctors. Joe looked up as his own personal grim reaper barreled towards him. "Oh shit."

"Miss me, Joe?" Lisa screamed as she shoved into him, causing him to be pushed back towards the bed.

"What are you doing, you clingy bitch?" He yelled back as he pushed back against her.

"You are not going to get away with this so easily. You think you're just going to walk away and not pay for your sins? Oh no, buddy. You've got another thing coming." She informed him as she continued to shove him back.

"You're weak, Lisa, just like you always were." He said as he gained footing and moved back to the doors.

"We're losing him!" A doctor shouted as they continued to try to save him.

"You're going to live a long, painful life in prison, and then when the sweet kiss of death finally reaches you, you will find no peace. You will rot in hell for eternity, along with that psychopathic brother of yours. You think you're above it all and you've gotten away with all of the evil you've done in your life, but you have no idea how cruel life can be." Lisa yelled as she struggled with all do her might to keep him in the hospital room and closer to his body.

Her struggling eased slightly when Doris appeared and helped Lisa shove him to the bed. He fell onto the bed and looked up at the new person in the room. "Who the fuck are you?"

"Seriously? You fucking killed me on the beach and you don't know who I am?" She asked as she held him down with Lisa.

"Just a long line in many. Sorry sweetheart, you're nothing special." Joe tried to stand up again, but found that he couldn't. "What's wrong with my legs? Why can't I move my legs?"

Jodie looked to her friends, then back at Joe. "It's working. His body is paralyzed from his base of his spine."

"What? No! I'm fucking paralyzed?" He screamed out as he tried to stand up.

The doctors were using the paddles on him to bring him back to life. The closer they came to reviving him, the more he was tied to his body. The three women stood over him as he struggled to pull away from his corporal form. He screamed in pain and frustration as he merged with the meat of his body, his eyes bouncing between the three women.

"Don't worry, sweetheart," Lisa said over his agonizing screams, "I'll see you again. And just know that the next time you see me, really see me, it will be right before you're dragged to the bowels of hell, you piece of shit."

The sound of his heartbeat on the monitor rang out through the room as the medical staff successfully resuscitated him. His eyes opened and focused on where the three women were standing, but he saw nothing but the medical staff as they fussed around him and checked his vitals.

***

Three months later, almost on the year anniversary of Jodie's death, the Rappaport brothers stood trial for murder. The investigation into the brothers brought out a slew of charges for their crimes. The search of their properties brought forward written plans for their plan to kill their parents, along with files of information for their search for Joe's son.

Amanda and Ben sat in the courthouse with Jodie's and Lisa's parents as they waited for justice for the victims of the brothers. The District Attorney had entered into evidence a box of trophies that they found in Joe's belonging; a collection of trinkets from his victims, which was mostly compromised of panties. Forensics matched the DNA on the material to some missing persons and cold cases.

Jodie watched on with Lisa and Doris as the story of their heinous crimes were spelt out the judge and jury. The courtroom reacted in outrage as each torrid detail was explained, starting with Lisa's abuse and death, the murder of their parents, to the attempted murder of a child and ultimately Jodie's death.

It was not long until the jury found them guilty. A sense of peace washed over the women as they heard the jurors read their verdict.

"In the case of the state versus Joseph Rappaport, we find the defendant guilty for statutory rape, conspiracy for first-degree murder, voluntary manslaughter, second-degree murder, and first-degree murder. In the case of the state versus Patrick Rappaport, we find the defendant guilty for manslaughter, conspiracy to commit murder, rape, and first-degree murder."

Jodie watched as her parents held on to one another and Amanda collapsed into Ben's arms as the verdict was read. The judged sentenced the brothers to life in prison without parole. The officers entered the court to remove the brothers from the room. Pat stood in his orange jumpsuit as he was cuffed and escorted out as Joe, who was permanently in a wheelchair was escorted by another officer.

The families somberly celebrated their victory with the lawyers as the courtroom began to empty. The girls stayed in the room until they were the only ones left. Jodie looked over at girls and asked, "Do you feel better now that it's over?"

Lisa nodded her head and smiled. "I do. He can't hurt anyone anymore. He's finally going to pay for his crimes." She then looked to Doris with a sad smile. "I'm sorry you didn't get justice for what he did to you."

Doris shrugged in response. "It's okay. My parents came to terms with my death with the explanation from the coroner. He is being punished for eternity for the other crimes he committed. I didn't need my name associated with him to know he'll pay for what he did to me."

"So, now what?" Jodie asked.

"I feel ready to finally move on. My loved ones are safe," Lisa said with a smile. "It will be nice to finally be able to do that."

"You can just choose to do that?" Doris asked.

"Yeah, once you feel like you're ready to move on, you can. But it's a one-way ticket. There's no coming back to check on anyone or send messages. You'll meet them again when the time comes, but not until then."

Doris nodded her head as she absorbed the information. "I think I'm ready too. There is nothing left for me to accomplish. My parents have each other, and my murder has been delt with."

"How about you, Jodie? You ready?" Lisa asked.

Jodie looked out of the courtroom window as she watched her grieving best friend and boyfriend stand with her parents by the cars in the parking lot and felt her chest ache at their grief. It was nearly a year since she had been gone, but they all cried as if it just happened.

"I don't think I can go. I think Amanda and Ben still need me. I need to watch out for them until I know that they are alright. My actions that night had a ripple effect and changed the course of their lives. I can't abandon them."

Lisa nodded in understanding as she approached Jodie. "I get it. I felt that way about you while that asshole was still alive."

"Does this mean I won't see you both anymore?" Jodie asked as she looked at her two friends.

"We'll see you again when you're ready. It will be before you know it. Time isn't the same for us as it is for them." Lisa said.

Jodie hugged Doris as tears welled in her eyes. "I'm so sorry, Doris. I never meant for any of this to happen. I should have never planned that trip."

"It's okay, Jodie," Doris said as she squeezed her friend. "It was my time. There was no preventing this. Don't carry the guilt for any of this. You saved lives because of that trip too, don't forget that."

Doris let go of Jodie as a bright light shone from the side of the room. Doris smiled at Jodie one last time, then headed towards the light, but paused to wait for Lisa. "You go ahead without me," Lisa said to Doris, "I'll be right behind you, I just need to say goodbye."

Doris nodded her head and walked through the warm glow. The girls watched on until Doris was no longer visible. Lisa turned her attention to Jodie, who sucked in a deep breath to stifle a sob.

"I'm not sure what is going to wait for me on the other side," Lisa admitted, "I did some bad things to make sure Joe got what he deserved."

"I don't understand," Jodie said with a sniffle.

"I manipulated you, I did it to Doris, and I did it to Joe. I'm part of the reason why Doris slept with Ben. And I'm part of the reason Joe killed her. I like to think my bad deeds served a greater purpose, but I can't change what I did.

"A word of advice to you. Don't interact with them too much while you are here. It's fine to watch over them, but don't do it too often. I made that mistake with you, and you were medicated because of it. I just don't want you to make the same mistakes I did."

Jodie nodded in understanding as Lisa grabbed onto her and held her tightly. "I love you, Jodie. I'm sorry for how everything happened, but I'm so grateful to you for helping me. You always were and always will be my best friend."

Jodie cried as she clung to Lisa, not wanting to let her go. "I'm scared. I'm scared I won't ever see you again."

"You will," Lisa assured her. "I'll be with you again. I might need to pay for my misdeeds first, but I promise you, we'll be together again."

Jodie nodded and sobbed as Lisa let go of her and headed to the light. Lisa looked back one last time and waved to her friend before she was engulfed, then the light dissipated, and Jodie was left in the empty courtroom.

She turned her attention to her family and friends as she watched Ben console a distraught Amanda. He seemed so strong and stoic through the events of the trial, and still offered his strength to her best friend as she fell apart. Guilt consumed Jodie as she watched Ben escort her to the back seat of her parents' car, as they watched from inside the car.

They all departed, and Jodie made her way to her old bedroom, where she sat around her familiar things and hoped they would bring her some comfort. When she realized that it would not help, she left.

***

Ben made his way home after the trial ended, forcing his empty shell through the day as he tried to stifle his emotions for Amanda's sake. She was barely holding it together as she suffered through the loss of her other best friend. The once strong and outspoken woman was now a weeping mess, and Ben was right there with her.

He entered his empty apartment and pulled the tie loose from around his neck and tossed it onto the table as he made his way to the bathroom, removing articles of clothing on his way. He looked at his sallow reflection in the mirror before he turned on the shower and allowed the water to heat up.

He climbed in and closed the curtain and stood in the water as he succumbed to the grief that had taken up residence in his chest. He sobbed as the water washed away the tears as quickly as they fell from his eyes. He leaned against the wall for support, then slid down and sat in his tub as the water pelted against his skin,

"Why?" He cried out to a God he did not believe in. How could he exist when she was taken away? "Why did you have to take her? I needed more time. Why couldn't we have more time?"

Jodie listened to his wails as he sobbed out loud. "Why did I fuck up so much? Did she really know how much I loved her?"

His cries drowned out the words he tried to choke out. His heart bleed out as he exorcised the grief and pain that infused his soul. "We didn't have enough time. I didn't get to love her the way I wanted to. I fucked it all up. Why didn't you take me?"

He sat in the tub until the water lost its warmth. He felt weak and drained when he finally managed to get himself out of the tub and wrapped a towel around his waist. He stood in front of the fogged mirror and braced himself against the counter. He hung his head, his eyes burned from crying. His phone lit up on the counter, and his eyes drifted to it, where he saw the time was eleven eleven. A smile formed on his face, remembering that Jodie would always say to make a wish whenever she saw that time.

"I wish you were here with me, Jode. I wish we had more time together, and I wish you knew how much I love you." He whispered into the room.

Jodie's heart ached for him, but soared when she heard his whispered wish. She moved next to him, and his head raised as if he could sense her. She smiled at him as she looked around, then took her finger and placed it against the fogged mirror.

Ben watched on in fascination and horror as a heart appeared on his mirror, as if someone had drawn it with their finger. Part of him felt scared, but the other part of him knew. He reached out and touched the heart as he whispered, "Jodie."

Twenty-Nine

Time passed slowly and at the blink of an eye as Jodie watched over her loved ones. She understood what Lisa meant when she said that time didn't matter to them anymore. She no longer saw minutes and hours or years. Everything just was.

Amanda dove head first into therapy, where she processed her trauma and the loss of her friends. It took some time, but she made progress and was able to address her feelings and get beyond her grief. As much as she tried, she could not get passed the damage that Pete caused her.

She doubted her ability to judge men, as she felt she epically failed when it came to her relationship with Pete. Her therapist tried to explain that Pete was an unmedicated bipolar personality who was brainwashed by his mother and wife to turn his back on her. The therapist drove home that Pete had loved her, and even reached out to Andrea to help her heal.

Andrea explained the horrible things their mother said to Pete, and corroborated the narrative the therapist told Amanda, but she did not want to hear it. She no longer trusted men in a romantic sense, and had trouble interacting with them.

She heavily relied on Ben's friendship, since she knew he was the only other person who lived through the trauma and new what it was to lose two friends on a weekend getaway.

She had postponed her master's degree for a year and changed her major to social work. Her fear of people hindered her, so she earned her degree online.

Aside from venturing out for her therapy appointments, she spent time with Ben as he opened his own restaurant. After the trial was over, Andrew inherited the Rappaport fortune. Andrea gave Amanda and Jodie's family five million dollars each, as a thank you for saving her son's life.

Amanda decided to take some of her money and invest it in the restaurant that Ben was trying to open. He had taken out a business loan, but was running into some issues with the building he purchased. Amanda came through with the funds he needed and became a silent partner.

She spent her free time with him as he built his dream from the ground up. It took almost a year to get the building ready and the restaurant opened. He named it JR's, after Jodie Rogers, and had a picture of her smiling with the flower in her hair from their night in Atlantic City.

Amanda often sat at the spot at the bar in front of Jodie's picture. The two of them had grown close over the five years since her death, but it was in the most platonic, family-like way. Amanda became a social worker and volunteered her time at a local domestic violence center.

She experienced the success of JR's first hand; the restaurant and bar became a hot spot for locals and the college crowd alike. The place had a family friendly atmosphere during the day, but became a popular bar spot at night.

Amanda watched on as one of the waitresses, a pretty girl with short blonde hair and a warm smile, would try to flirt with Ben during her shifts. Ben would smile at the girl and banter with her, but never fed into the flirting. He would watch her from afar when he thought no one was looking, but then would look up at the photo of Jodie and sigh.

"Ben," Amanda said as he saddled up to the bar across from her. "Why don't you ask her out?"

Ben looked confused. "What are you talking about?"

"Jillian, the pretty waitress who bats her lashes at you every chance she gets. I can tell you like her, and it's obvious she's into you."

Ben shook his head. "No, I'm not interested in dating. That part of my life ended with Jodie."

Amanda shook her head she looked at her friend. "You know she wouldn't want you to never have love in your life again."

"Look who's talking. Haven't you sworn off men?"

Amanda scoffed. "That's different. I need one of us to have a happily ever after. I'm too damaged for any of that, but I do help other people achieve it. Let me help you."

"Absolutely not."

"Why?" Amanda asked.

Ben shook his head. "You wouldn't believe me if I told you."

"Try me."

"Okay, but you're going to think I'm nuts. Any time I see eleven eleven on the clock, I see a heart somewhere. Whether it's a cloud, or a sticker, or a puddle, I always see one. And I know it's from Jodie. It's her way of telling me she's there, and that she loves me. It keeps me going, because my heart will always belong to her."

"It's a beautiful sentiment," Amanda said after a pregnant pause. "But Ben, it's been five years. I know you two loved each other in your own ways, but I think you're romanticizing the past. The two of you were oil and water most of the time. She always loved you, Ben, but she wouldn't want you to waste your life pinning away for something that will never be. You need to live for both of you now. I do what I'm doing while carrying her and Lisa in my heart. You need to do the same."

Ben shook his head. "I will never love someone the way I loved her. She was supposed to be my forever."

"And maybe in another life, you'll be that for each other, but in this one it wasn't meant to be. No one ever said you can only love one person at a time. You'll fall in love again, it just won't be the same love that you had for Jodie, and that's okay. Just think about it."

***

Ben and Amanda stood in a spot they never thought they would ever stand in again. It had been ten years since the night Jodie lost her life, and they decided to come back and have a small memorial service. The two of them stood under the pier and placed flowers near the base of one of the pillars, one bouquet for Jodie and one for Doris.

They shared some stories about the women that they tried not to speak about too often, but who were always in the back of their minds. They planned to invite Jodie's parents to the event, but they had sold their house moved not too soon after Jodie passed away and did not keep in touch with either of them. Ben understood the need to remove themselves from the house, but Amanda never forgave them from running away from their daughter's memory.

Amanda had taken it upon herself to upkeep Jodie's grave in their absence. She visited twice a year, once on her Jodie's birthday, and the other on the anniversary of her death. She felt that it was a way to take care of her friend when she was no longer around, and Amanda felt that her purpose in life was to help others since she couldn't save her friends.

It took a few years before Jodie visited Amanda in a dream. She was afraid to upset her since Amanda was in such a fragile state. Her visit was brief but comforting; she only wanted to let Amanda know that she was okay, and that she loved her and thanked her for still caring about her. Amanda found peace in that dream, and never sought Jodie out, just continued to care for her final resting place.

After the small service was over, Ben walked away and settled himself down on the sand for a moment to himself. He watched as the seagulls danced across the sky, then focused on the waves as they crashed against the sand. As haunted as this place was for him, he still found the surroundings peaceful.

As he sat there and stared out into the ocean, he felt someone sit next to him. He smiled as he said out loud, "Hi Jodie."

She smiled at him and responded, "hi Ben."

"It's been a long time," he said as his eyes still focused on the waves.

"Has it?"

He smiled at her response as he looked over at her, she hadn't aged a bit since the last time he laid his eyes on her. "God, I miss you."

She smiled at him, then looked behind her as two children played in the sand, a pretty blonde woman stood with Amanda as they watched them play. "They are adorable, Ben. They look a lot like their father."

"Yeah," he agreed, "they are the second-best thing to happen to me." He looked at her with a sad smile.

She chuckled softly. "I'm glad you're happy," she said as her eyes drifted back to the lullaby of the ocean.

"I named her after you, my daughter. They are Josh and Jodie." Ben told her.

"I know."

"You stopped visiting me. I never see hearts anymore at eleven eleven."

Jodie let out a sigh and then looked at Ben. "You don't need me anymore."

"I'll always need you, Jodie."

She slowly shook her head, "no, Ben, you haven't need me for years, and that's okay. It's the way it should be."

Ben went to argue, but she interrupted him. "I know you love me, Ben, and I'll always love you. But I need you to be here and love your family. I need you to live your life. I promise you that I'll see you again, when it's the right time. You'll be old and gray, with a lifetime of love and memories. And I'll be there, waiting for you on the other side."

She reached out and placed her hand gently on his face, he could feel a slight breeze and tingle where it rested. A bright light glowed from beyond the sand and sea, and it blinded him. He raised his hand to shield his eyes, but as he did so, the light dissipated, and so did Jodie's presence.

Amanda walked up behind Ben, and he looked back at her with tears streaming down his face. "She's gone," he said quietly.

Amanda nodded her head, "I know, I saw her."

Epilogue

Nearly a year later, Amanda received an email from Andrea. She informed her that two days before Pete was set to be released from prison, he was stabbed in the yard by someone who had ties to Pat Rappaport. They rushed him to a hospital, but he was pronounced dead when he arrived. The man who killed him was a recent transfer from the prison where Pat was incarcerated, and was rumored to be his boyfriend.

Pat lasted another twenty years in prison before he was killed in a gang fight in the prison. He was in his fifties at the time he died.

Amanda never married, and devoted her life to helping women and children of domestic abuse. She was very close to Ben's children, who called her Aunt Mandy. She also stayed in touch with Andrea and Andrew, who had grown into a wonderful man, and shared no traits with the monsters he shared genetics with.

Joe Rappaport served his life sentence in prison, and passed away at the age of eighty-three. He had a few health scares over the years, and each time he kept his eyes peeled for Lisa. Each time she did not appear, he sighed a breath of relief. But that last time when he laid in his death bed, Lisa peered through the surrounding hospital staff and corrections officers and smiled when he noticed her. He began to panic, and the machines beeped from his erratic heartbeat as he tried to scream out.

True to her word, she was the last thing he saw before he passed away. As he began to leave his body, she took a running start and headed straight for him, collided with his body, and dragged his straight to hell as she promised.

She told Jodie all about it when she returned. Jodie took a lot of joy in hearing that Lisa was finally able to deliver Joe to the eternal damnation that he deserved.

It took some time, but eventually Jodie and Lisa met Amanda when it was her time. She was ninety-five years old, and had led a fulfilling life helping a countless amount of people. Her non-profit had grown to at least one presence in every state, leaving a legacy of hope and protection for those who needed it. Amanda needed no time to take care of anything and joined them straight away.

A few months later, Ben was on his deathbed, surrounded by his wife, children, and grandchildren. He led a good life; he loved his wife and family, he ran a successful business, and provided a good life for those he loved. As he said his goodbyes to his loved ones, he saw Jodie standing off in the corner of the room. When she noticed that he saw her, she raised her hand in a silent wave, and he acknowledged her with his kind eyes.

He took one last look at his children, then his eyes settled on his wife, then he smiled and closed his eyes and took his last breath. He slowly stood up from the bed as he watched his family cry over his body. He stood there and watched them grieve when he felt a hand on his shoulder.

"This is really weird," he commented without turning around.

Jodie agreed with him, but let him process what was happening. After a few moments, he turned and smiled at the first girl he loved. "You haven't changed a bit," he said with a smile.

Jodie looked back at him and returned the smile. "You have, and I'm so happy that you did. Have you had a good life?"

"You didn't watch?" He asked.

She shook her head. "No, I wanted you to live. And it was a little hard for me to watch."

Ben looked back at his wife and children as he nodded his head. "I understand. I'm sure it would have been difficult for me in your position. But to answer your question, yes, I had a very good life."

Jodie smiled at him. "You have a choice. You don't have to come with me if you're not ready. If there is anything you need to do or watch over, you can. There's no time limit. But it is a one-way ticket, so if whenever you decide to move on, make sure you are absolutely ready."

He looked at his family one last time and smiled, then turned back to Jodie. "I'm ready."

Jodie looked at him in surprise, "are you sure? It just happened, and you might need some time to process."

He shook his head, "No, I'm ready, I've waited nearly sixty years to see you again. I'm ready."

Jodie smiled brightly at him as she reached out her hand and took his frail, wrinkled hand in hers and led him to the warm, bright light. When they crossed over, Jodie looked over at him to see him the way he looked the last time she saw him on the beach.

He looked over at her, then pulled her to him and kissed her. Jodie clung onto him as she returned the kiss, her soul finally felt whole. They broke apart to see Amanda standing there with Lisa at her side.

Ben walked over and hugged Amanda in a tight, long hug that Amanda returned just a fiercely.

Jodie watched as her two best friends and the man she loved stood together. She smiled and approached them, feeling at peace for the first time ever, all the heartache and pain a distant memory.

Author's Note

This book has been in the works for nearly 20 years. Inspired by a trip taken to Atlantic City with three of my friends back in the summer of 2005. Nothing bad happened on the trip, but we did stay at the seediest motel called the Burgundy Motor Inn. It closed, but do yourself a favor and google it... we had no idea about the history of the place either. And I absolutely have photos of the room from that trip.

I have been writing stories for a long time. Back in junior high I had a story that I wrote and my friend would read and beg me to write more. I've always loved creating stories, and it's taken me a long time to finally get here.

The catalyst that finally got me to take the plunge and publish was my niece, Elizabeth, who has discovered her love for writing. When she is asked about it, she says she loves to write like her aunt. How can I tell her to follow her dreams if I don't do it myself?

I have a bunch of people I need to thank for getting me to this point. To my husband, Tom, for always encouraging me to write the books, and traveling with me to AC and indulged me as I took pictures of all the place I wrote about. Thank you for being my number one supporter and location scout.

To my mom, for always supporting me and guiding me to stick with my strength, my ability to write. Thanks for being my rock. To my dad, for inspiring and enabling my love of books and reading, and who always taught me that there is always time for a creative outlet.

For my sister, Mary, and my brother, Michael, thanks for support and encouragement. I'm sure some of our antics will eventually wind up in a future book. For my Uncle Sal for always asking if I published my book yet. Yes, Uncle Sal, I finally published!

To my bestie, Lauren, who was my test subject and read a draft back during Covid. Thanks for giving it to me straight and admitting that you thought you were going to have to lie to me and say you liked it, but you actually did and to publish it.

For the countless others: my in-laws, co-workers, and friends who I spilled the beans to, I appreciate the encouragement and hope it was worth the wait.

And to anyone who made it this far into my ramblings, thank you for taking a chance on reading this story. I hope you found it entertaining. I look forward to publishing the next one!

About the Author

C.E. Maras is a Long Island native, who lives with her husband, Tom. She is a technical marketing writer by day, and inspired by her dreams and past experiences to write fiction at night. She has been writing fiction since elementary school, and was told by her first grade and seventh grade teacher that she was meant to be a writer. With many stories written and shared with her friends growing up, C.E. decided to take the plunge-publishing her first novel, Burgundy, in the summer of 2024; and fulfilling the answer to the question in her elementary school yearbook, what do you want to be when you grow up? Aside from writing, C.E. is a voracious reader, consuming around 150 books per year. She also enjoys knitting, crocheting, cooking, baking, spending time with family, and spoiling her niece and nephews.

Follow on Facebook and Instagram: C.E. Maras Books

Made in the USA
Middletown, DE
17 September 2024

61030269R00163